The Harrison

The Harrison

A Beautiful Place to Die

A Madeline Donovan Mystery

MADISON KENT

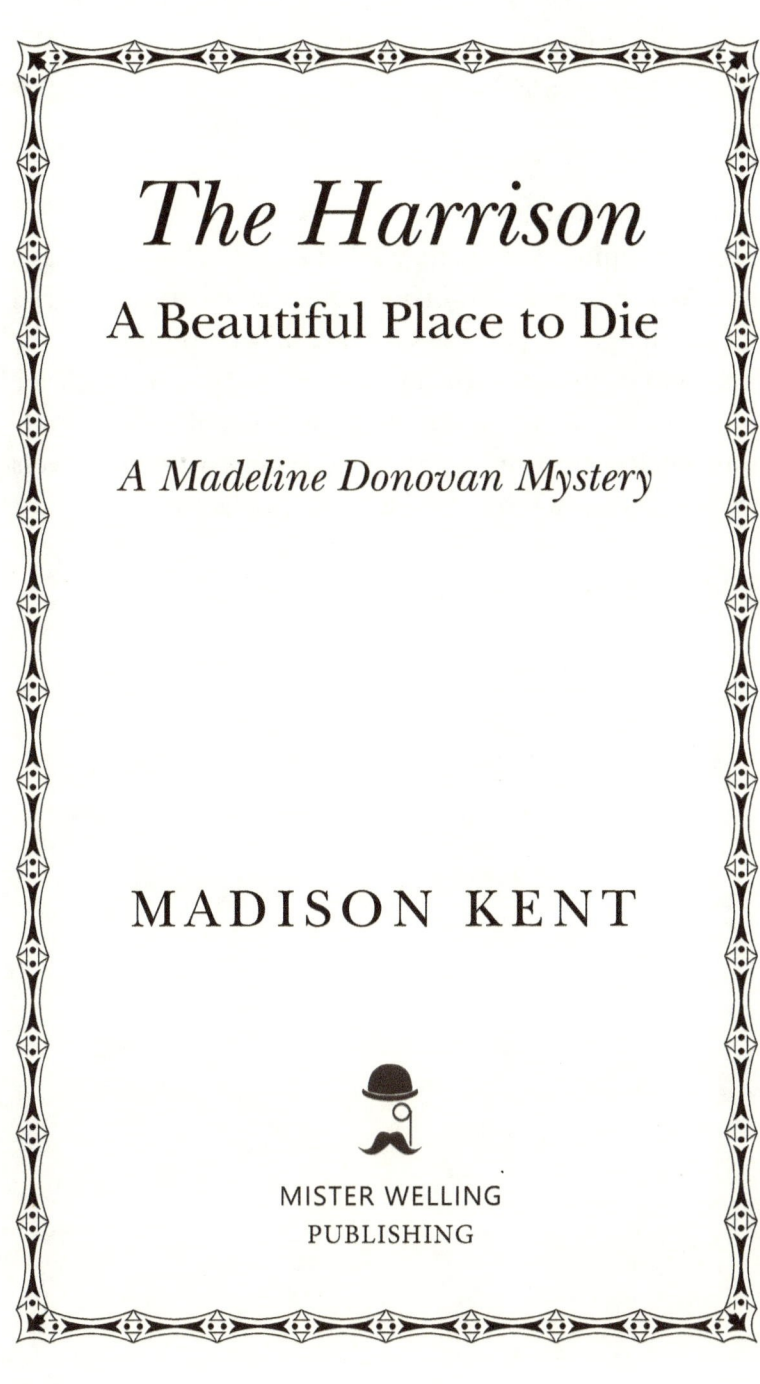

MISTER WELLING
PUBLISHING

To Army medic, John Francis, a decorated
Bronze Star recipient
Resulting from his heroic actions at the
Battle of Myitkyina in Burma-WWII

Contents

Contents

Prologue

After an extended time in London, Madeline Donovan returns to her hometown of Chicago. Her experience abroad created the desire to establish a detective agency. Madeline's unexpected adventure while traversing Whitechapel's streets, although dangerous, gave her a way to cope with life again and find purpose.

Her first case presents itself from a surprising source and has ties to a hotel within walking distance of her home. Young girls are disappearing in Chicago; it reminds her of the infamous Jack the Ripper. She begins to wonder if such a creature could exist in her backyard or is it, as the police think, just a case of young girls sowing their wild oats and looking for excitement in a bustling city.

Her two dearest friends Hugh Scott and Jonathan Franks will once again come to be by her side and assist her in her quest to find the girls. Although she believes she will never again marry or have another family, both men have romantic feelings towards her, and she is softening to the idea that maybe she can love again.

The eccentricities of the owners of The Harrison Hotel are many, but are they so peculiar that one could be the murderer? The Harrison itself is a building of secrets and confounds Madeline as to what it hides on its third floor.

Chapter 1

The Agency

June 1, 1889

Dear Hugh,

It does not seem possible that it has been nearly six months since I have seen your face smiling at me. I miss the pleasure of conversing with you at length about Jack the Ripper and all manner of things. I received your last letter with a grateful heart. I fairly ran up to our porch, without even entering the house, and sat on the veranda reading your welcome words.

There is not a day that goes by that I do not think of you and hope that all is well. Especially in the evening, when the moon shines directly onto our window seat, I think of you. The moon casts such a lovely shadow and reminds me so of looking out over the streets from my room at the Hotel George. It is at those times, whenever there is a knock at the door that I peek out and almost expect to see you or Jonathan standing there.

I am still looking for a proper rental place for my agency. I hope to find one that is reasonably priced and with access to the business district and walk-in traffic. Of course, Father is discouraging me at every turn, but my determination is strong in this.

There has been an epidemic of viruses that have afflicted the residents, and Father spends long nights attending to his patients. He has compelled me to assist him, and I do. However, it is hindering my initial effort to get my detective agency off the ground.

I do hope you and the aunts will seriously consider coming to America for the Christmas holidays. Wouldn't it be wonderful for all of us to be together again?

Please write soon.

Your dearest friend,

Madeline

Hugh Scott, the dashing young solicitor from London, who, standing at nearly six-foot, with short, silky black hair that always seemed groomed to perfection, was someone very dear to her heart. She had befriended him while residing in London for a few months in the autumn of 1888.

When she arrived in London, she was frail and in a state of mind so befuddled that her small frame of five-foot-three inches appeared even slighter still. She ate only to survive and nearly blew in the wind at just one hundred pounds. Her once lovely, long auburn hair was now just piled atop her head with a few pins. Still, somehow Hugh Scott and Jonathan Franks had shown a compassionate and almost loving interest in her.

She believed her appearance had somewhat improved from those times, but she knew she was guilty of still neglecting herself. She looked up from her reading to glance at her reflection in the porch window. She still had her streak of white hair cascading down the left side of her face, and she still looked undernourished. However, she now wore lovely, bright-hued frocks and even adorned herself with a rose-colored pearl necklace and earrings. She knew if she were to go into business, she would have to be more diligent about appearing fashionable and in the picture of health.

"Madeline," her father called out, "hurry," it is Mrs. Gardner. I think it's time—the baby is coming."

"Oh, Father, must I? You know how I dislike watching the mother's writhing like that. I was just about to walk down to the business district."

"I'm sorry, my dear, but Mrs. Abernathy is still not recovered."

Mrs. Abernathy, her father's nurse, an employee, was down with an ailment that produced fever and vomiting. Madeline thought she would bring her some chicken broth and do whatever she could to get the poor woman back on her feet, purely for selfish reasons.

She was certain now more than ever that she must get her detective agency off the ground. She did not wish to be readily available and at her father's beckoning. It wasn't that she didn't love him; it was because she didn't particularly take any fancy to the practice of medicine. She never liked the sight of blood. As for the birthing of a child, she could barely endure her own childbirth experience, let alone someone else's.

After her sleuthing experience in London, she had decided that the idea of being an amateur detective suited her. She loved the idea of tracking down the miscreants that plagued society.

Reluctantly, she helped her father carry his medical bag and other materials needed for Mrs. Gardner.

An old woman answered the door, throwing her hands up in the air; she exclaimed, "Oh, thank heaven you're here. She's in there, in the back bedroom."

Amidst the mayhem of the Gardner household, where three other children already had laid claim to the house and were running about shouting and playing boisterously, Dr. Donovan assisted the birth of a child, yet another boy, Mrs. Gardner's fourth.

"Thank you, Madeline," said Dr. Donovan, as they stood side by side, washing in the large basin of water the old woman brought for them.

"Yes, it is wonderful, at least the part when it's over and new life comes into the world. It always makes me think of my boys. I'm afraid, Father, I will have to leave you. I will return later in the day. I think I will go to the park," she said as she wiped away the few tears that had fallen upon her cheek.

"Oh, Madeline, what's wrong with me? I shouldn't have asked. I just thought as you have been doing so well…"

"No, Father, do not fret. I was glad to do it. I think, though, I would like to walk for a while."

He hugged her, and she departed.

Chapter 2

In Search of Maria

Madeline Donovan became a widow during the Christmas of 1887, when her husband and two beloved boys, Will, and Nate, died in a fire, presumably ignited by their Christmas tree. She had come a long way in adjusting back into society since then, but only after a period of grieving that all but took her life. Mrs. Gardner's son, crying out with loud, sweet bursts of life, brought back the memory of her first-born, Will, and the joy she and her husband, Russell, felt at that moment of birth, and then later when Nate was born.

Lost in thought, she continued walking and did not stop at the small park near their home. She instead found she traversed far enough that she was now in view of the Harrison Hotel on Erie Street. The three-story hotel was the grandest building anywhere near her home. It had been the talk of the neighborhood since the residents knew that such a place would come to rest in their humble surroundings. She believed it had been open perhaps two or three months now, and she had meant several times to walk about the place to observe its décor and clientele.

Arriving, her immediate impression was that the foyer was more impressive than that of the George, the hotel she had stayed at in London. The marble floors gleamed like starlight, boasting ornate pillars that designated the different entrance-ways. Upon entering, the nearest shop was a Parisian café that served beverages and delicate pastries. Seating was available outside the café, where you could view the activity of the patrons and staff congregating throughout the area. Lavish, red velvet draperies, with sheer white panels, adorned the panoramic windows that allowed you to see out into the street. It was lovely, and she felt it was a beautiful addition to her neighborhood. Chicago was stretching its arms and bustling with new construction and an abundance of new businesses were popping up everywhere.

Stopping at the French cafe, she chose to sit in its extension in the lobby. She sipped her Earl Grey slowly, stirring it with a spoon that made a tinkling noise when it hit the China sides. Darjeeling had been her choice of tea for many years, but recently, she took to drinking Earl Grey because it reminded her of London. It was what her dearest friends from there, the aunts and Hugh, preferred to drink.

She had yet to see the rooms, but she decided this would be the perfect place for the aunts to stay if they were ever to visit her from everything she saw thus far.

After an enjoyable hour of listening to and watching the bustling crowd at The Harrison, she slowly walked back down the quarter-mile of the road towards her home, looking up at the two and three-story flats, abundant with life flowing out from them.

Children were playing marbles and baseball; it was indeed a lovely Chicago afternoon.

She arrived at their two-story flat with basement lodging on Erie Street, feeling joy at the sight of her home. It was constructed only one year before and still had that lovely newness about it. The silvery-gray brick home boasted a decorative bay window on the main floor where they resided. She enjoyed looking up from the window seat, where she sat on many an afternoon reading. The ever flow of people and pushcart vendors traveling through the street was a portrait in motion. A floral brocade rug with autumn colors of green, brown, and light burnt orange lay over the parquet floor. In the same color scheme, three pieces of footed furniture sat so that the light of the day would shine upon them. The room was spacious, nearly two thousand square feet, and would have been considered a grand amount of space compared to the tiny rooms she had seen in London.

When leaving the main family room and entering the dining area, one would pass through two mahogany colored pillars on either side of the room. A beautiful oak table, a buffet, and a china hutch graced the room. All of twelve feet long, the table once had many a dinner at it, but no more. These were among the few pieces of furniture father had brought with him from her childhood home on Evergreen Street.

Their cook called out to her, "Mrs. Donovan, your father wishes you to dress in your finery for dinner," said Mrs. O'Malley, as she stirred the pot of broth in the large, clean, white kitchen.

"Is there a special guest coming?" asked Madeline.

"There is, Miss, and he said you would be particularly interested in who it was."

"You have piqued my interest, Mrs. O'Malley. I will do so, and will be in to assist you with the table after I dress."

"Thank you, Miss. I do appreciate that. I believe your father invited Uncle Hank."

"Oh, wonderful—I have not seen very much of him this week."

He wasn't actually her Uncle Hank, but a cherished neighbor who now rented the basement flat. A bachelor, he worked a rigorous day at the Chicago stockyards, his pencil-thin frame and drawn face showing every bit of his care-worn days. Whenever she dropped in for a quick visit, the only food items in his cupboard were a few apples and maybe a bottle of beer. Her father often invited him to dinner, but he was a proud man and rarely accepted the invitation. Mr. Henry Dabrowski was very dear to her, and she had taken to calling him "Uncle Hank" many years before.

Arriving downstairs in her maroon lace frock—her hair pinned back and adorned with two pearl combs for accent, she saw her father's approving smile. Her two-inch heeled black leather lace-up boots made her appear a bit taller, and she was aware her tiny frame needed that extra bit of height.

"Madeline," her father said, "we will be dining a little earlier, at six. I am pleased you are ready as I would like to speak to you in my study."

The study was a third bedroom that her father had converted into a quaint little area with hard-covered books on the shelves against the wall, two leather sitting chairs, a few miscellaneous writing instruments, and a pile of paperwork.

"A patient of mine, Mrs. Rosa Silvestri, came to my office this very day in hysterics, requesting medicine to calm her. A few weeks ago, her sister arrived from New York for an extended visit, and she is now missing. The police have done nothing about it, as she is of age, I believe— twenty-five. They think she decided to leave of her own free will to explore the city. But Mrs. Silvestri says that would be impossible, that her sister would never leave in such a manner that their relationship is close, with no problems. She also said her sister was on the adventurous side, but it wouldn't be like her to have departed independently. Besides, all of her belongings remain at their home."

"Father, what a remarkable story. But what is the reason she is coming here?"

"I invited her because of you, Madeline. This is your chance to get started. You may not yet have a storefront, but you now have a client."

"You are wonderful. I thought you disapproved of this endeavor. You would be the last person I would have thought would encourage me in this."

"No one is helping her, and she needs someone she can

trust, not some charlatan who will fleece her and end up just spending his time at the local drinking establishment."

"Do you know the sister's name?"

"She told me, but I don't remember it. She should be here at any moment. She might bring her brother with her or her husband. I gave her pills to calm her; so hopefully, she will be able to be questioned without crying or exhibiting too much anxiety."

Madeline was intrigued—not only had her father initiated a meeting that involved her possibly employing her sleuthing activities, but there was also this mysterious disappearance. Of course, there was always crime in any big city, and Chicago was no exception, but she had never involved herself before in this capacity.

She was busy arranging the floral centerpiece when Rosa Silvestri and another man arrived.

"Please come in. My father has explained why you are here. I am Madeline, Madeline Donovan."

"I am sorry if I do not behave properly. I am quite distraught over the disappearance of my sister, Maria. This is my brother, Louie Falco. I don't mean to impose, but I don't think I can get through this without him."

"Of course, it is no imposition. Father had already planned for an additional guest. We will be having simple fare for dinner. I hope you do not mind."

"I will probably eat very little, thank you just the same," said Rosa.

Of Italian descent, Rosa was slightly shorter than her, and Madeline believed her to be five-foot-one or so. Louie was somewhat taller, perhaps by two inches, but still shorter than most of her male acquaintances. However, he was dauntingly handsome, with raven, curly dark hair, black eyes, olive skin, and dressed fashionably in a bowler hat, dark gray dinner jacket, waistcoat, and trousers, all accented with an ascot tie. Rosa was also quite becoming, with lighter, chestnut-brown hair, and wearing a royal-blue, simple day dress.

Louie said, "Your father gave us the hope that you might be interested in helping us find our sister. The police have disregarded our concerns and believe she is in the city sight-seeing, or that perhaps she has found a male companion to spend her time with. This is all nonsense, of course, but they showed us their crime journal. The officer continued, saying every day that the amount of *real* crimes that come across their desk is overwhelming and suggesting that we wait a few more days and that we would probably hear from her by then. I can tell you I am in a state; my sister is gregarious, likes to flirt, and enjoys her freedom, but not to the extent that we would not have heard from her...impossible."

Rosa looked as if she were about to faint, just hearing Louie speaking about Maria.

"Rosa, may I get you a glass of wine?" asked Madeline.

"Yes, that would be very nice, thank you."

Madeline's father entered the room and took Rosa's hands, "My dear, I hope you are feeling better. Who is this you have brought with you?"

"This is my brother, Dr. Donovan, Louie—Louie Falco."

"How do you do, sir...welcome to my home. Please, let us go in for dinner. I believe our cook is ready to serve. We are just waiting on our tenant, Mr. Henry Dabrowski, to join us," said the doctor.

Madeline thought her father was a most distinguished gentleman. His fine, grayish-white hair was as straight as a line; but was puffed up a little across his forehead. Gold framed spectacles that slid down his nose gave him the habit of constantly pushing them back up to his eyes. He stood at five-foot-ten inches, hunched somewhat from worry and older age, but carried himself to her as if he stood ten-feet-tall. Always the gentleman and always living his life thinking of others, her father never acted in any way that would ever denigrate his integrity. She looked at him now, filled with pride, and felt grateful she had, at least, one surviving family member.

A knock on the door signaled that Uncle Hank arrived. His scarecrow physique and shy demeanor made him appear even more loveable as he smiled brightly at the dinner guests.

"I'm sorry I'm a bit late, but they worked us a little longer today. Business has been good. I don't mind, because it means a little extra money," said Hank.

After introductions, Dr. Donovan took his place at the head of the table, with Madeline and Hank seated at his right. Rosa and Louie sat on the left side of her father. It was a breezy, mild day, and they had left the window open in the dining area. The balmy wind blowing stirred the candlelight on the table to flicker. Dusk had come and given the room a shadowy, warm feeling.

Mrs. O'Malley served a hearty chicken soup; however, no one ate very much except for Uncle Hank. Madeline's curiosity was getting the better of her, and all she wanted was for dinner to be over so that Rosa and Louie could tell their story.

"Rosa, do you feel you can begin to tell us a little more of what has transpired with your sister?" asked Madeline.

"I have not seen my sister for two years—she lives with

my father in New York. After our mother passed away, she stayed with my Father to help him run the family bakery. Father was finally doing well enough to allow Maria to come for an extended stay here in Chicago. She arrived several weeks ago and had been in awe of the city, spending time at McVicker's Theater and traveling everywhere around Chicago.

However, after one of her days of sightseeing, she did not return. She previously never arrived home later than nine. I know she had made several casual acquaintances, both male, and female, but nothing more than to enjoy a visit to one of the museums or to have a meal with.

Several days ago, acting somewhat secretive and dressed in a most becoming gown, she left, saying she was attending the theater with a group of ladies. She said she was meeting them down the street at the new Harrison Hotel. We have not heard from her since."

"I agree with my sister, something terrible has happened to Maria, and no one in authority seems to care. They said they would send a police officer around to the hotel to ask about her, but that was about it," said Louie.

"Do you have a photograph of her?" asked Madeline.

"Yes, we had some taken as soon as she arrived. She is a beauty; I am sure you would agree," answered Louie.

He handed her a picture of Rosa, her brother, Louie, and Maria, in a studio setting. They were a handsome family, and as Louie said, Maria stood out among them. Although there was no color in the photograph—only shades of sepia—her striking features nonetheless compelled one to look at her.

"She looks like someone from the stage. Yes, she is lovely," said Madeline.

"Her hair is black as midnight, and she loves to wear brightly colored hats," said Rosa.

"She's quite athletic and can compete with anyone in tennis, which accounts for her shapely figure," said Louie.

"May I see the picture?" asked Hank.

Squinting, he stared at the photo. He held it for a moment, then said, "I could be mistaken, but the other day, when I was at the drugstore that is across from the hotel, I saw several women standing outside. I remembered them because they were finely dressed and, they stood out from everyone else. I think one of them might have been your sister."

"Yes, I believe she liked to frequent the shops there," said Rosa.

"So, I will start at the hotel. Do you have any names of anyone that she has met while she was here?" asked Madeline.

"No, not really—she mentioned a few people by their first names. I think I remember Felicity or Felicia and Rhonda," said Rosa.

"I think it was Wanda," said Louie.

"Perhaps you are right," said Rosa.

"If you could go through her things and find any receipts or any mementos from places she has been, it may help. If you could bring me everything you have that may have shown where she has frequented, I will start there," said Madeline.

"What is your fee?" asked Louie

Madeline realized she had thought of this but had never come to an answer, not knowing what her services would be worth, as she was not a tested detective.

"I will discuss that with you when you bring the items

to me, but I believe that one dollar per day would be a fair price."

"It is fair," said Louie as he shook her hand in a contractual agreement.

Madeline exchanged pleasantries with Uncle Hank, promising to have him over for tea and perhaps a card game later in the week.

After their guests left, her father sat drinking tea with her at the dining table.

"Madeline, it is a risky business that you undertake, but you are a grown woman, and I will not interfere. Perhaps you should try to engage a male participant if you are to go through with this business."

"Unless it is Hugh or Jonathan, I think not. That is my point, Father. Females must assert themselves into society in roles that are traditional to men. We must break ground in this; someone has to start it."

"You will, at least, let me know your whereabouts. I know I will worry, but you must go your own way, especially now. If this somehow relieves your burden of grief, I must stand beside you."

"I will try as much as possible to inform you of where I will be. Do not worry, Father. I am stronger than you think, and I promise you I will not take any unnecessary risks."

He looked at her still-trembling right hand, which she called her "opium tremor." She had slid into the undesirable habit of using opiates while in London, and she knew her father was worried that the stress of investigating a disappearance might bring her back to that state of mind. What he didn't know is that it never left her. Her cravings for opium were something she dealt with daily. Her father tactfully said nothing about her uncontrollable finger movements, but thankfully they did not occur with frequency anymore.

"I will begin tomorrow with the coffee houses, drugstores, and the hotel. Sometimes the news-boys have a keen eye and remember people. It is a beginning. If their account of Maria's actions is an accurate one, then she is most likely in danger. But we don't know if she might be more adventurous and did perhaps go away intentionally. However unlikely, it is a consideration.

"The autumn days still have long light, and I will be able to be out in the safety of daylight until late."

"Perhaps if either Uncle Hank or I am available, we can escort you."

"Thank you, Father, we'll see. If I am to do this, I must put myself into it and not be too reliant on others. But, I will see what I will find out and decide after that."

"All right, Madeline. Good-night."

Chapter 3

The Harrison

It was the custom in this day and age for women to make a change of clothing up to four or five times a day, and now that Madeline was no longer wearing her black mourning dresses, she appeared better in complexion. Donning a sea-foam-green dress, and adding a darker green hat with a placement of feathers, giving her what she thought was a fashionable appearance for the first time in a year.

When she reached the drugstore, located directly across from the Harrison Hotel, she made inquiries about Maria. No one was particularly interested in answering Madeline's questions; they brushed her off without her obtaining any useful information.

However, one of the newsboys, a boy she learned, was

called "Little Tony," had thought he might have seen Maria.

"She's a beauty, Miss. I noticed her right away. I think I remember her with two other ladies, but I saw her go into the hotel a few times," said Little Tony.

"Thank you, Tony," she said as she handed him a few pennies for his time. "If you will keep a watch out for her for me, I will buy all your papers. Her family is worried about her. If you should see her, please contact me."

"Should I say you're looking for her?"

"No, she wouldn't know who I am, but please tell her that her family wishes to get in touch."

Madeline was pleased that she had found some positive news so quickly. Perhaps that is the answer. Maybe Maria did meet some young man, and they had an impromptu rendezvous. Although she still did not think this idea likely. If Little Tony was correct, and Maria had been to the hotel several times, maybe there was someone in her life that Rosa and Louie did not know about.

Madeline entered the Harrison Hotel and again observed its uniqueness. An array of curiosity shops, a hair salon, a barbershop, as well as other businesses on the first floor were open to the public. The area reserved for hotel guests was on the second floor, and according to the young man at the concierge desk, business offices were on the third.

Two studious young women, each wearing fashionable spectacles and beautiful dresses, sat in the French café's extended dining area. There were about a half-dozen tables in a cordoned-off portion in the lobby. Golden ornate chairs and tables, and simple white tablecloths, with a vase of dainty flowers in the center, were a sweet, delicate sight. Madeline paid particular attention to the women because of what they were reading—scientific journals. She had found that not many women she met held any interest in being modern or competing with men. She was now quite curious to meet them.

"Excuse me, I'm Madeline Donovan, and I'm in search of a young lady who might have frequented this café or been in this hotel. I wonder if you might take the trouble to look at a photograph of her. Her name is Maria Falco."

"How do you do? I'm Marilyn Zajec, and this is my sister, Nancy. Of course, if we can help you, we will. Please be seated."

"If I may say so, you look like you might be twins," said Madeline.

"Yes, not identical, but close enough as you can see," said the flaxen-haired girl named Nancy.

"We have come here often since its grand opening. With all the industrial fairs held nearby, there are so many visitors to our great city that it is interesting to speak with them and hear their stories. It is like taking a vacation without leaving the city; to see their different way of dressing, speaking, and thinking is an education unto itself," said Marilyn.

"I couldn't help but notice what you're reading. I see you have an interest in science," she commented to Marilyn.

"Yes, my sister and I are students at Northwestern University. I am studying forensic science. It's not something most people are familiar with, but our father was a police officer and prompted my interest in this field, even as a young girl," said Nancy.

"Oh, it is wonderful that you have an interest in forensics! When I was recently in London, Scotland Yard had just recently begun using this science. I hope someday we may have luncheon together, and you will be so kind as to tell me all about your studies. I am fascinated by it, especially as I plan to pursue a career as a detective," said Madeline.

"That is interesting that we all have passion for subjects considered to be the male domain. Mine is chemistry, and I am one of only three young women in my classes," said Marilyn.

"That is wonderful. Your parents must be so proud of you," said Madeline.

"Our parents have passed on, but I do believe they would be. They were very supportive," said Nancy.

"Now, about this photograph of Maria—what do you think, Nancy?" asked Marilyn.

"There have been so many young women that pass through here; it is difficult to say. But now that we know you are looking for her, we will keep watch," said Nancy.

"I will leave my name and address with you in the event that you do. I do hope we will see each other again soon. I may one day require your expert knowledge," Madeline said.

"Of course, and we will meet for luncheon, as you suggested—perhaps sometime next week," said Nancy.

"Good day, ladies, it was a pleasure to meet you," said Madeline, as she excused herself and continued to the concierge desk.

Charles Winter, an older gentleman, perhaps in his fifties, with steel-colored hair, spoke with her, "I can't say as I recall this particular young lady, but it is strange, another young lady was here earlier looking for a friend of hers that also has gone missing. Two young women, and both seen in our hotel—it is peculiar. I will see that upper management is made aware of this."

Madeline was surprised and concerned about his statement.

"You say another girl has gone missing? Goose Island is one of the safest neighborhoods in Chicago and not the news someone is likely to hear."

"She was a lovely lass, as lovely as they come. I remember the photograph they showed me and remarked on it. Perhaps these two fine ladies have met young gentlemen and are just about the city enjoying its fine attractions," said Mr. Winter.

"I certainly hope you are right. Is there a possibility I may see the hotel registry to see if she had checked in?"

"I'm sorry, Miss. I'd have to get permission from the owners to let you do that. if you wait a minute, I'll look it over myself."

While Mr. Winter reviewed the last two weeks' registers, she gazed upon the many patrons walking through the lobby. There was an excessive amount of young ladies browsing the shops and gathering in the café.

"No, Miss, I don't see her listed. Is it possible she might have checked in under a different name?"

"That is unlikely. But if you could do me the favor of passing the information to the staff in the event someone saw her, I would be grateful."

"I will be happy to."

She left her contact information. However, in this bustling atmosphere, she doubted if anyone would consider two missing young ladies' plight as something of a concern.

It was a sea of women; she wondered if anyone would be able to tell one from another, even if they were intent on looking for just one particular woman.

After purchasing a copy of the Chicago Tribune, she walked back to the drugstore and looked for any news that might be relevant to her pursuit. On the third page, on the bottom, was a short article about discovering a dead woman's body near the stockyards. The paper stated they believed it might be a suicide. Her breathing rapidly increased as she went on reading the description. There were not many details. The unidentified dead woman was of average height, believed to be in her twenties, and dressed well. The death is under investigation, and the police asked for any information anyone might have as to who the victim was. There was always the possibility it was Maria.

She decided she must go to the police station to find out what she could. She hoped Rosa and Louie did not see the article.

A cabby took Madeline to the Maxwell Street Station. It was barely a year old, and according to the papers, was one of the finest police stations in the country. But Chicago was a growing metropolis, and compared to the population, policemen were in short supply.

When she arrived, people were everywhere, most of them arguing and demanding attention. She waited nearly two hours before a nervous, slender, young man named

Jimmy Parsons brought her to his desk.

"Now, what is it we can do for you today, Miss?" asked Mr. Parsons.

"I'm seeking information on behalf of a friend of mine. Their sister never returned from a trip into the city a few days ago. I have a picture of her with me. In light of what I read in the paper this morning about the poor girl from the stockyards, I wanted to be certain it wasn't Maria," said Madeline, handing him the photograph.

"I can probably narrow it down for you without even looking at the picture. Was she a blonde?" asked Mr. Parsons.

"No, she has black, wavy hair."

"Then it is not her. This unfortunate lady was a fine-looking blonde, a real stunner. What a terrible shame. Have your friends filed a missing person report?"

"I know they have spoken to someone, but they were to come back in a few days. It would seem that it would be a harsh request to make to a family panicked by this occurrence."

"Unfortunately, people come and go in a city like Chicago at a rapid pace. We barely have eight hundred officers for a city of almost a million people. Unless there is evidence of a crime, we simply don't have the manpower to investigate every young woman who has gone off sightseeing for a few days.

"Have you thought of hiring a private detective?"

"She did. That's why I'm here."

"You? I beg your pardon, Miss, but you are an unlikely person to be a detective."

"Perhaps for now, but soon women will hold many positions once thought of to be a man's job."

"I'll note your visit and try to follow up with you. It does seem we have had an unusual amount of people reporting young ladies that have not returned home. Most of the time it turns out they come home or have traveled elsewhere without their family being aware of it. Young ladies do not always like their family, knowing their every little secret."

"Hmm…to me, that scenario does not ring true in this case, Mr. Parsons. I would appreciate it if you would keep one of these photographs of Maria to show to the other officers."

"I will, Miss; I will post it on our board. I do understand your concern. I have a sister who has just turned twenty-one, and I don't imagine she would do a thing like that."

"Thank you. I'm sure I will return again. Should I ask for you?"

"Yes. As I have your information and will be aware of why you are here, I would be the best one to follow up with."

She left with a sense of relief that the deceased woman was not Maria, but she believed the young woman to be in danger. She would attempt to visit the places she felt a woman visiting the city might wish to see. Tonight, she would go to the McVicker's Theater.

Walking home, she found herself staring at every woman who passed her, but no one looked like Maria. The words Mr. Parsons spoke about missing women stayed with her and made her believe there was a greater possibility of foul play. She thought of the Ripper again, and it gave her a momentary chill that she physically shook off.

Arriving home, she found that her father was in the parlor with Louie Falco.

"Mrs. Donovan, excuse the intrusion, but I saw in the paper…"

"Wait, I know what you're going to say. It's all right, I just came from the police station, and the victim was a young blonde, and definitely not your sister."

With that said, Louie sank back into the divan, buried his head in his hands, and kept repeating, "Thank God, thank God," then added, "I could not bring myself to go. You don't know how relieved I am. Thank you for going. Your father was right to have introduced us. I see you do care about this, and despite being a woman, you may be able to help us."

She dismissed his comment about a woman's capabilities, knowing his concern for his sister caused him not to mince words. Besides, she knew that this was the consensus about women in business, and she would have to prove herself.

"Yes, I was also relieved. I will endeavor to cover more ground each day. You said your sister enjoyed plays so I will go to the McVicker this evening. It is the most well-known of the Chicago theaters and the closest to our area. I would think it might be a place she would have wanted to go."

"Rosa and I will continue our search in our neighborhood and then go into the market areas. Rosa, however, gets more despondent when we have no word from our Maria. Each day that passes now, I am more fearful that something terrible has happened to her."

"I know…that possibility certainly has to be met. How long has it been again?"

"It will be five days today with no word from her."

"I will contact you if I hear anything tonight, even if it

is late, I will get word to you. Otherwise, I propose that we meet again in the Sixth Street café in two days at six."

"I will try and bring Rosa with me if she is well enough," said Louie.

They said their good-byes, and Madeline watched him walk away with his eyes downcast to the street and his shoulders slumped. She imagined the fear that must be taking hold of him and hoped she could find something out that would lead her to Maria.

Her father was not home yet, and she wished she had someone to discuss all that had transpired. She decided she would write to Hugh. She gathered her writing materials at the window seat and began to write.

June 8, 1889

Dear Hugh,

I look forward to hearing from you soon and am anxious to know if you and the aunts have considered my offer to come and stay at Christmas-time.

Although I still have no storefront for my business, I have my first client from the most unlikely sources...my father. A brother and sister came to dinner the other night and told me of their sister's disappearance, who was visiting from New York. I believe she is in danger and have begun my investigation at a hotel built near my home. This story has a curious twist as I have also learned that several other inquiries were made concerning missing young women. Of course, the first thing I thought of was it possible that someone is preying on young girls, as Jack had done. As of yet, though, there have been no murders reported. Yesterday, however, a deceased woman was found at the Chicago stockyards. It is unknown whether this was an accident, by suicide, or by foul means that she died.

I wish you were here so that I could once again have your counsel on these matters and be in the presence of your steady on demeanor to quiet my mind.

She continued her letter describing her meeting with Marilyn and Nancy and her planned trip to the theater. She would write to Jonathan Franks, her friend, ally, and reporter at the New York Times, later in the day, and inform him of these mysterious disappearances.

Louie brought her additional photographs of Maria. She placed them in her satchel and prepared herself for her night out.

"It's been a long day, Madeline. I will enjoy our time together. If we hurry, perhaps we will have time to dine," said her father.

"That would be wonderful, Father."

It was socially compulsory that women's evening gowns show a woman's bare shoulders and be cut so that they reveal the bosom of a woman. It had been quite a while since Madeline had worn her provocative dark red gown, but accompanied by her father gave her the comfort level she needed to present herself in society in such attire again. The last time she dressed this fashionably, she was on the arm of her husband, Russell.

"Madeline, how beautiful you look! My darling girl has returned. It should not have taken the search for Miss Maria to bring you back to life. You must insert yourself back into the world again. You have taken such steps forward these last few months. I hope to see you enjoying the theater again soon, and without you father, but with a male admirer."

"I have thought about it, Father, but not just yet. Perhaps if Hugh or Jonathan were here, I might. I am all right. If it is to happen, it will. Besides, it adds intrigue to our evening out together, to be pursuing leads in my case."

Their carriage arrived at their destination on a moonless night. The air was warm and inviting, and the city's noise pervasive, making her feel a sudden excitement at the moment.

The words, William Shakespeare's *The Tempest,* was prominently displayed on a large sign outside. She had longed to see this play, but now the circumstances that brought her there had changed her plans. Instead of immersing herself in the excitement of seeing the play, she now sought to learn the whereabouts of young Maria.

After the Chicago fire of 1871, Louis Sullivan, the great architect, had designed the theatre to resemble an Athenian temple. The atmosphere created by his elaborate designs was one of awe. With a myriad of ornamental columns and at least a dozen mythological creatures painted on the walls, she felt she stepped into a lost place in time. Stenciled glass windows decorated the large auditorium. It was an attraction that lured the city's visitors, and Madeline believed Maria may have ventured to its captivating arms.

"Father, I would like to wait to be seated and mingle in the foyer for a bit. I'd like to show Maria's picture to the staff."

"I will have a glass of wine while I wait for you. I see Dr. Hill and his family. I think I will go over and pay my regards. I will wait for you at the main entrance," he replied.

She spoke to any employee who would give her a minute of their time, but they were scurrying about and reluctant to give her photo more than just a cursory glance. Then she approached an older man with thick white hair parted in the middle of his head and puffy reddish cheeks.

"Excuse me, sir. I wonder if you might look at this photograph. This young lady, Maria, has been missing these last few days, and her family believed she might have been here. I know you must meet so many people, but she is striking. Perhaps you remember her."

He stopped and handled the picture gingerly in his wrinkled fingers before scratching his head. He said nothing for a moment, then looked up at her and said, "Yes, I think it's her. Yesterday—no, wait, the day before yesterday—a young lady came up to me who became separated from her group of friends. She was quite frantic as she said she was not familiar with the area and was from out of town. New York, I think she said."

"Yes, yes," she interrupted him with a touch of his arm. "That must be her."

"She stayed with me for quite a while, both of us watching for her three friends. I believe she said there were two ladies and a gentleman. We never saw them; she thanked me and said she would take a carriage home. I remember her saying she hoped she had enough money to pay the fare and looking worried. I don't like to see a young girl alone without an escort, and I offered to accompany her if she waited till I was off duty—even told her I'd loan her the fare, but she would have none of it. She said if anyone inquired about her, to tell them she had returned to the hotel. After that, I remember seeing her leave through the main entrance and didn't see her again."

"You remember her specifically saying she would be returning to her hotel?"

"Yes. She didn't give me the name, and I assumed they might be all staying there together and would know what she was referring to. I do hope the young woman is all right. She was a delightful young woman."

"Thank you, Mister...?"

"Sam Thompson, and may I ask your name?"

"Madeline Donovan," she answered as she scribbled her contact information on a piece of paper and handed it to him.

"Please, if you should see her or if there are any inquiries about her, I would appreciate it if you would let me know. It is of critical importance."

"I will. I promise you; I will."

The theatre bell chimed, indicating the entrance doors were about to close. Madeline made her way back to her waiting father.

"I was beginning to think we would be locked out. I have not had the pleasure of going to the theater in a long time. I am looking forward to it," said Dr. Donovan.

"Yes, I am happy we are here together," said Madeline as she thought of Maria's family and the torment they must be going through.

Although a masterful work of art, *The Tempest* could not hold her attention, and Madeline found herself looking at every face that she could clearly see in the dimmed light of the theater. She knew it was a fruitless task, but she could not stop herself from staring, hoping to see someone who resembled Maria.

When they returned to the lobby during intermission, she said, "Father, one of the doormen believed he may have seen Maria. A small miracle, no doubt, but I think it was her. He said she became separated from her companions and said she would return to the hotel. Curious, don't you think that she said she would refer to a hotel instead of her sister's home? The Harrison Hotel has become my focal point now. Something untoward must be going on there."

"I believe this endeavor to be a detective is filled with risks, and the prospect of finding out the information you need is like threading a needle with a piece of yarn—an impossible task. Perhaps you should rethink this matter."

"If I can make a go of it, I will hire other females to help me, and perhaps even a man."

The doctor laughed as she took his arm and reentered the theater.

Instead of enjoying herself, her mind's eye only saw young girls being pulled from their rooms or abducted in the street.

At the end of the performance, she requested they enjoy Mrs. O'Malley's leftover stew instead of dining out.

She felt in a rush to return home.

After a hasty meal, she kissed her father good-night and hurried to her room. Her thoughts were twirling around in her head about the missing girls. Tomorrow she would return to the hotel, but tonight she would write to Jonathan and ask his opinion about the strange events happening so close to her home. Sitting at her writing desk, she began to write,

June 9, 1889
Dear Jonathan,
The most peculiar events have occurred over the last week. A family has employed me to find their missing sister. While attempting to do so, I have discovered that several other ladies have also been reported missing in the area. I wish you worked at one of the Chicago papers so that I could speak to you as we once did about Jack. I feel there must be a sinister presence that is connecting these disappearances. It seems unlikely to me that these missing women do not, in some way, have a direct link to each other.

She asked his advice on what he might do and requested that he write to her soon. She hoped the *Times* might send him to her city for some reason. Chicago was always making news of some kind, and it was not unusual to have journalists from around the country reporting on some sensational new invention or building going up.

Chapter 4

Felicia and Wanda

The morning found her with a renewed spirit to revisit this hotel, where all things seemed to converge.

The doctor had already left for his office when she came down for breakfast. Mrs. O'Malley smiled at her as she set her cup of tea down and said, "Miss, you had a visitor who came shortly after you left last night. Mr. Falco, the man from the other evening. He said it was important that he speak with you. He said he would be here before the noon hour."

"Oh...I had planned an early morning trip, but now I suppose it will have to wait."

"Did you enjoy the theater?"

"It proved a delight in every way. It was wonderful to be with Father. We so seldom go out together, and I may have gleaned some useful information pertaining to our missing Maria."

"I'm sure your Mr. Falco will be happy to hear that."

"Will you prepare a light lunch for us, Mrs. O'Malley? Nothing fancy, perhaps just some simple ham cuts and vegetables. That will do nicely."

"Of course. Will there be anything else?"

"No, I think I will try to put some thoughts on paper and see if I can organize a plan."

She returned to her room, musing over why Louie wished to see her. Perhaps Maria made contact with him. As she began writing in her journal, she hoped that was the case.

The Tribune reported that the identification of the woman found in the stockyards was still unknown. The report said that the manner of death was undetermined.

It was not quite eleven in the morning when she saw Louie hurrying up the steps of their home while sitting at the bay window.

"Come in, come in," Madeline said. "Mrs. O'Malley told me of your intent to visit us. Luncheon is ready, and I hope you will join us."

"Thank you. I would enjoy a cup of hot coffee if you have it," said Louie.

Seated at the dining table with Madeline, Louie pulled from his coat pocket several crumpled pieces of pink stationery.

"I wanted to bring these to you as soon as possible. Quite by accident, I found this piece of paper, with notations made by my sister, stuck inside one of her books. I believe these may be the names of the two girls she recently met. Rosa thinks she remembers hearing her say one of their names."

"That is, indeed, valuable information. May I see your paper?" asked Madeline.

The ink was somewhat smudged, and it was difficult to be certain, but it appeared the names were *Felicia Zugaj* and *Wanda Gapinski.*

"The names are clearer to read than the address, but perhaps someone in the area will know them," said Madeline. "I have to say I was hoping you had some good news and perhaps had heard from Maria."

"If only that were true, I would not be in the state I am. I'm sure you've noticed I have not been well. As each day passes, and there is no contact from her, I grow more alarmed. I cannot sleep and find myself walking the streets near the hotel, hoping to see her."

"I do understand your concern. I, too, believe her disappearance may have something to do with her being at the Harrison. These names, however, could prove very useful. How is Rosa holding up?"

"She is frantic. She also has spent time in every corner store and speaking to people in the street. The police have finally declared Maria a missing person, but do not give us much hope in resolving anything soon. They say there has been a rash of young girls reported missing. The only information that gives me hope is that he said most of the females were blondes, and of course, Maria is black-haired. If someone is assaulting fair-haired women, my sister should be safe."

"Well, certainly something is terribly amiss if they have given you such information. Did they say anything else?"

"No, he seemed reluctant even to give me that much information."

"I can see if Father can give you something for your nerves if you like, and I can assure you I will spend the rest of this day searching for clues. I will also see if I can find anything about the girls mentioned in your sister's note."

"Yes, I can come by this evening when your father is at home. Perhaps something for sleep, if he could do that for me, I would appreciate it."

"I will see you this evening, and I hope I will have some news for you."

She called to Mrs. O'Malley that she would be at the Harrison Hotel and that she would not return until the dinner hour at six. She hurried from her home as if someone was chasing her, feeling compelled to hasten her footsteps in her newfound pursuit of the girls Wanda and Felicia.

She had a partial address for Felicia. The words looked hurriedly written and read *Felicia Zugaj Hern-Goose.* Being unfamiliar with the area, Madeline assumed Maria meant to write Huron. Her neighborhood, named Goose Island, did have a street called Huron, which sounded close enough to Hern. She hoped she was right in her supposition that is what the note meant. For Wanda, there was no indication of a street address. Most of the area consisted of Polish and Italian immigrants, with a smattering of others, like herself, from various places. She decided to would walk to Huron Street first before going to the Harrison.

She began knocking on doors, hoping to find someone who knew the Zugaj family. People were friendly in Chicago and usually were not only aware of their neighbors were but knew all the gossip about them and would congregate in little huddles to talk about them.

There was one such group sweeping the streets, laughing, and speaking in broken English and Polish. Four gray-haired women, with plain day dresses, were gathered together on Huron.

"Excuse me, ladies; I am looking for the home of a friend of mine. She told me her address, but I have lost it, though I know her family lives on Huron. Would you know the Zugaj family?"

There was a flurry of talk in Polish among them, which she did not understand, but she did realize that the name of Zugaj caused them all to react.

A portly woman with kind eyes spoke, "Yes, yes, Felicia. We know her. Her family is most unhappy these days. Felicia has not come home."

Madeline was startled by her words and said, "She is missing! I am also looking for a young lady who has also gone missing, and her family is in great distress."

The older lady took her hand and said, "Yes, it is terrible news. We are all looking for our little Felicia. We would see her walk by all the time, always a kind word. I will take you to her house, but her mother is not good, but maybe if I go with you, she will speak to you."

The group of ladies followed behind them, continuing to chatter in high pitched nervous voices.

"We have all been very worried. We think something may have happened to her. She would never be one not to speak to her Mama. I am Mrs. Grotski," she continued as she shook Madeline's hand.

Mrs. Grotski introduced her other friends, and Madeline politely exchanged pleasantries, but her mind was whirling with this news of another missing girl, and could barely keep up with any of the conversation.

"This is it, dear," said the lady who said her name was Elsie Posninski. "She may not talk much; she is in a bad way these days."

"I can understand that. Perhaps just a few questions," said Madeline.

Elsie knocked several times, but no one came to the door. This time, she leaned over the stair railing and tapped on the window.

"Cecilia, it's me, Elsie. I have a visitor, and we would like to speak with you."

After a few minutes, they could hear rustling, and a drawn-looking stout woman wearing a stained apron that existed over her dark blue dress, said, "Come in…come in. I will be no good company but sit. I have coffee brewing, and I will get some for us."

Elsie shook her head in empathy for her friend Cecilia. "If it were my daughter that was missing, I'd look the same or worse. I don't understand it; this is a fine neighborhood. Everywhere you go, you can find a helping hand and a friendly face."

"I know. I don't recall anything like this happening before. It is strange and gives everyone cause for worry," said Madeline.

Cecilia returned to the room with a tray of demitasse cups and a silver pitcher of coffee. She was clutching a lace handkerchief in her hand and periodically stopped to wipe her eyes.

"My Felicia's now been gone for two days. She and her friend, Wanda, went out for the evening. I believe she said they were going downtown for supper. She said she wasn't certain what time she would be home, but that it would be before midnight, as she had to get to work early the next day.

"We asked all of her friends, but no one has heard from her. All the police said is that they will send someone out to look for her. They said not to worry, as these situations almost always turn out all right, with the girls showing up at a friend's or relative's house.

"I know it is the worse. Felicia and Wanda would not wander off. It is the worse," she said again, her voice trailing off as she buried her face in her hands.

Elsie put her arm around Cecilia, trying to comfort the woman, but she could not do so.

"If you will wait here, I will get Mrs. Gapinski. She lives right around the corner," said Elsie.

Madeline offered some hope as she said, "I am employed to seek the whereabouts of another young lady, and I shall look for your daughter as well. I promise I will do all I can to help."

When Mrs. Gapinski arrived, Madeline retold the story.

Mrs. Gapinski pleaded, "Please...please do what you can to find our daughters. We have done what we can, but we have no money, and the police do nothing."

With that, Mrs. Gapinski began to weep.

"I will stay with them," said Elsie.

"Yes, I will go. Here, this is my contact information," Madeline said as she hastily wrote down her information on a corner of a newspaper in Cecilia's home.

Things were going in the wrong direction. Not only did

she not have any concrete clues to Maria's whereabouts, but she'd also discovered more girls were missing. Madeline wiped her brow from the summer's heat and found she was not only flushed from warmth, but her left hand was shaking. This new development meant some menacing presence had drifted into their once-quiet neighborhood, and she felt a shiver of fear run through her.

She was walking back in the hotel's direction when she saw the familiar face of her dear Uncle Hank. He was speaking with some similar-clad men, all with dirt-stained shirts and wet, slick backs. He was wringing a grungy hat in his hands and speaking while waving to one of the men.

She called out to him, but he did not hear her. He began walking, and she hurried to meet up with him.

"Uncle Hank, wait! It's me, Madeline."

He finally turned, smiling and looking embarrassed about his appearance.

"Madeline, I was planning to come up for a visit once I got myself cleaned up. I hope you don't mind me," he said, trying to brush off some of the grit from his trousers.

"I've been out looking for Maria and have found out some startling facts. It's good to see a friendly face."

"I've found something out just this morning, and it's not good news."

"What is it?" she said, as she peered at his downturned face.

"I'd hardly like to be the one to tell you. I was coming home from work, taking my time, just walking, slow as I could be, stopping to talk to the street vendors, when I come across a crowd of folks in the street. Some of them were crying and carrying on, so I went up to see what the fuss was all about.

"There she was...a sight I never want to see again."

Uncle Hank stopped speaking for a moment, his eyes not meeting hers. Madeline touched his shoulder and said, "Please, go on. Oh...please, go on. Is it all that terrible?"

"They were all gathered around a young lady who was run over by a carriage. She just lay there, broken, not moving. Some ladies were crying, and the men were all yelling.

"Madeline, I think it was Maria—the Maria you were looking for. I have her picture and have watched for her as you asked, and I do think it was her."

"No, it can't be. Perhaps you're wrong."

"I suppose I could be. Will you go to Maxwell and find out?"

"Yes, I had planned to return home, but now I will go straight there first. This is the most upsetting news, Uncle Hank. When you arrive home, will you please tell Mrs. O'Malley that I'll be late coming home?"

"Of course, I will. I never heard of nothing like this going on before. Are you sure you will be safe?"

"There is still daylight for another hour or so. I should be home by dusk."

She watched Uncle Hank walk away; hoping that the news he brought her was not true. She secured a carriage and was bumping along the uneven road, overlooking the city go about its business; most of them unaware there was reason to fear the evil that had set itself on Erie Street.

She sat in the Maxwell Street Station for over an hour, waiting to speak to someone. This time, she had written confirmation from Louie Falco that she was able to represent the family. When she finally was able to speak to Officer Parsons, he confirmed that they believed it was Maria.

"She didn't have any identification on her, but she had several embroidered handkerchiefs with the initials *MF*. We have sent someone to the house of the family. I remember you; you were the one that was looking for her," said the officer.

"Yes, this is regrettable news, indeed. Was it an accident? Do you know anything about the circumstances?"

"We will be investigating that fact. We have many witnesses to the incident, but at the moment, we have conflicting information."

She went on to discuss with him her news of Felicia and Wanda's disappearance.

"It is a strange thing, indeed. We have an onslaught of reports of missing young girls. We have taken a great interest in this phenomenon. I agree with you that it cannot be just a coincidence. At the moment, we have no leads."

"I will go now to speak with the family to see if I can be of any assistance. They will require help. I will continue to search for the other girls."

"Be careful. If you were my sister, I don't believe I would like it. You might be putting yourself in the path of danger."

"Perhaps, but I will continue just the same. Thank you for your concern."

She shook his hand and left the station. She walked with her head down, consumed now with thoughts about Maria and a past case involving a young woman named Polly. She remembered distinctly how it felt to deliver the news to the girl's aunts, that Polly, one of the Ripper's victims, was gone. She would have to face Rosa and Louie, look into their eyes, and meet the torment she knew she would find there when they discovered the terrible truth.

Hailing a cabby, she looked out over the city she loved, wondering now if she could ever see it in the same way after these recent events.

She planned to go straight home but abruptly stopped the driver when she saw the Harrison Hotel come into view. She thought she might question the concierge again about Wanda and Felicia.

The doorman greeted her warmly, and she attempted a forced smile in return. Still immersed in thoughts about Maria, she was surprised to hear her named called from a distance.

"Madeline, hello, Madeline," said Marilyn as she walked closer to her.

"Marilyn, how are you? I see you are here with your sister, in your favorite spot at the café."

"Yes, we are here often. We enjoy doing our studies here. It is a pleasant way to do the work, and it is not very busy during the mid-day, so the owner does not mind us taking up the space.

"I can see by the look on your face that you are quite troubled," proclaimed Marilyn.

"May I join you, and I will tell you both about it?"

"Of course, it would be my pleasure."

They walked back to the table where the twins were partaking in their afternoon tea and pastries.

"I am so happy to see you. My head is swimming with unhappy news. Do you remember the young lady, Maria, who I said I was searching for? I learned an accident occurred. The wheels of a carriage crushed a woman. I have just returned from the police station, and an officer I spoke with confirmed her death.

"It all seems strange. First, she goes missing with no contact with her family and then meets with this tragic end. It doesn't make any sense. I know there must be more to it than that."

"I cannot imagine how the poor family will take this news. In the past day or two, there have been times when you could overhear people passing and speaking of these missing girls. It has reached a level of concern among the people in the neighborhood. We all are seeking answers to what has become of them," said Marilyn.

"If there is any way we may be of assistance to you, Madeline, please tell us," said Nancy.

"I may well do so. As you are frequent visitors to the hotel, you are unique to have intimate knowledge of this establishment. I am certain now that this hotel holds many secrets and is in some way involved in their disappearance," said Madeline.

"Truly, do you think that? But it seems such a respectable and notable hotel. Perhaps we should not frequent this place. I am not so brave as to put myself or my sister in danger," said Nancy.

"As long as you are together and only come during the

daylight hours, I don't believe you could be in danger of any kind, but, of course, it would be wise to be on your guard nonetheless.

"Perhaps I am wrong, but I think I will spend more time here, and I will try to speak with the management to see if I can find out anything more," said Madeline.

"You can count on us. I believe that is Mr. Thomas by the concierge desk. I think he is the assistant manager of the hotel," said Nancy.

"Thank you. I will see if he will speak to me. I hope to see you both soon," said Madeline as she excused herself from the table.

"Mr. Thomas…Mr. Thomas," Madeline called out.

A short, stout man with salt and pepper curly hair responded, "Do I know you, Miss?"

"Oh…no, a friend of mine pointed you out and informed me you were in a management position, and I wondered if I could have a word with you."

"Certainly…there is an empty table for two by the window. We shall have a lovely view while we speak."

"I'm sure you are aware, Mr. Thomas, that several young ladies, who have recently gone missing, frequented this hotel. One of the ladies is deceased while the whereabouts of the other remains unknown. Could you tell me if there has been an event or some reason these girls would have been here at the hotel?"

"Young lady, The Harrison has deservedly been named one of the best new hotels in the city, if not the best. Its reputation is impeccable and has the finest clientele. Chicago is booming and draws all to its welcoming arms, as does the Harrison.

"There has been a fair recently near here, as well as some historical exhibitions. The number of people coming in and out of our doors, just for refreshments and shopping is inestimable. Now, does that answer your question?"

"Not exactly...did you know if any of the girls were frequent visitors?"

"That would be a question I would answer only from the authorities. I hope you do not think me rude, but that is hotel business."

"I do understand, of course. I am only here at the request of family members. I will convey your sentiments on the matter," she said sarcastically.

"Now, let us not be too hasty. Let me see what I can find out for you."

"Is it possible to speak with the owner?"

"My dear, the three brothers who own the Harrison are rarely here...business, you know. It takes them all around the city and out of the country. However, I will note your request and see what I can do when one of them is available."

"Thank you."

He left to speak with a young man standing near the elevator, who she later learned was the brothers' assistant, Alfred.

He returned a few minutes later and said, "Apparently, there were a considerable number of young women here two weeks ago for some fashion event. Perhaps you can start there. The business that ran the event was...let's see...oh, here it is, House of Morgan. Here is their contact information."

"And my other request...to speak to one of the brothers?"

"I will let their personal assistant know of your request, but I believe it unlikely. We here at the hotel, of course, aspire to know what happened to the girls and are hopeful they shall all return to their families without incident."

"Yes, of course. That is what we all wish. Good day, sir."

Returning home, she seemed to arrive at her doorstep as if without knowledge of how she got there; her thoughts occupied with the inevitable conversation she would have with Rosa and Louie about Maria and her growing concern over the other missing girls.

Her father met her at the door, embracing her and saying, "Madeline, Henry told me what happened. It is too awful. I am so glad you are home safe. I was so worried about you knowing you had such news. Those poor dear souls, their lives will never be the same. Will you be going to see them?"

"I must, Father. I may be an unwelcome visitor. They may wish to be alone with their grief, but I must go and offer my condolences and see if there is anything at all that I may do to help them."

"Then let me grab my bag. They may require a sedative or something medical that I may be able to help them with."

"Thank you, Father. I think you are right, assuming, of course, that they already have been told by the police about their sister."

"Yes, of course. It certainly wouldn't be our place to do that. If they do not know, I think perhaps you should suggest you take a trip to the Maxwell Station to check on any current information."

"Good idea. Let's hurry, Father. We will be back as soon as we are able, Mrs. O'Malley."

Chapter 5

A Time to Cry

Dr. Donovan hailed a cabby and patted her hand several times while they rode together.

"This is a tragedy...a tragedy, Madeline. Promise me you will be extremely careful while you pursue these missing ladies. I agree with you now that there must be something more going on than a few young ladies caught up in the fervor of the atmosphere of the city and innocently staying away."

They lived within close proximity to Rosa and arrived within a short time.

"Father, our question as to whether they know about Maria has been answered for us. Look, an officer is standing on their porch and another at the foot of the stairs."

He squeezed her hand as they descended from the carriage and proceeded to Rosa's home. The officer stopped them and said, "I'm sorry, no one is allowed inside without the family's expressed permission. It is a private matter."

"I see. Will you please say Madeline Donovan is here with her father? He is a physician and is here to help if it is requested."

The tall, thin, youthful man strode up the steps and returned within moments.

"You may go in," he said curtly, nervously pulling at his jacket. Like Madeline and her father, she assumed that the people here were uncomfortable with the task at hand. In some way, all sharing in the family's loss, knowing that although they could sympathize and comfort, they could never understand the profound grief the family was feeling.

Louie came out to meet them, looking dazed, wiping his forehead where drops of sweat accumulated.

"We have just learned the news. I have not gone to identify that it is our Maria, but the officer had her picture with him and confirmed it was her. Rosa is in a state of shock, as you can well imagine. She has all but collapsed upon her bed. Perhaps Dr. Donovan, if you could look in on her," requested Louie.

"Of course, I will go at once. I anticipated Rosa would need something for anxiety and someone to comfort her," said the doctor.

"Madeline, I must go to the coroner's office. Would you accompany me?" asked Louie.

"Yes, I will assist you in any way that I can. Our housekeeper, Mrs. O'Malley, is making soup and stew for you.

"Our carriage is still here. I had asked the driver to wait if you did not wish to see us," she replied.

"I cannot think. It is overwhelming. There is a part of me that wants to believe it will not be my sister, but I know that is unrealistic. I was concerned but made myself think she had gone off and had a romantic rendezvous. I suppose I never allowed myself to think the worse, and now it has arrived."

"I don't know what to say except how truly sorry I am. I had hope also for a positive outcome."

They continued speaking while riding in the carriage, Madeline relating to Louie what she had learned.

When they arrived, they were ushered in quickly to a waiting area. Momentarily, the coroner came, a stern-looking older man with trimmed brown hair and a bushy mustache.

"Please, come in. Rosa is in here. It is not an easy thing to do. Do you need a moment?" asked the gentleman.

"No, please, I need to see this through," said Louie.

"Come then," replied the man.

The area was ripe with death. Seven or eight cadavers were lying beneath stark white sheets. Madeline trembled as she walked past them, noticing the toe of one person, tagging and falling out from beneath the sheet. She would be glad to leave with as much haste as was possible.

The man pulled back the cover, and Louie grabbed onto the table, leaning over his sister's now deceased body. He moaned but did not cry or say one word for several minutes. The man and Madeline stood beside him, respectively, giving him this moment.

"What exactly killed her? Did the carriage crush her?" he asked.

"It appears so. You can see here," the coroner said as he pointed to her neck and what appeared to be a bulging where the break occurred.

He pulled back the sheet and asked, "She has jewelry, which I am sure you might wish to remove."

As Louie retrieved her rings and necklace, Madeline touched his arm. "Look there, her wrists. There are bruises around both of them. Certainly, the accident could not have caused that? Bruises don't form that quickly."

"You are right. We have not yet done a full autopsy, but the markings on Maria's wrists would have no bearing on her death."

"Would they be from some type of struggle or having her wrists bound?" asked Madeline.

"I suppose that is a possibility. Why? Was she accosted in some way before her accident?" asked the man.

"She was missing for many days," replied Louie, "we don't know what may have happened to her."

"Now that you have made the identification, we will call you within a few days with a full report. Again, we are sorry for your loss," said the coroner.

Louie held the few jewelry items that he had taken from his sister and a lock of hair he clipped from her head.

"This is all, Madeline, all that I have left of this once vibrant, beautiful woman. I had not seen her for so long, and when she finally arrives, the most unspeakable of events happen," then he added with an urgent look on his face, "You will go on investigating. I must know what happened. I do not believe this was an accident. These events are peculiar."

"Yes, the bruises. It doesn't make sense…possibly made

by binding the wrist. I will do my best to find out what happened to her. Have the police told you anything?"

"I don't know if they will follow up. Supposedly, it was a simple accident. The police believe that possibly drink or drugs incapacitated Marie. At least, that is what I overheard one of the officers stating. I don't believe with that attitude that they will be thorough if those thoughts are at the forefront of their thinking. I am dismayed by everything that has happened. I am not thinking clearly, and I will need to be Rosa's support. I am asking you to continue the search to find out what is going on here."

"I will. You have my word on it. I'm sure my Father will give you something to calm you should you need it. I will contact you if there are any new developments. In the meantime, call on Father and me if you just need someone to talk to."

"Thank you, Madeline. We will have to plan her funeral now. There will be much to do. Take care, and I am sure we will be speaking soon."

She hugged his slumped-over body, feeling helpless that there was nothing she could do for him now except to find the truth about what happened to his sister.

When she arrived home, her father had already returned.

"Miss Rosa is in a state. She did calm down somewhat after I gave her a small draft of opium. What an unspeakable thing to have happened! That poor girl, I wonder what state of mind she was in to have put herself in such danger."

"Father, I don't believe it could have been an accident.

What if she ran to get away from someone, which caused her to run in front of the carriage? Was about pushing her?

"Madeline, this is not London, with its madman, Jack the Ripper. It is Erie Street, a peaceful, lovely community of friends and neighbors. I think you are letting your imagination run away with you."

"We'll see. Perhaps I am assuming the worse for no reason, but something is going on within our community, and it is neither healthy nor peaceful."

"By the way, you have a letter from your gentleman friend."

"How wonderful! I miss them all so much, Father. It is a treat to hear from any of them, but especially Hugh."

"I did not say it was Hugh. It may have been Jonathan."

"Oh..."

"No, you are correct. It is Hugh," he said as he watched her blush at the mention of his name.

"So, he is the one who has captured your attention. I thought you said you liked them both the same."

"I do. I suppose I had been thinking of London so often; I assumed it was from Hugh."

"Hmm....well, go on and read your news. I am leaving for my office."

She retrieved her letter and a cup of tea and went onto the porch. Her letter from Hugh would be a welcome respite from the events of these past days.

She could hear Mrs. O'Malley humming in the kitchen, and somehow, her familiar lyrical tones made the world a nicer place to be.

She opened the letter carefully, as if not to disturb its contents in any way.

June 2, 1889
Madeline,

I have been so busy of late that I have neglected to write to you. But I hope you will be pleased when I tell you of my startling news.

A cousin of mine, twice removed, who I had been very close to as a child, met with a riding accident. Unfortunately, it resulted in his death. Unexpectedly, he has left me a considerable amount of money. At least, substantial enough that it will make a significant change in my life.

I plan a leave of absence from my law practice and will come to your native Chicago for an extended visit. I hope to purchase land there to spend time both in London and Chicago in the future.

I have been diligently working on the plans to come and already booked my passage on the City of New York. Now I will get to see her as you did, not just at a glance, but as a passenger. Phillip, of course, will be working, and I will have him for company. He also is planning to stay a few days in Chicago with me until he is required to return to the ship.

I hope this news that I will be coming to see you will be as delightful to you as it is to me. I have told the aunts, and they are already busy embroidering something or other for you. They say they still plan someday to come on coming to see you sometime soon.

Please write back at your earliest convenience. I hope to hear from you before my departure, which will be in three weeks.

Your dearest friend,
Hugh Scott

What wonderful news, she thought. If ever she needed the sight of a friendly face and a confident, it was now. It had taken almost ten days for Hugh's letter to arrive, so she decided to write back immediately in the hopes he might receive it before he left.

June 12, 1889
Hugh,

I received your letter and read it with such happiness as I have not had for a while. As I have told you about my recent escapades into a female detective's life, I'm sure it won't be a complete shock that some very unpleasant news has happened. The young woman I had been seeking was found dead. I will go into greater detail when I see you. Many mysterious events are occurring in my once-quiet life on Erie Street.

I hope you will consider staying with us. We have a three-flat, and the upper floor is vacant. It is not large and not furnished in the grandest style, but I hope, nonetheless, that you might wish to stay with us. It is large enough to accommodate both you and Phillip.

I will look forward with great anticipation to your safe arrival.
Your friend,
Madeline

She thought it necessary to post the letter immediately. The post office was within a block of the Harrison Hotel, and she could stop there as well.

As usual, the Harrison was busy with a crowd of people perusing its shops and partaking in a meal at one of its three cafes. She was disappointed to see that neither Nancy nor Marilyn was at their usual spot at the French café.

Madeline again asked the concierge if it were possible to speak to one or more of the three brothers who owned the hotel but refused. She purchased a newspaper outside and now went to the cafe for a cup of tea. She could read the paper as a guise while observing the people. She was about to be seated when she felt a tug on her arm.

A heavyset, elderly woman, with gray hair piled high on her head and silver spectacles sliding down her nose, was staring at her.

"I've seen you here several times, and I heard you asking about my boys again. What is it you want of them if you don't mind me asking?"

"Your boys? I'm not sure what you mean," replied Madeline.

"You keep pestering, my friend, Mr. Thomas, and I have to tell you I don't like it. What do you want with them, the Harrison boys?"

"Do you mean the owners of this hotel?"

"None other."

"Are they your sons?"

She laughed then, a belly laugh that made her plump stomach jiggle beneath her elegant beaded gown.

"They may as well be, for they treat me like their own mother, and I love them as my own. I lost my own boy many years ago to the polio. I knew them and their mother when they were young, and they have let me stay here for such little money, you'd think I was their mother."

"I see. I meant no offense. I am sure they are great men. Certainly, they are successful men. But you see, there are missing young ladies—perhaps in some danger—and many of them seen at this hotel. I feel the Harrison's must look into it. At the very least, to have their staff look into it, to see if someone who's staying here may have some connection to these disappearances."

"You can ask me. It would be just the same as asking them. I know everything about the goings on here. I don't stay in my room much. I like to mingle with the people. If there's anybody who would know anything, it would be me. Ask away."

Madeline took the pictures she had of Maria and the other girls and showed them to the woman.

"These are the girls I am looking for. By the way, may I ask your name?"

"It's Mary Brooks, but they call me Lady Mary around here. That's respect—they all know I have my connections with the Harrisons," she said with an air about her and a tilt of her head upward.

"Now, let me get a good look at these girls."

She held the pictures in her hand, tracing her fingers over the lines of their faces. She kept her head down for several minutes, turning and shuffling each picture back and forth. Madeline thought it odd the way Mary concentrated on each one, but given her personality, Madeline then dismissed it.

When Mary finally looked up, she didn't look her in the eye and said, "No, quite sure. I can tell you none of these girls have been in this hotel. I'd stake my life on it. Quite sure, yes, quite sure."

"You seemed a little startled when you first glanced at the pictures. Are you certain you have seen none of them?"

"Startled—heavens, no! That's just an old lady's nerves coming out. I tell you I would remember fine-looking girls like these. Now, you see, you have no reason to talk to the boys."

"I appreciate your time, Mrs. Brooks...I mean, Lady Mary. May I get you a cup of tea or a pastry?"

"No, it's my time to sit out on the patio. The sun is almost setting. It's the best time of the day, and everyone stops to talk to me."

"Well, thank you again. I'm sure I will see you again when I come to visit the Harrison."

Now Madeline was captivated. There was no doubt that Lady Mary was lying, but was it as simple as she felt the need to protect "her boys," or was it more than that. Madeline felt sure Lady Mary had seen either one or all of the girls. She had watched her body language. Although she could not see her face, the way she reacted when she looked at Maria's picture gave her pause to think Lady Mary had seen her. She felt clues to what happened to these girls were at the Harrison.

Walking home, she felt a new purpose and resolve in getting to the bottom of this mystery. What she believed was only supposition had now turned into a reasonable belief. She knew the Harrison brothers were guilty of misconduct, but how far did that go? Could it include murder?

It was after seven when she arrived home. Her father, Uncle Hank, and Mrs. O'Malley were all gathered in the dining area, enjoying their coffee and some leftover cherry pie.

"Madeline, we waited dinner for you, but when you did not come, we dined without you. I had Mrs. O'Malley save you a plate of food. Would you like it now?" asked Father.

"No, thank you. I ate a salad at the cafe. I wasn't very hungry, but I do think I will join you for some dessert."

"Louie came by and said they would have a private closed-casket wake tomorrow, with only immediate family invited. He said the news reporters have already been diligent in their attempts to interview him. He asked that you call on him in a few days after she is at rest," said her father.

"How did you find his sister?" asked Madeline.

"She was inconsolable and incoherent. "She muttered, 'It can't be true.' " over and over again. But she gave in to sleep quickly after I gave her the sedative of opium. Opium can be destructive, but in small amounts can be a blessed relief from pain."

Yes, Madeline thought, remembering the times when she used opium to reduce the sting of her bouts of grief. For her, though, she was still paying the price from the withdrawal of the drug. Her headaches were constant, and she still had moments like these when she craved to use the drug again.

"I'm certain it will be a while before she can cope with her loss, but I think Louie will be strong for all of them. When we went to view the body, the most curious of things she had marks on her wrists, which appeared as an injury from being constrained. There was a delineation of a circle around both her wrists," said Madeline.

"I don't understand how those horses trampled her. The noise is so loud, how could she have run in front of them?" said Uncle Hank.

"You were there just a short time after the incident. Do you remember anyone who was there that might have been witness to the event?" asked Madeline.

"There was much commotion—people were screaming and running, but the usual couple of men, the street vendors, were there. I think one man's name is Jacob. He's the one who sells potatoes and watermelons. He's always singing when he pushes his cart along the street. He's not one you likely forget. I would start with him," suggested Hank.

"That is useful information. I will seek him out tomorrow. I think I will retire now and write to Jonathan and tell him of this latest news."

She told her father earlier about Hugh coming to America, and she inquired, "You are certain you will have no objection to Hugh staying with us?"

"How could you even ask? That young man was so hospitable and kind to us when we were there. How could we do otherwise?"

"I have not heard yet whether he has accepted. I hope he will, but sometimes he can be very British and may think it improper."

"He did not feel so when taking you in when you were ill. I certainly hope he will stay. I look forward to seeing him again."

"I'm happy to hear that. He is a special friend. I think you will like him also, Uncle Hank."

"If he is a friend of yours, of course, I will," he said as he smiled at her and squeezed her hand.

When she was in her room, she held the pictures of her family...now gone from her for almost two years. Russell, Nate, and Will would always be the last faces she would see every night as she kissed the photograph of them that sat at the table by her bed.

"Sometimes, I miss you all so much. I think I cannot tolerate another day on this earth. But I know I am fortunate to have Father, Uncle Hank, and Mrs. O'Malley. They are all so good to me. Still..." she said softly.

She had hoped to rest, choosing to read some poetry by candlelight, but she was consumed with the thoughts of the missing girls out there somewhere. She was still not asleep by midnight and decided to return to her favorite window seat in the main living area. Taking her stationery with her, she positioned herself within the moonlight that cascaded into the room. She was comforted by the thought that Hugh would soon be here. She could once again seek his counsel on all manner of things. But for now, Jonathan Franks, her other dear friend, and advocate was on her mind.

June 19, 1889
Jonathan,

I hope this letter finds you well. One of my father's patients has employed my services as a detective. My first case has seen me in the midst of the most unusual of circumstances. I can tell you that I have often thought of you and wished I could speak to you about it. I believe it would be a story you would cover if you were here in Chicago.

A man hired me to find his sister, who had gone missing while on vacation here. The most unfortunate of ends found her meeting her death in a gruesome way—trampled under the wheels of a carriage. There are also several other girls missing. I don't suppose you would have heard of this news in New York, as it has barely made the news in Chicago. The article referring to it is hardly even noticeable, placed on today's paper's twentieth page.

My other news is more pleasant; Hugh Scott is coming to America and should be here within ten days or so. I wish you were also here so that we may have a reunion of sorts.

She continued for two more pages describing the city with all its summer festivals, dotting the landscape, and wrote an entire page about the Harrison and its unique atmosphere. She ended with,

Please write soon and let me know if you might visit our fair city anytime soon during the time Hugh will be here. I believe he will stay through October.

Your faithful friend,

Madeline

She stayed another hour looking out the bay window onto the street. Now and then, a couple walking hand in hand went by, or a stray cat scampered by. She remembered the times she and Russell would take strolls after midnight before the children were born. Sometimes now it seemed as if it never happened. She wished again for the intimacy of a relationship. She had once thought she would remain a widow for the rest of her life, but she had begun to rethink those thoughts.

Returning to her room, she nodded to the photograph of her family one more time before drifting into sleep.

Chapter 6

Investigation

The next few days she spent speaking to any person she could find might have witnessed Maria's accident. The street vendor Uncle Hank mentioned, Jacob, proved to have given her valuable information. He stated that he had noticed Maria immediately; that she stood out not only for her beauty but for the frightened look that was upon her face. He said she moved through the street, almost in a frantic zigzag manner.

Madeline planned on returning to see Jacob that day and brought the other missing girls' pictures with her.

Jacob was not hard to find; he had a booming voice and dressed as if he were a troubadour touring with a stage production. His handlebar mustache—trimmed to perfection, and his scarlet red vest and patchwork pants compelled one to look at him.

"Jacob," she called out, "Do you have a moment to talk?" asked Madeline.

"If you wait a few minutes, Miss—I'm almost sold out, and then I can speak to you."

He continued calling out, "Po-tay-toe—wa-ter-me-low" as his customers came up to him for their purchases.

She was close enough to the Harrison that she could observe the people lingering outside the hotel. She thought she saw Marilyn walk in, but there was a stream of people moving in and out of the ornate doors, and she couldn't be sure. She thought again of what Lady Mary said and how certain she was about not seeing the young girls. It seemed an impossible statement to make, one Madeline felt could be said only in defense of someone. There were too many people that frequented the establishment. People sometimes gathered outside just to look at the structure of the building, a masterpiece of architectural design. She thought, *How could she be so definitive about her reply. She was only trying to protect the Harrisons. I'm sure of it!*

Jacob pulled his cart back from the street and motioned for her to come toward him.

She handed him the pictures as he wiped his brow with a bright red handkerchief.

"I can't say for certain. I wish I could tell you I saw them. This one," he said, pointing to Wanda. "I may have seen her. She has the unusual color of blond hair that is almost white and those fancy glasses. I may her saw her walking about. That probably won't help you much, but now that I have seen them, I will make it a point to watch for them.

"One thing further, I do remember. I'm glad you came 'round. The more I think about it; I think there may have been someone chasing her. Maybe it is just my imagination, but I recall now a man coming up behind her. It happened so fast—I couldn't tell you much more than it was a man. I tried to remember if he was tall or large, and I couldn't say for sure."

"Did you happen to see what direction he walked away?"

"No...to tell you the truth, after that, I had put my cart down and went to see if I could be of any help to the poor girl."

"Do you think it possible that he may have interfered with the girl? I mean, could he have pushed her or in any way caused the accident to happen?" asked Madeline.

"I couldn't exactly say that. I'm not even certain of what I saw. I suppose he could have, but there were so many people in the street and carriages moving about, I think it would be hard to tell something like that. Of course, unless you were standing right beside them, but if that were the case, I suppose someone would have told the police."

"I suppose you are right, but it is not the type of accident that is common. Especially if I may offer my opinion, women tend to be very careful around the street, much more so than men. I do hope it proves to be just an accident after all."

"Do you think it might be otherwise?" asked Jacob.

"There are too many unusual things going on in our quiet little neighborhood. Because of that, it makes me wonder if it was an accident at all, but perhaps done deliberately."

"I will keep an eye out. You can count on me," he said as he turned back to his cart.

She would pass the Harrison on her return home and knew she must stop if only to observe. As she walked by the doorman and then into the lobby, she hoped she might be fortunate enough to see Marilyn or Nancy there.

An event was in process; a local artist was displaying his paintings for purchase and was in the process of painting a young boy sitting on his mother's lap. It was the type of scene that brought smiles to the faces of the onlookers. A gathering of twenty or so people had formed a circle to watch him paint.

Madeline could not resist taking her place and observing him. Someday, she promised herself, she would return to her passion for painting watercolors and oils, but she still did not feel she was in the state of mind to produce anything of beauty. The artist was shamefully young and did not appear to be more than seventeen or eighteen years of age. But, she surmised, he must have studied abroad because he was masterful at what he was doing. Immersed in watching his long, beautiful brushstrokes and the way he was capturing the light around the boy's face, she did not immediately respond to the tug on her arm. The next time, it was more forceful, and she turned to see Lady Mary peering at her as if she were an interloper in the old woman's living quarters.

"You're here again. Why? I hope you have a good reason, and you're not just trying to mind everyone else's business."

Madeline was about to speak when Marilyn appeared between them and grabbed her hand in welcome.

"I was hoping to see you today. I thought perhaps Vincenzo's art display might bring you here. Many on my street have come to watch him at work."

"Lady Mary, this is my friend, Marilyn. I am here to have lunch with her, so please set your mind at rest as to any devious plot on my part," Madeline said as she laughed, trying to put Lady Mary at ease in the hopes she would not continue her hound-dog pursuit of watching her every move.

"How do you do? I've seen you here. I'm sure you're a good girl, so studious. I'll leave you both to be," Mary said as she walked away.

"What was all that about?" asked Marilyn.

"I have much to tell you. I see Nancy seated in your favorite spot. May I join you for a cup of tea?"

"Oh...please. We are anxious to hear any news about your investigation."

She took her seat among the two girls, grateful for a familiar face and to share their company.

"Tell me about that old woman. She has such a sweet appearance, like a cuddly little lamb. I've often seen her here, but the way she spoke to you startled me. What brought on her hostility towards you?" asked Marilyn.

"I've been here many times trying to speak with the elusive Harrison brothers. They are never here, or if they are, it is unlikely anyone would allow me in to speak with them, but I keep trying. I thought that perhaps if I became an annoyance, they might agree, just to be rid of me. Lady Mary has a personal connection of some kind with them. I presume she feels I am, in some way, a threat. She has overheard me speaking with the concierge and inquiring about the missing girls. She is a permanent resident and claims she is a fixture around here and knows everything," said Madeline.

"I can certainly attest to the fact that I have seen her here many times," said Nancy.

"Has she ever spoken to you?" asked Madeline.

"No, not that I recall. I've seen her just wandering about, sometimes taking tea at the outside courtyard with an elderly gentleman," continued Nancy.

"Tell us about your other news. Have you had any progress in finding your Maria?" asked Marilyn.

"Yes, unfortunately. It was not a good outcome—Maria is deceased. She was trampled by a carriage not far from here. My Uncle Hank was coming home from work and was one of the first people on the scene. He recognized her from the photograph we had of her. As you can imagine, the family is inconsolable."

"But at least she did not meet with foul play; there must be some comfort in that," said Nancy.

"I'm not at all certain that the death was accidental. I spoke with Jacob, one of the street vendors, and he observed the entire event and had the impression someone followed the woman," said Madeline.

She did not tell them about the marks on Maria's wrists or that she thought it was Lady Mary who had been pursuing her. She believed the family would not want her to reveal specific personal facts.

"It is disturbing. There is uneasiness in the air. I hear people sometimes whispering about the missing girls," said Marilyn.

"There is a request I have to make. I don't know whether you will fulfill it, but I was present at the coroner's and viewed Maria's body. There seemed to be a light spray of white powder on one of her sleeves and near her collar. I know Louie has preserved everything; in the hopes there might be some hidden evidence. I was wondering if I brought you the dress, would you be able to analyze the powder in your lab at school?" asked Madeline.

"I'm not sure. I've never done anything like that, but what a challenge. I certainly will try."

"I'll come with you. We can use the lab after hours," said Nancy.

"Then I will call you when I secure the clothing. Perhaps we can meet back here at The Harrison," said Madeline.

They continued their visit for a little while longer, with the twins said there were an unusual number of young girls who came in groups to the hotel. They didn't stay long and sometimes whisked off to another area. Both girls considered it peculiar. When she left them, she felt grateful for their assistance and their observations. Madeline wrote this in her notes. She would be glad when Hugh arrived, and she had someone to speak to about the Harrison and its curious activities.

When she arrived at her residence, the aroma of baking apples and cinnamon lingered in the air. She knew Mrs. O'Malley must have baked her father's favorite apple pie. It was good to be home.

Mrs. O'Malley walked through the swinging kitchen door into the dining area and said, "Your father will be home shortly, Miss, and you have a special-delivery letter waiting for you."

"Thank you, Mrs. O'Malley, and thank you for baking Father's favorite pie. It smells wonderful."

"If ever a man deserved it, it's your father. He's a saint of a man, that one."

"You won't get an argument from me on that, but you are too. The way you take care of us is nothing short of saintly."

Mrs. O'Malley smiled a broad, sheepish grin as her shoulders moved back in pride. "Now..."

"Don't even try to deny it. You know there's no one quite like you."

Madeline sometimes was remiss in appreciating the treasured Mrs. O'Malley and decided she would be more forthcoming with praise for her. These disappearances had made her think of her family and friends and how important they were to her.

She went back to the main room to the table stand, where Mrs. O'Malley left the incoming post. There she found Hugh Scott's ship-to-shore telegram awaiting her.

June 24, 1889

Madeline,

I was delighted to receive your letter. It arrived right before I left to embark on my journey to America. I would be happy to accept your invitation to stay for a few days until I can secure lodging, for I would not like to impose for too long a time.

The seas have been rough, and I stay in my cabin with a severe case of seasickness, but Phillip tells me tomorrow should bring calmer seas. I hope so; I do not wish to arrive looking like a bedraggled dog, which I feel like now.

I am anxious to hear of your adventures on Erie Street and look forward to seeing you and your father. Please give him my regards.

The ship is due to arrive in New York on or about June 26th,
and my train trip to Chicago should have me arriving on the 29th.
Your friend,
Hugh

Today was the 28th of June; the weather had cooled just
enough that the breeze blowing through the open window
made the rooms comfortable. Hugh would be here when
the weather should prove enjoyable and stay until the
advent of autumn and its cornucopia of changing leaves.
After reading the news that he would be there in just one
day, her excitement was evident as she ran to tell Mrs.
O'Malley.

"Mrs. O'Malley, he will be here tomorrow. Imagine that,
after so many months, I will see my friend again. Through
the darkness, there is a wondrous light that gives us such
reason to live. May we have something special for dinner?"

"Is this Mr. Scott you are referring to?"

"Yes, of course, the most charming, Mr. Scott. You will
think him quite the gentle, kind soul; I am certain."

"It is good to see you smile and have some spark back
in your eyes. Your father will enjoy having the young man
here. He has spoken of Hugh with great praise."

"As he deserves. I feel guilty to have such joy in my heart
with all the pain the Falco's have laid at their door."

"Nonsense. You have taken on this job of detective to
help others, but in that, you cannot deprive yourself of all
happiness. It would be an unwise choice to continue, for
I'm sure you will find many a fallen tree in the forest you
are entering."

"Of course, you are right. Joy brings us strength so
that we can go on. I must look into my wardrobe to find

something suitable to wear when I meet him at the train depot."

After laying her clothes out for her meeting with Hugh, she decided to visit Louie and Rosa. It had been several days since the funeral, and she hoped they might be ready to speak with her about Maria.

When she arrived, the house was eerily quiet, and a lady, who said she was a cousin, seated her in the living area. Even though the draperies remained open, the house was as dark as midnight. It began to rain, a light rain, but the tapping of it on the window finished an embracive gloom effect.

"Madeline, how are you?" asked Louie in a hushed tone. "Rosa is lying down. She spends most days in repose, barely eating. Sometimes I think I may lose her too from grief."

"I understand. The days immediately following a tragedy like this can be very painful. I have come on an errand and hope it is not too soon to speak with you about it. I was hoping to acquire Maria's clothing and take it to be analyzed. I have a friend who may be able to ascertain if there is anything of note on the clothing."

"Yes. I have the clothes preserved as you had asked. I will gladly give them to you. Come with me into her room, and I will show you what I have."

It was a lovely room, the kind you decorate for a very feminine girl. Lacey curtains and plush pillows adorned the bed coverings. Maria's things were laid upon the satin as if they were still waiting for her return.

"This is what had interested me when we were at the coroner's office. Do you see these random specks of white that look like some powder? I am hoping this may tell us something."

"I hadn't paid attention to that before, but yes, I can see there is some on the sleeve of her dress and around her collar. One other interesting thing has occurred. Rosa tells me this ring does not belong to Maria. At least, she had never seen her wear it before. Her jewelry consisted of some fine pieces left to her by my grandmother in Italy. The rings she possessed had antique settings. They were beloved by her as it was a gift to her from her Nana. That's why this ring stands out. It doesn't seem likely she would purchase a piece such as this."

Madeline held the ring in her hand. It appeared to be white gold with small diamonds set in a row.

"It is lovely. It almost looks like a betrothal ring."

"That's what we both thought, also. The type of ring one usually gives or gets when romantically involved. Maria did have a boyfriend in New York, but it was nothing serious. We have already contacted him, and he did not give her the ring."

"Perhaps she did meet someone, and this was a promise ring."

"That's always a possibility, but Rosa and I both feel that is an unlikely answer."

"Yes, sometimes in war-time you hear of such occurrences of instant attraction and marriage, but I agree that, under the circumstances, it does not seem likely. It will be invaluable as a clue to her disappearance; I'm sure of that. It may have been an enticement used by an unsavory character to win her favor. If it was against her will, she might have been trying to escape when she ran into the street."

"It is too difficult to speak about her. Take her clothing, and please let us know as soon as possible what you discover."

"I will, and I hope that Rosa will be better soon. Do you need my father to come and see her?"

"Yes, the medicine he gave her has relaxed her. Perhaps if he could bring her additional opium, that would help."

"I will tell him about your request, and I'm sure he will be able to see you before the end of the day."

"Thank you, and take care. Remember, whoever harmed Maria is still out there."

"Unfortunately, that is true, but now we have some useful information to find him."

She carefully laid Maria's clothing over her lap as she drove home in the carriage. Now that she had seen the ring Maria had in her possession, it steered her thoughts in a new direction. It seemed to her highly improbable that Maria's death was nothing but an unfortunate accident. She would contact Marilyn immediately, hoping to see that she had Maria's dress as soon as possible.

For the rest of the day, however, she would concern herself with her guest's arrival from London.

She stopped at the florist to buy flowers for the table and Hugh's room. Even a man could appreciate the scent of fragrant flowers. She believed it had a way of making one feel welcome and at home. She had cut catmint from her garden, with its beautiful lavender color and spicy scent, along with white roses; she felt this would make a suitable display. She found herself humming as she arranged the flowers and thought that she couldn't remember doing that for a long time. Perhaps at long last, she was getting better.

After dinner, she took her place at the window seat to continue reading The Mystery of Cloomber, a novel by Conan Doyle. Although it did not feature Sherlock Holmes, she still found the writing style and plot-line to be superb. She hoped there would be another Holmes mystery coming soon. Immersed in her reading, she did not immediately respond to the soft knocking on the front door. Then a familiar face tapped at the bay window. It was her Uncle Hank. She wondered what would bring him to her door at this late hour and hurried to answer the door.

"Uncle Hank, is everything all right?"

"Oh...I'm fine. It's nothing to do with me. It's the paper. I was out with some of my friends from work, and on my way home, I got the late edition of the *Tribune*. I was looking for my horoscope when I came upon this article. Look here; *Unidentified Women Found Floating in Chicago River.* I knew you would want to see the article; it just may be one of the girls you're searching for."

"Please come in. Sit. I will get you a cup of coffee. It feels like déjà vu. I remember seeing the headlines in the paper in London when the Ripper struck. I know this is different. It may be accidental, just like Maria...still...I'll be right back with your coffee. Thank you for bringing me the paper."

The doctor heard them talking and came out in his robe, his hair somewhat ruffled.

"What's this? Anything wrong?" he asked.

"I bought the paper with me, and there's news of a girl floating dead as nails in the Chicago River. What's happening to our neighborhood? It must be a worry indeed to any lady walking about that she might be in danger," said Uncle Hank.

"Good heavens," said the doctor. "May I see the story?"

Uncle Hank handed him the article while Madeline returned to the room with a tray of coffee and a handful of finger sandwiches.

"Thank you. I am hungry. It was another hard, long day, and I haven't had much besides beer to sustain me," said Uncle Hank.

"Sometimes, I think you will blow away in the wind. You may come up anytime and join us for dinner. You know you are always welcome, and when my friend Hugh arrives tomorrow, you must come and meet him," said Madeline.

"What does the article say, Father?"

"There is a vague description of a young girl. A fisherman saw her and brought her to shore."

"It doesn't say much at all...just that a woman believed to be between twenty and twenty-five years of age was found fully dressed in the river. They say it appears there was no foul play involved. They believe she may have accidentally fallen in.

"I think I will go to Maxwell Station and see the same officer that I spoke with about Maria, and show him the photograph I have of Wanda and Felicia."

"Let's talk about more pleasant things, like our visit from Hugh. I will be glad he will be here. Perhaps he will accompany you when you are out about town. I know that with this latest development, I will feel much better if he does," said her father.

"It will be wonderful to have him here, but Father, you will have to adapt to my position as detective. You know there will be some risk involved."

"I know, but still...I am happy he will be here."

"And me, too, Miss Madeline. Erie Street is not the place it was just a few weeks ago. I would have said you could walk safely at two in the morning, but not now," said Uncle Hank.

"I will be cautious. I don't for a minute believe that these two deaths are either accidents or unrelated. Thank you for bringing the paper," she said before bidding them good-night.

Her father hugged her in a way that he had not for a while—more of a protective embrace than just a casual good-night.

She knew that when she awoke the next day, her friend Hugh would be here, and that gave her courage and strength. She would now have an ally to confer with about the disappearances.

The morning brought a hearty rain, with black clouds converging over the area like an umbrella. Madeline was disappointed that her friend, Hugh, should have to arrive on such a day like that, but it was a familiar sight to him living in London.

She had hoped to see Marilyn and give her Maria's dress, but she was worried the garment might get wet in the rain. She would wait for Hugh, and they could go together. It would allow her to introduce Hugh to them.

"You look lovely, my dear," said Mrs. O'Malley. "That blue color suits you. I have not seen that dress before."

"I confess that I wanted something new and less conservative-looking to wear today."

She had chosen a princess line day dress that was gathered at the back in layers, dotted with tiny gold leaves against a sharp periwinkle blue dress, with white lace across the bodice.

Her father had wished to join her in meeting Hugh, but he had an emergency surgery that would now prevent him from doing so. She brought writing material to busy herself if it might be a long wait before his arrival.

When she arrived, the rain had not let up. She could hear the sound of the train, and her excitement at seeing Hugh made her maneuver about the other awaiting people to see if she could position herself closer to the platform. She waited under a covered area, her clothing damp and the front of her hair becoming frizzier, but that was the style now, and she didn't mind.

She could see the passengers begin to descend from the train. They moved along with great haste, all anxious to meet loved ones or to reach a new place they had never seen finally. In the sea of men and women hurrying to leave the train, it was hard to distinguish him through the dark coats pulled up close to their faces. But then she saw the familiar red tea rose flower, placed upon his lapel, a feeling of joy came over her, and she ran into the rain, waving to him.

He smiled at her, that familiar smile that she knew so well.

"Madeline, it is so good to see you, and also to be done with traveling. I am weary of it. It seemed forever to arrive in New York and then another journey by train to Chicago," he said as he took her hand in welcome.

"You are a sight for my eyes to see. How many times I have seen you or one of the aunts coming to see me in my mind's eye and now here you are. You do look a little done in. We will have a day of peaceful rest, hot soup, and good conversation."

"From here, Chicago looks considerably like London; wet, gloomy, and crowded."

"Oh...I know. How I had hoped you would have arrived on one of our lovelier days. Tomorrow the weather forecast is much better. But where is Phillip?"

"I gave him your address. He had some things he wished to do. He will bring the luggage and come later."

"Come, a cabby is waiting for us."

In the carriage, Madeline commented about the tea rose.

"I see you have that lovely flower in your lapel. That is how I was able to spot you amongst the large crowd," said Madeline.

"I know how much you liked the flowers from my mother's moonlight garden. I have brought you some plants from there. I hope they might thrive here as well."

"How wonderful! I don't know what will grow here. The winter comes in strong and seems to destroy my chances of building a garden, but I will certainly try my best."

"There is so much to talk about; I don't know where to begin. I am anxious to hear news about the case you are working on."

"And I wish to hear about your plans for buying land in Chicago."

She looked at him as if for the first time, thinking she had never appreciated how handsome he was. Looking the fine English gentleman in his gray suit, gloves, and top hat, he seemed to embody both grace and dignity.

Her father, Mrs. O'Malley and Uncle Hank were all waiting in the dining area when they arrived.

"Hugh, good to see you. I hope you had a pleasant journey to America. I hear it is your first visit. I hope you will find it as interesting here as we found London to be," said her father.

"I already know I will like it because of the good company I will be in," said Hugh.

Her father smiled.

"Now, Mr. Scott, I hope you will like a bowl of hearty Irish stew. It is a favorite in our household and a native dish we are most proud to call our own. We also have some homemade broth that sits well on a night like this. It is the day for it—the thunder is shaking the house. I have made the coffee strong and the stew a little spicy. I hope you will enjoy it," said Mrs. O'Malley.

Their conversation focused on Hugh and the news he brought from London, speaking about the aunts and their adjustment to the death of Polly, a Ripper victim, and the general conditions of Whitechapel and other political talk. They did not speak about the young women's recent deaths, believing it to be too difficult a subject to breach over dinner—especially a welcoming dinner—but she would speak to him about it later.

She showed him upstairs to his room, where he lingered by the flowers, commenting on the lovely aroma. She was pleased to hear this. It was nothing grand, but it did have a good, clean kitchen and tiny dining area beside the main living room.

"This is wonderful. It is somewhat larger than the quarters Phillip and I share. I'm certain he will like it also."

"Then, you have decided to accept my invitation to stay."

"Yes, for a while."

"Please get comfortable. Change into your casual wear, and I will have tea ready for us by the seating area at the window seat. It is my favorite place to muse and put the day's events to rest. You will join me?"

"I would be delighted. Phillip should be here soon. I am sure he will be hungry and in need of a hot bath also."

"I will look for him and see you back downstairs in a while."

She sat near the window seat, peering out, watching for her friend Phillip. He had been her first contact with the *SS City of New York* on her way to London. He attended to her as if she was family, and she would never forget that.

She heard the noise of a carriage and looked out to see Phillip bound from it, dragging a large trunk.

"Father, Phillip is here. Could you come and help with the luggage?"

The doctor came out in his smoking jack, partaking of his one vice, a pipe of tobacco that he had on limited occasion. He put it down and said, "I'll be right there."

Madeline held the door for them as they lifted the trunks inside.

"Phillip, my dear friend. How good it is to see you? Welcome to our home," said Madeline.

Hugh had heard the commotion and had come down. "Here, I will give a hand with those. They will go upstairs where we are staying."

"Come down quickly when you are through so that we may have a visit," said Madeline.

"If you don't mind, Miss, I would like a hot bath and to rest a bit, but I am hungry," said Phillip.

"We'll have something to eat waiting for you," said Madeline.

"After I get Phillip settled in, I will be down for tea," said Hugh.

Madeline brought the serving table and tray with tea and biscuits over to the window seat. Hugh came down momentarily and joined her.

"I can see you sitting here with the moonlight cascading in, throwing light over your Sherlock Holmes novel," said Hugh.

"The Mystery of Cloomber, to be specific," she said as she laughed. "It is a new novel by Doyle, although it does not feature Sherlock, it is as provocative a read as Sherlock, and I am enjoying it. Perhaps we will have our reading circle of two sometime."

"Before Phillip comes down, please tell me what happened to your Miss Maria, the girl you were looking for?"

She described the recent events, including the most recent finding of the unidentified girl in the river.

"Perhaps you would like to go with me when I deliver Maria's dress to Marilyn, the girl who has agreed to try analyzing the cloth."

"I would like that and a chance to see some of this new city."

"There he is!"

"It's been a long day, and I would be most grateful for a cup of hot tea," said Phillip.

"Come. Sit in the dining area. We have some Irish stew, freshly cooked bread, and some cakes. If you are still hungry after that, I'll find something else for you," said Madeline laughing.

"The tea is excellent," said Phillip. "It is Earl Grey, not your Darjeeling."

"I confess I began to drink it in remembrance of you and your cousin, and now I have taken a liking to it," said Madeline.

The doctor and Mrs. O'Malley joined them.

"Son, you must have a hundred stories of your adventures at sea, and I insist on hearing some of them," said her father.

"More like a thousand, sir, and I would be happy to accommodate you."

Phillip held their attention, especially Mrs. O'Malley's, who had never ventured from Chicago, with his tales of the sea and the quirky people he encountered. It was a lovely two hours of light banter and laughter, and now it was nearing midnight.

"Well, I haven't stayed up this late—except for duties from my medical practice—in a very long time. I don't think since our New Year's dinner aboard the *New York*. I look forward to dinner tomorrow with everyone," said Brian Donovan as he said his good-nights.

Phillip went to the upstairs flat, but Hugh remained with her returning to the window seat.

"Now, you must tell me all about your inheritance and your plans while you are staying in Chicago," urged Madeline.

"I will, but tonight, may I be allowed the luxury of your company for a short while before we retire and reminisce about our time in London."

She smiled and said, "Oh...of course, that would be most pleasant. We have many tomorrows ahead to speak of many things. Today is the first of what I hope will be many moonlight talks."

Chapter 7

A Pinch of Sugar

Madeline had a good night's sleep—something rare for her—not waking once with any dark visions.

"Good morning, Mrs. O'Malley. The clouds have dispersed, and the sun is peeking through. I feel it will be a good day."

"I can see that. I'm sure you will have many good days now that your friends are here."

"I believe you are right. I hope you do not mind cooking for the additional people."

"Not at all, it will be good to have the company."

She heard them both coming down the stairs and welcomed them inside.

"Good morning, gentlemen," said Madeline.

"I meant to tell you yesterday, Miss, that you seem to be quite recovered and look the picture of health," said Phillip.

She was grateful for his words and said, "I hope that is true. There were times of great stress during our attempts to look for the infamous Ripper, but that is all behind us now."

"I hear not completely, for you have ventured into the investigation business," continued Phillip.

"You are quite right, but I cannot imagine involvement with anything as dangerous or heinous as what happened in Whitechapel. Now I am searching for what appears to be at least three or four missing girls. I hope to engage your cousin, Hugh, to assist me," said Madeline.

"I see. I plan to take a tour of the city. Some of the lads from the ship and I are interested in taking a walking tour of the downtown area."

"I will join you on another day, Phillip, but today I promised Madeline I will go with her," said Hugh.

"I contacted Marilyn, and she will meet us at the Harrison. The hotel seems to be at the forefront of these disappearances in some way. Some of the girls were known to have frequented there before they disappeared. It may mean nothing; after all, everyone in the area has visited this hotel. It's luxurious motifs, the cafes, and the shops bring everyone there," said Madeline.

As they entered the palatial Harrison Hotel, she saw the twins immediately and waved. Madeline marveled at the beautiful decor each time she visited. She supposed it was only natural that no one suspected anything could be amiss in such grandeur. Sometimes she wondered herself if her suspicions were unfounded.

"We have many beautiful hotels in London, but this... this is more modern. I don't believe we have any that have shops like these on their ground floor," said Hugh.

"Ladies, may I introduce my good friend from London, Hugh Scott."

Madeline was proud to be on his arm. He was such a distinguished-looking man and displayed impeccable manners. She reminded him of what little girls would imagine a prince would be like.

After a few minutes of polite conversation, Madeline opened her satchel and pulled out just a part of Maria's dress, the sleeve.

"This is the white substance I found in several places on this dress, and I would like to have it analyzed," said Madeline.

"Do you think someone drugged her?" asked Nancy.

"I think it a consideration," said Madeline. "I appreciate your doing this."

"Anything that we may do to be able to help, we will gladly do so. It is the concern of all of us to find these girls," continued Nancy.

"There is Vincenzo again happily painting, and now he has a young girl with him. Would anyone like to walk over and view his latest work?" asked Madeline.

"I will stay here and watch over the parcel, but you go ahead," said Marilyn.

The three strolled over to where the artists had drawn a small crowd to watch them paint.

Vincenzo painted in a more traditional sense, but his companion's work was brighter in color and had an almost illusion-like quality as if the characters she painted were nymphs.

"Miss, I have seen you here before. Would you like to sit for me and have a portrait done? Or perhaps by my assistant, Miss Sobon....Joanie Sobon from Paris," said Vincenzo.

"I greatly admire your work, Mr. DeFrancesco, and Miss Sobon's is also unique, but we are here as observers. It is a credit to you that you have created such a stir. Your audience has grown," said Madeline.

"We survive, that is all. Between us, we can afford a place to stay in this hotel, and we both feel fortunate for that. The Harrison is a magnificent addition to this great city," said Vincenzo.

"For you, perhaps, poor Vincenzo. He was not born in a unique place as I and still does not understand culture, I'm afraid. I cannot say that I think this is a great city after where I was born. After Paris, I cannot say that any city can compare to it," said Miss Sobon with a teasing nod to Vincenzo.

"I am from London, and I do agree as far as art is concerned that Paris draws all the great painters, but do not most of them hail from Italy? Isn't that where you are from, Vincenzo?" asked Hugh.

Vincenzo laughed and said, "Yes, of course. See, Joanie, be it British or American, everyone knows where excellence comes from where artists are concerned."

"I think Miss Sobon's work is quite original and beautiful," said Nancy.

"*Merci, mon ami,*" said Joanie.

"Perhaps another day, we will return to sit for a portrait," said Madeline.

They were about to leave when three well-dressed men appeared in the lobby. By the way, everyone scurried around and began straightening themselves; she surmised it might be the elusive owners of the Harrison. *At last*, she thought, after a glance at them.

"Excuse me," she said to her companions as she hurried across the room to the concierge.

"Sir, are those men the Harrison brothers?"

"Indeed, they are, Miss."

Without thinking, she walked quickly toward them and caught them as they were about to enter the elevator.

"Pardon me, gentlemen, but I have sought an interview with one of you for several days now, and the staff tells me you are never available. I feel I must press my case and ask if you are aware that several missing girls who have frequented your establishment are now missing."

"What importance is that to us?" asked the shortest, whose pudgy body and thin, tight smile made him the least attractive of the three.

"I was curious if you might have done your own internal investigation to see if perhaps a hotel guest might have had something to do with their disappearance?" asked Madeline.

"Nonsense! What impertinence. If I hear you even implying such a thing about our hotel, I will thwart your actions. That is incredible and scandalous," said the lanky, handsome brother with the silver-streaked hair. He looked at her with hatred, even though they had just met minutes before.

"I do not wish to be insulting in any way. I am trying to find some answers, and I believe people connected with this hotel may have seen the girls and may shed some light if questioned," said Madeline.

"If that were true, the police would have been here long before you," he responded. "Now, I must ask that you step aside. We are on our way to an urgent meeting," he added.

She watched them leave her, and she thought it curious that the one brother, who was equally as tall as the one with the silver hair, did not even lift his eyes to look at her or address her in any way. Instead, he continued to read the newspaper he had in his hand, without diverting his gaze at all. This action offended her, even more than the other's coarse remarks. He was athletic in build and attractive enough to rival any theatrical star. She wondered if this, plus his apparent wealth and position, made him behave the way he did.

She returned and told them of her conversation with the men.

"I wish I could identify them by their first names," said Madeline.

"I can help you with that," said Marilyn. "The shorter, heavyset man is Patrick. The tall one I saw you speaking with is Joseph, and the quiet one is Christopher. I identified them through an article in the newspaper, but there is also a bronze plaque engraved with their names on it located on the second floor, where the hotel guests reside."

Walking boldly toward them was Lady Mary, with a younger, rather dashing man following behind her.

"Oh no...," said Madeline.

"What is it?" asked Hugh.

"You'll know in a minute."

"I thought after our conversation that I might have persuaded you to curb your pursuit of the Harrisons. It is unacceptable. I will speak to the management to try having you barred from coming into our lovely home," said Lady Mary speaking with an irritatingly high-pitched tone.

"I have told you that I am not trying to cause anyone any inconvenience, but I feel I must ask the questions. Do you not care about these girls?" asked Madeline.

"They are the worry of their families, not ours. Your continued actions can ruin the fine reputation of this hotel. You are not welcome here," continued Lady Mary.

"Lady Mary is distraught. I'm sure she does not wish to sound unkind. Allow me to introduce myself; I am Alfred O'Connor. I am the personal assistant to the Harrisons, and they have entrusted me to watch over our beloved, Lady Mary. She is overprotective of the brothers; that is all."

He then took Lady Mary by the hand and said, "This young lady means no harm. It is all right."

"If you think so, Alfred. I trust you.

"I need my coffee—where's my coffee?" said Lady Mary.

"It is waiting for you on the patio, and your friend Willie is there right now," said Alfred.

Lady Mary walked away, looking somewhat befuddled, but left without further incident.

"Thank you, Mr. O'Connor. I am Madeline Donovan, and these are my friends."

After introductions, she added, "I understand her feelings. She naturally wishes to defend anything to do with the Harrison's and the hotel. She is right, I have no authority to ask, and I depend on the hotel's goodwill. I would think it in their best interest to also want to know what happened to these women seen in your hotel. I'm sure they would like to know if some unsavory character might be residing in one of their suites."

"I'm sure there was no intent to try to inhibit your search, just the hotel protecting the privacy of the people who stay here and attempting not to create any rumors that might be harmful to business," said Alfred.

"If I am unable to speak with any of the Harrisons, would you consider letting me interview you?"

"Let me see what I can do. I will endeavor to secure you an interview. If the brothers do not have an objection, I will be happy to speak with you," said Alfred.

"Thank you. That is what I have been hoping. Will you contact me, or should I return tomorrow?"

"They are expected to be in town for the next few weeks. Tomorrow may be too soon, but the day after, on Saturday, you can return then. I will have an answer for you one way or the other. And...by the way, I will speak to Lady Mary and see if I can't smooth her feathers."

When Alfred left, everyone began speaking at once. Marilyn and Nancy both blushed when they spoke of Alfred, Madeline believing they thought him attractive. Hugh seemed to be at a loss as to what was going on, and she said she would explain everything later when they took tea together in the evening.

"What did you think of Lady Mary?" asked Madeline to all who were present.

"She is an unusual woman to be sure, but how lucky for her to have such a delightful man escorting her around," said Marilyn.

"I don't remember seeing him around before, and he is not wearing a wedding ring. I think I would like to see him again, perhaps invite him to join us for tea at the cafe?" said Nancy.

"Sister, he must have made an impression on you. You don't usually notice men at all; you hide your eyes in some book," said Marilyn.

"You must admit that he is the most handsome man," replied Nancy.

Her comments seemed to make Hugh uncomfortable, and when Nancy realized this, she began to cough and fidget.

Madeline changed the subject to Maria's dress.

"Ladies, I am sure we have taken enough of your time. Should we meet you back here at any specific time for the results? I know it might be a few days...," said Madeline.

But Marilyn interrupted her.

"No...not at all. This is important. We will leave right now and obtain permission to be in the lab tonight. I should be able to have your answer by tomorrow. Perhaps we can all dine together."

"That is a wonderful idea, and you shall all be my guests," added Hugh.

"Hugh, would you mind going to the coroner's office with me. I'd like to see if I can find out anything about the body that turned up in the river."

"It wasn't exactly what I had in mind when I thought of seeing the sights with you, but I know you have serious work to do. I will gladly accompany you," said Hugh, touching her shoulder in a familiar friendly manner.

"I know they won't let me in to see the body, but I am hoping I may obtain some information as far as to her identity."

When they arrived at the coroner's office, they could hear the staff talking about the deceased young girl as they walked by. It was on everyone's mind.

She was unsuccessful in her attempt to view the body. She wasn't even permitted to speak to anyone in authority as she was not a blood relative but did listen to what was said in the waiting office.

When she heard a woman speaking about it with her friends, she stopped her and said, "I am looking for a friend of mine who went missing, but I am not family. Is there anything at all you may have heard? I have her picture with me and wondered if you might look at it."

She showed them the pictures of Wanda and Felicia.

The woman said, "I couldn't say about the appearance. None of us have seen the body either, but I did hear one particular thing. It seems there was what appeared to be an engagement ring on her finger. Was your friend engaged?"

"No, she wasn't. Thank you for your help," said Madeline.

During the carriage ride home, Madeline said to Hugh, "I suppose it's impossible to think it has any connection, but Maria had what looked like an engagement ring when they found her. Her family has no idea who gave it to her. I would love to get a look at that ring."

"Let's go back to your home, and after dinner, we can go over your findings. I would like to hear about what you have uncovered," said Hugh.

"Wonderful. And you can finally tell me all about coming to our fair city and how that came to be."

Mrs. O'Malley prepared a lovely brisket of beef with her specialty stewed onions and tomato side dish. Phillip and Uncle Hank joined them, and it was a lively conversation about immigration, including some of the problems the Irish faced in the United States.

After dinner, Phillip, Hugh, and she strolled down Erie Street taking in the local neighborhood sights.

"The city's architecture is so different from London. All these new buildings are going up with a distinctive modern look. I heard of someone called Frank Lloyd Wright, who is designing unique homes. I believe his work is internationally known," said Phillip.

"Yes, I have been seriously thinking of purchasing a home designed by him," said Hugh.

"Truly? Was your inheritance that substantial?" asked Madeline.

"It was, and even though Phillip was not in the will, I intend to share my good fortune with him."

Phillip smiled and said, "You are like a brother to me, but I can make my living at sea."

"Yes, but I'm sure you would like a home to come to in London and perhaps in Chicago," said Hugh.

He smiled and said, "I can't say that wouldn't be grand. I am intrigued by this man Wright. I heard about the opening of the Auditorium Building. I would like to see that while I am still here. It also has captured the attention in the news; we heard about it even in London," said Phillip.

"Chicago is growing into a city that I think one day will hold its own against the most prominent cities in the country. Of course, with that comes the problems of a big city...the crime," said Madeline. "Just a little further down this side street is the home of one of the missing girls, Wanda Gapinski. Do you gentlemen mind if I stop to inquire if they have any news about her?"

"Certainly not. I cannot imagine the distress these families are going through from not knowing what has become of their daughters...a frightful business," said Hugh.

A young girl answered the door, her eyes red from weeping, "Yes, can I help you?" she asked.

"What is the matter? Are you all right?" asked Madeline.

"It is my sister, Wanda. My parents have gone to attend to business about my sister."

"My poor girl...," Madeline said as she instinctively went to cradle the girl in her arms.

"Did you know her?" asked the girl.

"I did not, but I was assisting in the search for her."

"She was the girl in the river. We had hoped and prayed it was not her when my Mama and Papa went to the office where people go for that. I'll never see her again. She was my only sister. I don't know what I will do now. She always took care of me and was there for me."

The three exchanged glances of dismay. Hugh and Phillip attempted to console her also.

Madeline had thought it might have been one of the missing girls but had held out hope that it was not Felicia or Wanda.

She asked the child, "Is someone here with you?"

"No, I am alone."

"Would you like us to stay with you until your parents return?"

"Would you?"

She didn't feel it appropriate to enter the girl's home, but they could stay on the porch with her and try as best they could to calm the child.

"I am Alice, her younger sister. I am just twelve—my birthday was last month. It was the last time I saw my sister," said Alice.

"I am so sorry.

They all tried to comfort her, reassuring her of how things would get better, but she was too young to appreciate those words and continued to weep in intermittent intervals.

She seemed cautious about being around men and stayed close to her while Phillip and Hugh walked down into the street area, Phillip taking the opportunity to smoke.

"Your family will find a way to help you get through this. They will need you now more than ever. If you ever need someone to take you out for ice cream or just a walk, please ask your parents to contact me."

She continued to speak to her while Alice nodded her head and held onto her hand. A short time later, her mother and father arrived.

At first, they were startled to see their daughter with strangers. Then the mother recognized Madeline.

"You're the lady who is looking for the missing girls. Why are you here?" asked Mrs. Gapinski.

"I was in the area and wanted to check to see you if you had any news. Alice told me the rest. We volunteered to stay with her. She seemed in such a state."

"Thank you for that. We did not wish her with us. It was an ordeal even for me. I would ask you in for coffee, but I do not feel well."

"We would not dream of imposing any further. I am still trying to find out all I can, and if you do wish to contact me, I have my contact information here."

"When the funeral is over, I am sure I will need someone to talk to, and I would like to know what progress you have made. She didn't just fall into the river as the police have assumed, that much I am sure of," continued Mrs. Gapinski.

"Come, Mother, that is enough for now. Let us get our Alice inside. My wife told me about your inquiry. I hope we may speak again in the future, but for now, I believe we need to be alone," said Mr. Gapinski.

Hugh and Phillip had been listening and looked somber.

"I didn't mean to involve you both in something that should darken your spirit right upon your arrival. We will talk of other things—we certainly can make a plan to see the Auditorium Building."

They smiled at her, and Phillip said, "It is all right. It is just that it reminds me of what happened in Whitechapel. That is a chapter in our history. I'm sure we all wish never occurred, as I am sure this will be for your lovely neighborhood. We can do both, try to assist you, and discover the sights of Chicago."

"Mrs. O'Malley will be awaiting our return for lunch," said Madeline, linking her arms with both men as they walked toward home.

Upon their arrival, Mrs. O'Malley informed her that Marilyn came by. She had left a message that she would be at the Harrison Hotel at six and that she had the results.

"Now we know where we will dine tonight. Mrs. O'Malley, will you attend with us?" asked Hugh.

"I have been planning to do some mending of clothes, but perhaps I will go," she replied.

The evening brought them together at the Harrison. This time instead of the French cafe, they met at Michael's Italian Bistro.

After they had all been seated and ordered, Madeline said, "Marilyn, you are an indispensable ally. Thank you for doing this. I know I am anxious to hear your results. Is it drugs as I suspected?"

No one at the table spoke, waiting to hear what Marilyn had to say.

"I think you will all be surprised to hear that it is nothing more than sugar and salt. Most likely, particles falling onto the garment from the eating of a bakery item."

Madeline was the first to speak, "It is more than a surprise—it has completely upended my theory that they gave the girls drugs."

"If I can be of further service, let me know," said Marilyn.

As they continued in conversation, Madeline did not see Alfred approaching them until Hugh touched her hand and nodded in his direction.

"Mrs. Donovan, I am happy to see you here. I thought I would see you tomorrow, but I already have the news you wished for. The brothers have relented and apologized for their rather coarse behavior. They will see you next week on Tuesday if you are available," said Alfred.

"Of course, I will be there," said Madeline.

"Fine. If you could meet me in the lobby around two in the afternoon, I will take you up to their conference room."

"As for Lady Mary, she has agreed to be more hospitable."

"Thank you for everything, Alfred. Your efforts are appreciated."

"It is nothing, and I have taken the liberty to absorb the payment for your dinner."

"That is not..." said Madeline.

"Nonsense. Please do not protest. That is the least we could do for treating you so shabbily. I will leave you now and look forward to seeing you on Tuesday."

"How curious!" Madeline said when he left. "That is the last thing I expected to hear, besides, of course, that the powder was sugar. Life is unpredictable."

"There is Lady Mary, looking as exotic as ever. Look at the plume coming from her hat; it looks like it extends into the air a good foot," Hugh laughed.

"Is that the woman you were all talking about? Why... she's my age. Let me have a go at her. I'll find out what's going on with her," said Mrs. O'Malley.

Madeline felt if anyone could coax some information from Lady Mary, it just might be Mrs. O'Malley. She could disarm the most grudging soul with her frankness and her sincerity.

What a contrast, Madeline thought—plain as she could be, Mrs. O'Malley, with her solid brown dress and sturdy shoes, and Lady Mary, dressed in scarlet red, with sprinkles of purple and white flowers in her oversized hat.

"These meetings you have are more interesting than my sight-seeing. I will be curious to hear what your Mrs. O'Malley has to say about Lady Mary," said Phillip smiling.

They had finished dinner but decided to order a bottle of red wine to sip and savor while waiting for Mrs. O'Malley's return.

Nancy and Phillip were deep in conversation and seemed to take an instant liking to one another. They were close in age, Phillip being just seventeen and Nancy just having turned eighteen. Meanwhile, Hugh and Madeline talked about London and the memories they had during her stay there.

"I remember being so worried about you when you went into Whitechapel alone, and then when you were hurt, I felt somehow I had let you down. I should have been there to protect you at all times," said Hugh.

"How kind of you to say something like that, but you know I took chances that I might not today. I was in a different state of mind back then. I hope I have learned my lesson and will be more cautious in my approach to this case," said Madeline.

"I think it is an important step, from what you have told me so far that you have the opportunity to speak with the brothers. I wonder why they did such an about-face in their attitude," said Hugh.

"Perhaps it is nothing more than their attempt to be rid of me and any attention I might have caused."

"According to the paper, the police have questioned the staff and feel it is just a mere coincidence that someone saw the girls here. There's something about this place...I can't say what it is exactly, but it seems there is an aura of mystery. I suppose it is a house of secrets, as any place would be with so many people coming and going on its premises."

"I suppose if we knew what went on behind all those closed doors, we would both be shocked."

"Here is Mrs. O'Malley, and she looks pleased with herself," said Madeline.

"I can tell you this, that lady has more secrets than a peacock has feathers. She talks in riddles and almost seems to want you to think she's daft so that you can't tell what's true and what isn't," said Mrs. O'Malley.

"She sounds fascinating," said Hugh laughing.

"Were you able to get any information about her connection to the brothers?" asked Madeline.

"Not this time, but I plan to have luncheon with her this week," said Mrs. O'Malley, appearing quite satisfied with herself.

Phillip raised his glass in a toast, "Here's to a productive and busy week."

Chapter 8

Hidden Clues

M adeline and Hugh spent the next few days in relative calm, renewing their friendship and enjoying their evening talks by the window seat.

They had spent Sunday planting the moonlight garden florae Hugh had brought from London for her.

"Do you think they have a chance of surviving the harsh winter?" asked Madeline.

"They are hearty, but you may have to dig them up by Christmas and keep them inside to be sure they don't die. Our winters can equal the chill to yours so they may stand it," said Hugh.

He had brought her different plants that thrive and bloom in moonlight, including the Night Phlox, Moonflower, and the Queen of the Night. She had been fascinated by them when she saw them in his mother's garden—not having any knowledge beforehand that such flowers existed.

Now they were both seated, looking out at the flora. The light of the moon pierced through the trees and cascaded upon the plants, highlighting their beauty. The Queen of the Night's fragrance was bold. The flower's aroma drifted to their open window some twelve feet or so above the garden. The Night Phlox aroma was unusual; it had a smell of sweet vanilla candy, causing them to desire the delectable chocolates Mrs. O'Malley had left for them.

"How beautiful! I cannot thank you enough for such a thoughtful gift. I will spend many hours enjoying their beauty—it will give me a kind of peace."

"I am happy they please you."

"We have spent so much time talking about other things and still have not spoken of your inheritance. How did it all come to be?"

"A cousin, who had moved to Scotland, left me a substantial amount of money. We had been close as children, but for the last few years kept in contact only through correspondence. He never married and was thoroughly absorbed in business, but that's what he enjoyed. None of us ever realized his financial worth. I suppose he must have been a wise financial investor. He had a good size estate, but that he bequeathed to another cousin. I received his financial holdings, and I decided that there was more to life than the law while I was still young and have the opportunity. I have some fondness for it, yet it was more my father's choice for me. I had always wished to be an architect, but it was a frivolous choice in my family.

I had dreamed someday of visiting America, but knowing you are here made a choice relatively easy. I had read about Frank Lloyd Wright and his unique home designs. I believe I have enough funds to purchase one of the homes designed by him."

"You are fortunate indeed to be able to live independently and choose how to spend your time without the worry of money."

"I will not be idle. I hope to travel and perhaps design my own home someday. I would like to attend university to acquire the knowledge to do so."

"That sounds wonderful. My goals are to get my little business off the ground."

"I think you are amazing. You had to overcome personal tragedy, and it is not easy for a woman in this day to be taken as seriously as a man in any business. I admire your fortitude and spirit. I have never met anyone like you, Madeline."

Madeline felt a sudden uneasiness at his comments and replied, "You are a flatterer, Hugh, but I'm sure you are exaggerating."

Changing the subject, she added, "I just am not satisfied that I could be so completely wrong about the dress. I think I will have another look."

Hugh lit up a cigarette and poured them each a glass of wine. It was nearly midnight; the time escaped her without notice. When she was with Hugh, the hours passed like minutes.

"What do you hope to find?" asked Hugh.

"Honestly, I don't know—something—anything, a clue of some sort."

She laid the dress on the floor and spread the folds out. Kneeling on the floor, she touched the fabric as if it were made of glass, going over every part of it to see if she had missed something. Hugh knelt and joined her in the search.

"I don't suppose there is anything. It was just my imagination hoping there would be something," said Madeline.

"Wait, what is this, shoved inside this torn area?" He pulled out two small items. "It's chocolate pieces. Why in heaven's name would anyone put chocolate in the folds of their dress?"

"Unless it was what I suspected all along. This is where the drugs are in the chocolate. She probably hid them to make her captor or captors think she had consumed the candy, and possibly she would then either sleep or be in a malleable state of mind that they could control her."

"It does seem a likely scenario; no one would hide something like that in their clothing without an unusual reason."

"I'll get something from the kitchen to wrap them in and bring them to Marilyn. Tomorrow is my meeting with the brothers, so I will be able to do both."

"I hope you don't mind that I have made other plans for tomorrow. I plan to take a carriage tour through some of the neighborhoods."

"Of course not. I will be busy also. Good-night then."

She looked through the window one last time to admire her moonlight garden, thankingHugh again for bringing her the plants.

She said goodnight to the photograph of her family, ritualistically tracing her fingers over their smiling faces. She felt somewhat guilty for enjoying her time with Hugh but knew that she had to move away from her grief if she were to survive.

The next day found her feeling jubilant that she had secured the interview, and she thought it would give her a chance to assess the brothers. She arrived early at the Harrison to see if perhaps Marilyn or Nancy were at the French cafe. She saw Nancy as she entered.

"Good afternoon, the man we met the other day, Alfred, was here looking to see if you had arrived," said Nancy.

"It is good to see you. Thank you for telling me. I will tell the man at the concierge that I am here. Is Marilyn with you?"

"Not today. She had some a class to make up. Can I help you?"

"I have some exciting news. Hugh and I combed through the dress yesterday, seeking any additional clues, and to my delight, Hugh found two pieces of chocolate in the gathering of the dress. The seam pulled apart to create a small pocket, and there they were. I think this time; Marilyn might find there had been drugs injected somehow into the candy."

"Amazing. Certainly, if she took this action to conceal them, it sounds like the most plausible answer."

"Alfred is coming this way. Please do not let anyone know about this. I believe it to be prudent to keep this amongst our small group."

"Of course. I will tell my sister about this. If you have the chocolates, I will take them to her."

"I do."

She turned her back so that the approaching figure of Alfred could not see what she was doing. It was an inconsequential action; still...she did not want anyone to observe her.

"Thank you, Nancy. If you have access to a telephone, you can call with the findings. Otherwise, may we meet again tomorrow at this time?"

"Yes. Either way, my sister or I will be here."

"Mrs. Donovan, so good to see you," said Alfred.

"Good afternoon."

"I believe we must delay your interview, but not by very long. They are meeting with a new business owner that plans to open a shop here soon."

"I don't believe there is another hotel in the city that has the same atmosphere. Is it true that guests only stay on the second floor?"

"It seems to be working to their advantage. The shops on the main floor maintain a steady flow of customers. Many patrons proceed to book a room for an anniversary or some such event. Because of the limited number of rooms, they are almost always full, which creates a rather wanton lust for the rooms. There is currently a waiting list to reserve a room. The third floor is for business and also has private areas such as billiards and exercise rooms. It also has a grand dining area, where they have private parties for associates and family."

"How interesting! I am sure I would like to stay for the weekend sometimes."

"I am certain the experience would meet with your approval. Will you join me for a beverage while you wait?"

Under other circumstances, she might have declined such an invitation. She was amused at the words he used "*wanton lust*" when referencing the hotel—not the typical talk a man would use in polite company. It was apparent his grandiose style conveyed that he thought he was the most handsome man in the room, or for that matter, the city.

However, she could not fault him for that because he just might have been. She thought he probably was accustomed to being treated well. Still, something was charming about him that drew one in. However, the reason she said "yes" was to see if he might inadvertently tell her something of importance.

He had a presence there, for when he waved over the waiter to their table, the man practically flew over in haste, seemingly out of breath when he asked for their order.

"May I take the liberty of ordering you absinthe; it is the most popular cordial at the moment. Many of the ladies have a fondness for it."

She almost said no, but then reassured herself that absinthe once in a while could certainly not hurt her. Her addiction to its sweet nectar was something she had to fight against while in London, but now she felt she had that part of her life back in control.

"Yes, I have tasted it, and it is the most pleasing flavor. Thank you, I will have one."

"So tell me, what is it you do that you should be so concerned with these girls?"

"I developed an interest in becoming a female detective after trying my hand at it while I was in London. As a widow, I searched for a career path for myself, which presented itself to me. I find it quite stimulating, and feel it is a worthy way to spend one's time, in the assistance of others."

"How did you like London?"

"I found the fog beautifully enchanting. It gave you the feeling you were walking about inside the home of some great mystery. The people were different from Americans, and I enjoyed the differences in behavior.

"How did you come to be the Harrison brothers' assistant?"

"It had to do with Lady Mary, but that's a story for another day. My assistant is waving us into the elevator—they must be waiting for us."

She went to the third floor. Alfred continued chattering about the hotel's construction, to which she paid little attention, for she was mesmerized by the maze he took her through. They wandered down different corridors, some areas filled with staff talking and moving about, and others eerily quiet. An excessive number of doors were along the way, and almost every door was ornate somehow. Some were elaborately carved. Still, others had gold and silver adorned handles. Door knockers displayed jungle creatures such as the lion and jaguar.

She remarked on this to Alfred, to which he replied, "It's is quite like any other hotel, just more elaborate."

Almost everything she said to him, he responded by making some defensive remark, even such an innocuous comment about the unusual doors.

She believed she would never find her way back to the offices if she had to do it on her own. She thought someone designed it deliberately confusing and designed to make it difficult to find the Harrison brothers' offices.

Once inside, she saw they had their private elevator, which explained how they avoided the complicated path.

The Harrison men were all similarly dressed, with only slight differences to their garments, all in the color gray. They all wore spectacles, but in this, they were different. Patrick wore a monocle, Christopher had gold, circular frames, and Joseph wore silver frames. But although they were all similar in attire, their looks and even how they carried themselves significantly varied.

With just a casual observance, it was evident to Madeline that Christopher was the head man. He stood with authority, rigid and without even a glimmer of a smile. Patrick, the stocky one, bumbled about, straightening his coat, and squinting every few minutes. Joseph was the most relaxed but still fidgeted with his glasses, taking them on and off, wiping them and putting them back on. He was the only one who looked her squarely in the eye and spoke first, "Mrs. Donovan, as you know, we are busy men, but we have taken steps to allow this interview. We have heard little of these missing women, but we will try to answer your questions."

"The newspapers report as many as six missing women, all of whom were at your hotel. It's a possibility that a guest who resides here, or even a staff member might be culpable of interfering with these ladies.

"I would like to see your registration book to see if any of the girls may have stayed here or participated in the events that you showcase, such as the recent fashion show. I would also like your permission to question the business owners."

"It does not seem an unreasonable request. If you do it discreetly, I do not see the problem with it," said Patrick.

"There is a question of the privacy of our guests. I don't want any of them bothered by you and assaulted with your questions," said Joseph.

"I will be discreet. You have my word on that, and I agree that I will not question your guests," said Madeline.

Joseph stood and walked in front of her. "If Alfred is available, I would like him to accompany you whenever you are here. Then we will have an assurance of your conduct. You understand we are doing you this favor out of deference to your desire to help these girls somehow. We, however, think it is mere coincidence that they may have come into our facility. Since we have opened our doors, the people of this city have come through just to see the place. If they were among those, it would not be surprising," said Joseph, with a mixture of curtness and kindness that made her unable to discern his true nature. Still, the brother Christopher did not speak her name or even offer a greeting. He looked sternly out the window and barely moved, standing stoically during the entire time she was there.

She was about to leave when she heard what sounded like a muffled scream.

"That was a woman screaming, did you hear it?" she asked.

Patrick walked out of the room ahead of her and said, "There is nothing now. It may have been one of the staff acting out."

Then again, she heard someone cry out. Alfred ran out of the room and continued down the corridor until he came to a bamboo door and pushed his way inside.

Patrick and Joseph followed him while she stood there under the watchful gaze of Christopher. She couldn't leave even if she wanted to, for she would not know the way back to the elevator.

A few minutes later, Alfred returned and said, "It's all right—it's Lady Mary. She fell, and it appears she has sprained her ankle. She was afraid no one would hear her and was more vocal than necessary. She knows I always check on her. She sometimes comes up here to sit and read. It is the library room."

She saw Lady Mary peek out from the door and knew Alfred must be telling the truth, but she was mystified by what just happened.

Alfred returned her to the lobby with a smile, saying, "It is a large hotel, with a hundred stories going on at any given time. She is eccentric and sometimes can panic. That is why, of course, she has acted the way she did with you."

"I see," was all she replied.

"Are you happy with the outcome of your meeting?"

"Yes, I am. Apparently, you will be my guide. I hope you don't mind."

"Not at all. We have nothing to hide. I'm sure you will find it a fruitless outcome. This is a grand place, and only the best of people do business here."

"I hope you are right."

"Please notify me through the concierge whenever you are in the hotel next and wish to speak to the business owners."

She bid Alfred good-bye and began to exit when she saw Joanie Sobon setting up her painting easel.

"Miss Sobon, do you have a minute?"

"I am quite busy, *mon ami*. I must get ready, or I will not make any money today."

"I won't take up but just a minute of your time. I am searching for information regarding some missing girls; perhaps you have read about them in the newspapers."

"Oh...but no, Vincenzo and I, all we do is paint and make beautiful love," she said, laughing. "We do not look for trouble or seek it out. That is for the Americans."

Madeline tried to ask the artist about the girls again. But all Joanie did was wave her off and repeat that she had seen no one. She imagined it might be the truth if Joanie and Vincenzo were so engrossed in their painting that they probably did not pay much attention to their surroundings. She departed the hotel and left for home.

She had taken a carriage to the short distance to the hotel, as she did not wish her clothing or boots covered in dust, but now she decided to walk home, thinking about her time spent with Alfred.

She hoped Hugh had returned so that she could speak with him about the brothers.

When she entered the house, Mrs. O'Malley called out, "Your gentleman came around, and a post came for you."

She walked over to the table Mrs. O'Malley always laid their correspondence on. The Cook had put her letter on top, and when she saw the postmark from New York, she clutched it to her and went to her room to read it. It was from Jonathan Franks.

July 25, 1889

Madeline,

Everyone in New York in the news business has been talking about some of the special interest stories happening in your backyard. The Auditorium Building sounds as if it will be one of the sights to see when traveling to Chicago. We have all heard of Hull House and other businesses that have found a home there.

As it turns out, our editor wanted to send someone to do a month-long feature about these stories to send it to our readers in New York. New Yorker's always felt in competition with Chicago and have a keen interest in trying to do better. No one, in particular, wanted to go—if it isn't murder, it doesn't pique their interest. But as you can guess by now, I volunteered straight away (I think that expression stayed with me after London), and I will be coming by train, arriving in Chicago this Friday.

*I hope to find that Hugh is already there. I have your address,
and as soon as I secure a place to stay, I will come to see you.*
Your friend,
Jonathan Franks

She could not wait to tell her father and Hugh the good
news. Besides Hugh, Jonathan was the only other man she
became close to since the death of her husband, Russell.
After meeting him aboard the SS City of New York on her
way to London, he had gained her trust and respect. They
began their friendship reading Arthur Conan Doyle's first
novel, *A Study in Scarlet.* He had been sent by the *Times* to
report on the Ripper crimes in Whitechapel. They both
had interacted on the case, at times with Hugh by their
side. The three had formed a strong bond together.

She came out to the porch to soak in the afternoon sun,
the letter still in her hand, when she saw Hugh coming
down the interior staircase that led to his and Phillip's
upstairs flat.

"Madeline, I was looking for your carriage through the
upstairs window, but did not see you arrive and had just
now come down to ask Mrs. O'Malley your expected time
of arrival."

"I had quite an unusual afternoon, and this...this is a
most welcome letter from our friend, Jonathan. The *Times*
is sending him here to do a series of articles about some of
the new businesses that have come to Chicago. He will be
here on Friday."

"How wonderful, our trio will be back in full form. We
shall have a proper celebration. I will take us all to a fine
restaurant in celebration of our being reunited."

"That would be lovely. The evening is almost upon us, the breeze rushing in through the trees, and I have sat on this porch many nights imagining you both here with me. Now it will come to be. I am thoroughly delighted."

"I am anxious to learn about your adventure this afternoon, and I shall tell you what I have been about."

"Shall we plan our conversation for after dinner in our usual spot with our bottle of wine?"

She nodded and said, "It is pleasant and calming to sit there with you, an intimate setting that I have come to look forward to."

At dinner, Phillip spoke with gaiety about his journey through the city. Mrs. O'Malley reminded them of her luncheon with Lady Mary the next day, which she was looking forward to. It was, once again, a pleasant gathering of friends and family. Madeline did not speak about her meeting with the Harrisons, preferring to talk with Hugh about it later in the evening.

She had brought candles into the room, as there was no moon that night. They spoke by the flickering light, enjoying the warmth of the wine and the company.

"I have been to Beverly to see some of the homes designed by Mr. Wright. They are amazing. Although the prairie-style home is interesting, I prefer the Victorian, probably because of my upbringing. I have secured an interview with him through his business associates. If the price is within my means, I hope to employ him to design my home in Oak Park."

"That is a lofty goal, indeed. To have such riches must give you a feeling of power that you can choose your path on your own terms."

"And perhaps one day begin a family."

His comment and how he was looking at her as he said it somehow made her feel uncomfortable. Was it possible that he had feelings for her of another kind than just friendship? She hoped not. She admired him, and he was in her heart, but still only as a friend.

"Would you want to live in America when all your family is in England?"

"I suppose I would like to divide my time between both places. Many people do such things all the time and have successful lives."

"It makes me happy to think that I will have the pleasure of your company whenever you are in America. I'm sure Father will also feel the same way."

"You will come with me to Oak Park some time to see the homes Mr. Wright has designed?"

"Yes. Oak Park is a grand neighborhood, and I have only seen pictures of Mr. Wright's homes in the news and not ventured to the actual houses. It will be a fine way to spend a day. Perhaps in the near future, but for now, I feel I must put my time into this case."

"Yes, yes...tell me what happened today. I thought about you all day, wondering how you got through it."

"Alfred was exceptionally kind—almost too kind—but I will try to remain neutral where he is concerned. The office they took me to on the third floor looked designed to elude whoever might be trying to find their way. There were many short hallways and detours that he led me through. With so many doors, it didn't seem possible that there could be something behind each one of them—the rooms would have to be as tiny as a closet. And the doors, I have never seen anything like it. Each one carved or decorated elaborately, almost something you would see in a child's playhouse. It was fascinating. Alfred stated that the Harrisons were just unconventional and designed it to fit their surreal imagination.

As expected, Christopher again did not speak to me, observing the room from the farthest point, smoking a cigar, and barely exhibiting an expression of any kind. Patrick was again nervous. Joseph was the most amiable of the three. Although even he displayed curtness in his actions towards me."

"Everything you told me so far holds with our impression about the brothers, but the doors and the intricate winding of the corridors, well, that is interesting. I would like to see it sometime. Did you get their permission to inquire about the missing girls?"

"Surprisingly, they did allow me, but with the stipulation that Alfred must accompany me. But beyond the unusual myriad of doors, something else proved even more perplexing. Right before I was about to leave, a lady screamed. I looked at the brothers immediately for a reaction. I was wondering whether they were going to deny that they even heard it, but they, like me, seemed genuinely startled to hear it. In the next moment, we heard more of a moan. Alfred jumped up and disappeared while we all sat there saying nothing. He returned a few minutes later, saying it was Lady Mary, and she was in the library room. She had gone up the library ladder and, when coming down, faltered and twisted her ankle. I thought it a preposterous lie and had visions of some girl being trapped in another room. However, as I was leaving, she peered out through the door of the library."

"It sounds like a work of fiction. It is a strangely beautiful place, this Harrison. It looks as beautiful and inviting as a cathedral, but inside holds elusive secrets."

"The Harrisons and their hotel, whether intentional or not, have created with their eccentricities a place of mystery, and maybe more than that—murder."

She finally said it aloud, what she had been thinking these last few days.

Hugh stopped and looked at her, this time with a serious face, the kind she had witnessed in London after finding a Ripper victim.

"Madeline, do you truly believe it may come to that—murder?"

"I feel foolish saying it aloud, but it has been in my thoughts. I'm afraid everyone, but you may think I have lost my mind. That I am trying to create something that isn't there because of what happened in London."

"No, I can feel it too. Something is going on in that hotel, it may not be murder, but something."

"I saw Nancy and gave her the candy, so soon we will hear about that matter. I do believe that we will have a busy few weeks coming up."

When they stood to say good-night, he reached over, took both her hands in his, and said, "You are the right person for this. Your empathy and compassion for people is a wonderful thing. With the gift of life comes the burdens of life. You have known more than most, and somehow I think you will get to the bottom of this."

She blushed—it would have been impossible not to—for instead of pulling away quickly as she usually would have, she let him hold her hands and felt renewed by his touch.

"Thank you. Until tomorrow then..."

Chapter 9

It's Murder

In the morning, Hugh and Phillip once again set out early to see something of her Chicago. She mused that they probably would see things she had not seen herself or had not seen for a while; such is the benefit of being a tourist. Her schedule included returning Maria's dress to the Falco family and updating them with what she had discovered, such as the chocolates in the dress. She knew if she were right, and they contained drugs of some sort, she would then be obligated to take the information to the police. She wanted to speak to them about that also.

But before she left, she wanted to ask a favor of their cook.

"Mrs. O'Malley, are you still meeting with Lady Mary today for luncheon?"

"I am looking forward to it. She's a wonder, that one... not the sort of person I get to meet. It will be something to talk about in the market afterward."

"I did not mention this at dinner, but something odd happened yesterday while I was meeting with the Harrisons. As I was about to make my departure, a lady screamed, and then shortly after that, I heard moaning. I was quite unnerved by this and believed perhaps a crime committed, but it turned out to be Lady Mary, who had screamed. She was in the library down the hall. Supposedly she had fallen and hurt her ankle. Could you possibly discover if any of this story is true? I mean, I saw her in the doorway of a room. I don't know if it was a library, or if it was she who did the screaming."

"I can see life will be much more interesting now that you have become a detective, Miss. I don't suppose it will be that difficult to find that out. I hope to gain her trust and find out all I can, but I think we cannot underestimate her. I don't know how much of it is just play acting. We'll see."

"I am sure either way, it will be an entertaining lunch. Have a wonderful time. I will see you this evening," said Madeline as she left the home.

She hoped sufficient time had passed and that perhaps it was easier for Louie and Rosa to speak about Maria. When she arrived at their home, Louie met her at the door.

"It is good to see you. I suppose you are here because you know."

"I'm sorry...know what? I am here with some news, so I am not certain what you mean."

He picked up the newspaper that was laid open on their dining room table and pointed to the fourth page's article. It was short, just one short sentence and a few paragraphs of news, but the headline certainly caught Madeline's attention. In bold letters, it read, *"It's Murder...Maria Falco's Death Now Ruled Homicide"*.

She read the brief article that stated an eye-witness had now come forward to testify he had seen an unidentified man push Maria into the carriage path. He had been reluctant to come forward, believing he might then be in danger, but his wife persuaded him to do so. They described the man as having a short, stocky build, but because his long coat pulled up around his neck and a bowler hat pushed down across his face, the witness could give no further details. The person's identity is not known.

"Like you, I have believed foul play possible from the first reporting of this incident," said Madeline.

"My poor sister, to have met with such an end, still...It is a relief to know the police will look into it and find out what happened to her.

"You said you have news for me?" asked Louie.

She had brought Maria's dress back with her and now showed Louie the separation in her dress where the chocolates were.

"The powder on the dress was nothing more than sugar and salt. I had believed it might have turned out to be some type of drug...perhaps someone manipulated her through drugs. I was surprised that it turned out to be nothing. Then by chance, we discovered that Maria had hidden these chocolates in her dress. I am having them analyzed as we speak. I suppose that perhaps she knew the pieces of chocolate contained an opiate or something that dulled her ability to escape her captor. Perhaps this is how she escaped; her kidnapper did not know she had her wits about her and had not taken the drugged candy. Whoever held her prisoner might have believed she was in a drugged state of mind and would pose no threat. Of course, this is all conjecture for the moment, but it seems a good possibility."

"That is the most unusual news. There must be some logic behind such a gesture; no one hides chocolates in their clothing. And now, with this new turn in the case, it seems, as you say, that someone held my sister against her will.

"Rosa and I both want you to continue investigating. She had a two-thousand-dollar life insurance policy in which she named my sister and me as benefactors. We would like to give you two hundred of it to continue to work on this case."

"That is a great deal of money, Mr. Falco. I am not certain I should accept it. I cannot guarantee that I will find the answers you are looking for."

"Nonetheless, we believe in you. From the first, you were the only person who took an interest and had the correct supposition about what might have happened. Rosa is a little better; your father has been to see her several times. Most days, she remains in her room, but she does come down for dinner now. That is an improvement. Perhaps next time I see you, she will come down and speak to you also."

She shook his hand and said, "I will do everything that I can and will endeavor to report back to you every few days. If there is anything else that you discover, please send word to me, and I will come to your home."

"This is a beginning. There will be no peace for us until the person who did this is in jail."

"I understand."

She left their home feeling that all newly discovered facts were leading in the same direction. There was indeed a murderer loose somewhere in her neighborhood.

In light of this news, she decided to return to the Erie Street market area. She would try to engage Jacob, the street vendor, in further conversation.

"Jacob, may I speak to you?" she asked when she saw his familiar, friendly face.

"Miss, I know what you are here to talk to me about, and I don't think it best for me to talk about it."

"May I ask why?"

"You don't know these streets as I do. It's not always safe, but now, it's not wise to talk to anyone when there looks to be a murderer about them. You can get a reputation of a snitch, and that's never healthy."

"Can I ask if it was you who contacted the police?"

"Miss, that's exactly the kind of thing I'm talking about. It wasn't me. That's all I can be saying."

"If you do see something, I am willing to pay for the information, and I promise you no one will know I spoke to you."

"Pay for information? Hmm...now that's another matter, I will think on it."

She wrote her name and contact information down and handed it to him.

"If you don't feel comfortable coming around, I will be back within the week to check with you."

"All right. I'll keep my eyes open for you."

The hotel was now within walking distance, so she decided she would just stop in for a minute to see if Marilyn or Nancy might be there. When Madeline did not see them, she took a seat, and when the waiter came by, she found herself saying, "An absinthe, please."

She almost called him back to change her order to tea, but then surmised this was only the third time in many months that she had partaken of the forbidden substance. She rationalized that the stress of these past few days had made her believe she had earned a brief respite from abstaining. She wondered if she would always fight this demon, and then sometimes didn't think it was a demon at all, being only natural to partake in substances that helped alleviate one's suffering.

"I see you also like the lovely *fée verte*. In my country, it is well-liked," said Joanie Sobon.

Madeline had not seen the artist come up behind her. The scent of oil paint was a welcome one, as she also had a passion for painting.

"Yes, the 'green fairy' it is well-liked here also. I learned of it while in London, becoming addicted to this smooth nectar of the gods."

When Madeline was in London, absinthe, a green-colored liqueur, was all the rage, and people nicknamed it the 'green fairy.'

"May I join you," asked Miss Sobon.

"Certainly. Where is the inimitable Vincenzo?"

"Here is somewhere that I do not know of. It is extraordinary, indeed. Someone hired Vincenzo to paint for them, but with the understanding that their identity be unknown. Vicenzo says he doesn't know where he goes. But with the generous monies received, we can leave here and perhaps return to my beautiful city of light, Paris. Or, if not there, we will be able to rent a loft somewhere. It is not where a true artist paints, in the lobby of a hotel; it is what you Americans call crass."

"I understand that sentiment, but everyone here admired you both, and it is one of the finest hotels in the city."

"Yes, that is true. I suppose that is why we tolerate it for now, but soon, we shall have money. That will change everything."

"That sounds interesting. There seems to be no shortage of secrets that surround this hotel."

"I must go now. Alfred is waving to me to get back to work. Ahh...that is life."

Madeline walked home, stopping in the park to sit and watch the pigeons and the children play. She chastised herself for consuming the absinthe, and then in the next moment, thought of her lost children and believed perhaps it wasn't so dire that she ease her mind somehow.

No one was home when she returned. She retrieved her Conan Doyle mystery book and sat reading by the window seat, looking up periodically with the hope that Hugh or Mrs. O'Malley would return soon.

Mrs. O'Malley arrived first; her usual easy-paced walk became a quick bound up the steps. She knew she must have something interesting to tell her.

"Miss, I'll get us some tea. Oh...she is a character that one. I think she has had an unusual background, not one like my lady friends and I have cooking and sewing all the time. She is the kind of person we would talk about in whispers."

"I'll make the tea. You freshen up, and then we can meet in the dining room."

"I'll be there in a few minutes. I would like to change my shoes. I'm don't like such tight boots."

When Mrs. O'Malley sat down, Madeline was leaning forward in her seat, pouring her a cup of tea and waiting impatiently for her to speak.

"I don't remember when I have seen you in such a state. You look flushed. You must have had an exciting time," said Madeline.

"I've never played the part of a detective. I found it rather stimulating. She is not the type of person I might have otherwise associated with. Not that there is anything wrong with her— she's just a little too modern and bold for my taste."

"Yes, go on...," said Madeline, trying to hurry her to speak about their luncheon details.

"It took two drinks of bourbon and soda before she opened up about anything. She seemed pleasantly surprised that I was treating her—the money you gave me helped initiate some goodwill with her. When she did start talking, however, she told me things that were quite private."

"For instance..."

"She said she was a dear friend of the Harrison's mother. They had played together as children and even went to boarding school together. When Lady Mary's sister had a child out of wedlock, and as the Harrison's, could have no further children, agreed to raise the child."

"So, one ofthe Harrison boys is adopted?"

"Yes, the bulky looking one, Patrick."

"That explains his physical differences from his brothers—but he does resemble them. Perhaps, it is as they say that you begin to take on the appearance of those you spend so much time with. Maybe it is his mannerisms, but I would never have guessed by just his appearance that he wasn't a blood brother. He fits in with them like any group of brothers I have ever seen."

"It gets even better. Alfred was an orphaned boy, left on their steps. The Harrison's had always been a prominent family, known for their investments in the rails, and whoever left him felt they would care for him."

"And did they?"

"They took him in, and a nanny cared for him. Of course, the brothers were a good ten years older than him. They didn't adopt him but cared for his financial needs and sent him off to boarding school. When he finished, he returned and became their assistant."

"That certainly explains her protective nature of them, and them for her. Did you find out anything about that day in the library?"

"She was the most reluctant to speak about that, but eventually, she did. She said she likes to go to the library because sometimes she sneaks a cigarette up there. She likes to look through the old books, especially the racy romance books. I can tell you she did not sprain her ankle. I admired her boots and asked to have a better look, and she was right as rain...no swelling, and she did not walk with any limp or pain. Of course, I didn't want to mention the scream at all because I didn't want her to know you might have asked me about it.

"She said she had quite the fright the other day when she went into the corner of the library, into a little-used nook, and there she saw a hanging skeleton."

"A skeleton? Did she call the police?"

"No, she said Alfred told her its use was for the education of the bone structure and nothing more."

"I do suppose a library might have such things when you have such unusual owners. So that's why she screamed. I wonder why Alfred lied about it though, why wouldn't he have just told the truth. It would make an amusing tale.

"What a great job you did. You found out more than I could have hoped for."

"I enjoyed doing it. I suppose I have made a new friend in Lady Mary. I'm sure I will see her again."

"Did she happen to mention the missing girls?"

"She said that she thought they must all be low women, especially if they were about the city without an escort. She said she did not pity them."

"That's a rather cynical view and not one I think most women would have."

"I dare say not. How could anyone help but have anything but sorrow for what happened to those girls!"

"I agree."

"I'll be attending to the dinner now. I was happy to be of help to you."

She would have much to tell everyone at dinner this evening. This time she would share her news.

Hugh and Phillip returned, packages in hand; Phillip having purchased gifts for his family back in England.

At dinner, Mrs. O'Malley retold her story about her meeting with Lady Mary.

"It does seem odd that there would be a skeleton hanging there, even if it was for study purposes. What do the Harrisons do that would involve needing that? Of course, as pointed out, they are a strange lot. I suppose we don't know enough about them yet to judge whether that is just normal for them," said Hugh.

"Alfred mentioned to me that they each had different things they collect. Patrick is an avid hunter and mounts his dead birds in a room somewhere. He, at some point in his childhood, became interested in taxidermy. Joseph and Christopher each have their collections as well. I think he said Joseph's was stamps and Christopher miniature statues of horses, or the other way around. But apparently, their interests are diverse and include many different things," said Madeline.

"I wish I could sneak up to the third floor or see what's behind all those ornate doors," said Phillip. "They sound more compelling to see than the shops on the first floor."

"Jonathan will be here in two days—I wonder what he will have to say about this. As a journalist, he will have a particularly keen view."

"Yes, it will be good to see him," said Hugh.

They bid each other good-night, except, of course, for Hugh, who remained for their nightly visit. She enjoyed ending the day with him, talking about the day's events, and sipping on tea or a glass of wine. It had given her a peacefulness she had not known for a long time.

She had not written in her journal for quite a while. Life had been so busy. When Hugh left her, she spent a few moments before retiring writing in her journal.

There has been a witness to the murder of Maria Falco. The public does not know who it is, but nonetheless, it is as we all suspected. Wanda Gapinski, I believe, will also be found to have been murdered and not accidentally drowned. I am planning on visiting the family tomorrow. Mr. Gapinski agreed to meet with me. My primary interest is learning about his daughter's suitors.

It is wonderful to have Hugh and Phillip with us. Although Phillip will be returning to sea shortly, Jonathan will be here, and at least I will have two of my best friends with me.

I also hope to continue to be a presence at the Harrison and try to uncover some of its many secrets.

She had sent word to Wanda's father that she hoped to meet with him tomorrow, and he had sent back his agreement to see her.

The next day, Hugh escorted her to Wanda Gapinski's home.

"Do I understand correctly…that there is a dead woman in the river?" asked Hugh.

"So it is believed, but her best friend, Felicia, who was with her at the time of her disappearance, is still missing. I find it unlikely that she will be found alive. A fisherman found Wanda. There didn't seem to be signs of any struggle, but she also may have been drugged. I doubt there was an investigation into that. I don't think the family would press the matter and ask for an autopsy, as they do not want their daughter's body disfigured in any way. It has something to do with their religious beliefs. I had spoken briefly to them about it, and they were against the idea of it. The police have shown no interest in examining the body further and are satisfied that it was a drowning."

"I suppose the family would find the idea of a drowning easier to deal with than the prospect of murder. The family might not want to believe that this could have been their daughter's fate."

"My thoughts exactly…I think it would be much less painful to think it was an accidental drowning, but nothing explains how she happened to fall into the river without identification.

"The house is just a few doors down."

Mr. Gapinski opened the door and stepped outside to speak to her.

"If you don't mind, can we walk down to the park to talk? My wife is not in the state of mind to hear us speak about our daughter. I don't know when it will ever be the case when she will hear her name and not weep. It is also true for her sister, Alice."

"Have the police spoken to you at all since our last meeting?" asked Madeline.

"Not at all. They think it was an unfortunate accident."

"What do you believe?"

"I know that Felicia is still missing. Two girls don't just vanish, and one ends up in the river without a black hand involved in it. My wife should think she drowned, so I do not discuss it with her, but I don't believe it for a minute."

"The police mentioned that they believed your daughter was engaged. Did she have a fiancé?"

"No, she wasn't involved with anyone. She had her group of girlfriends and seemed content with that. She was more interested in finding ways to make money and pull herself out of our continued life of painful poverty. We came to this country from Poland with nothing, and now we have little more than that, but we always had hope...that is, until now."

"What is the relevance of her having a fiancé?" asked Hugh.

"I think I know why you are asking," said Mr. Gapinski.

With that, he pulled a ring from his pocket. Madeline's eyes widened. Maria had the same ring, a platinum band with a row of diamonds that resembled an engagement or wedding ring.

"What is it?" asked Mr. Gapinski.

"It is nothing; it is an unusual ring to have for someone that is not engaged. It looks expensive," said Madeline.

"It is not something she would have had. If she owned something like this, I never saw it. The way she was, if she had obtained something like this, she would have sold it to help the family...that's the kind of girl she was. Who could she have met that would have given her such a valuable piece of jewelry in the short time that she was missing? And if she met someone who gave her such an item, why would they then harm her? None of it makes any sense," said Mr.Gapinski.

"Did you speak to the police about the ring?" asked Hugh.

"I did, but they dismissed it by saying young women do not tell their parents everything and that if she had a secret love, she might not have told us about it."

"It does seem as if your constabulary here is satisfied with easy answers and not inclined to dig deeper into these matters," continued Hugh.

"Yes, our city is understaffed for such matters, and because there is no clear evidence, they are content to leave it alone," said Madeline. "I believe this ring may be of some importance."

"I will keep it safely locked away in the event it is evidence," said Mr. Gapinski.

Riding back in the carriage toward their home, Hugh asked, "What was that all about...the business of the ring?"

"It is the same ring found with Maria's things. I will tell Louie and leave it to him to take the information to the police. There is no way they can now dismiss the connection between these two girl's deaths. I will ask Louie to confer with Mr. Gapinski—I thought it was best to let Mr. Falco present this information to him."

"I see why you didn't say anything. That could be a blow he might not be ready for."

"I'm hoping that Louie Falco might bring his ring to Mr. Gapinski to confirm it and then go from there."

"You are knee-deep in it now. I can't imagine Jonathan not wishing to throw himself into this investigation with you when he gets here. Do you wish to stop at The Harrison?"

"Yes, you are as in tune with my thoughts as you were in London."

The carriage let them off on Erie Street's corner, where Little Tony, the newsboy, was busy peddling his papers. In his loudest staccato voice, he rang out, "*Another three gone missing—disappearance frightens neighborhood. Read all about it—one murdered, six missing*".

"Tony, what is this all about?" asked Madeline.

"Two tourists visiting and one more local girl...vanished. The papers selling like hotcakes off the griddle—my best morning in two weeks. Where'd ya' think those girls got themselves to?"

"It is a mystery, Tony, and hopefully, someone will find out before anyone else goes missing," said Madeline as Hugh paid him for two papers.

Just then, Patrick Harrison came out, flushed-faced with beads of sweat on his forehead, and yelled at Tony, "Take yourself away from here, young man. It is a place of business. People don't wish to be bothered with your screaming. Out—out."

"All right, mister...all right," said Little Tony, as he moved across the street close to where Jacob was.

Patrick Harrison strode past Madeline and Hugh without even looking up at them as if they were invisible. He marched through the doors spitting angry words to the doorman, demanding he keep Tony from reentering the space in front of his hotel.

When they entered the hotel, an excited Marilyn leaped from her place in the French cafe, where she sat with her twin sister. Waving to them, she held a piece of paper in her hand, "Madeline, it is opium, just as you had guessed. Imagine...what a discovery."

Madeline leaned over to embrace her and thank her for what she had done.

"Will you go to the police with this information?" asked Marilyn.

"Of course. I must. There is other startling news also."

She went on to tell Marilyn and Nancy of what she discovered about the supposed engagement rings.

"Did you see Mr. Harrison run out to the street and chase poor Little Tony away?" asked Madeline.

"Yes, the missing women...at least, I think that's why he acted the way he did," said Marilyn.

"All the brothers were in the lobby. They huddled around together over the paper," said Nancy.

"The tall one, what is his name?" asked Hugh.

"That is Christopher, the one with a little gray at the temples."

"He appears to guide the others. They do all the talking, and he barely says anything but seems to control them just the same," said Hugh.

"He never said one word to me when we had our meeting. I don't know if it's arrogance or just pure pride that he feels he is so far above the mere mortals who come to his hotel," said Madeline.

When the three brothers left through their private elevator, everyone returned to their familiar chatter.

"I think they are finally feeling a little pressure about the girls. Have you or Nancy heard anything about the new ones who are missing?" asked Madeline.

"When Little Tony began calling out, most people went out to buy a paper. I only know what we read...two of the girls missing are tourists, the other is local. The two girls were visiting the Auditorium Building. The other, it is not known where she was last," said Nancy.

"Then the brothers should not have been concerned if they were not associated with their hotel," said Hugh.

"Perhaps they know the police will be more likely to be vigorous in their search as the numbers of girls gone missing will have the city's residents demanding some action," said Madeline.

Marilyn handed Madeline the remains of the chocolate and the results.

"I suppose the police will question me now," said Marilyn.

"I can't imagine that they wouldn't, you don't mind, do you?" asked Madeline.

"No, of course not. I would like to help in any way I can; those missing girls could be any one of us," said Marilyn.

"There is Lady Mary on the outside patio. She is with an older man I have not seen before," said Madeline.

"I have seen him with her. I think he is a hotel guest. He, like Alfred, appears to take a protective watch over her."

He was short, with a bulging chest area that protruded through his coat jacket. For a moment, she wondered about what the witness had said about the person who pushed Maria. He fit the description, as did Patrick. But, of course, there were a hundred people within her neighborhood who probably would fit that description.

During their return ride, Hugh and she both sat reading the article about the missing girls.

"When Jonathan arrives and writes about the Auditorium Building, he will find he has another story as well now to write about," said Hugh.

"I think I will go to the police station," said Madeline.

"And I back to meet with my building designers," said Hugh.

She found that this time, the police officer was interested in what she had to say. They took the chocolate and said they would investigate the situation with the rings. She left, hoping that now the story of the missing girls would receive the attention it deserved.

Tomorrow Jonathan would be there, and they would be able to hear his thoughts on these matters.

Chapter 10

Jonathan Arrives

They were all anticipating Jonathan's arrival with joy, as another member of their cherished group from London would join them. Jonathan sent a telegram stating they should expect him at five at the latest. His train arrived in Chicago around noon, but he had things he needed to attend to before meeting with them.

Madeline would not see Hugh and Phillip until the late afternoon when they planned to gather for tea to welcome Jonathan. She would use that day to prepare the house, picking flowers from her moonlight garden, and purchasing additional radiant roses from the market.

She had visited Louie Falco, who had agreed to meet with Mr. Gapinski to tell him of the similar rings found in both their daughters' belongings.

Perhaps tomorrow, she would go to the hotel and ask Alfred's assistance to do her canvassing of the Harrison's businesses regarding the missing girls.

She had spent more time on her appearance, hoping to garner the approval of her male friends. During her time with them in London, they almost always saw her in a mourning dress. Choosing to wear her burgundy satin dress—the back accented with bows on the decorative flocked purple paisley, she was pleased with the way she looked. It was the latest fashion seen on State Street, and she had recently acquired it as a gift from her father.

Mrs. O'Malley was away for the weekend visiting an ailing friend, so it would be up to her to serve her guests. As yet another baby decided to be born on that rainy day, her father could not join them. Just as with Hugh's arrival, the early autumn weather produced dark clouds and steady, dripping rain to invade their happy reunion.

Promptly at four, Phillip was the first to arrive.

She was pouring the attractive young man a cup of tea when he remarked, "You look very lovely, Mrs. Donovan."

"Thank you, Phillip."

"What news of Jonathan?"

"Jonathan sent a telegram stating he should be here no later than five. It will be grand to have all of you here with me again.

"How are you, Phillip? Are you still enjoying your time at sea?"

"Fine...fine...and yes, I don't suppose I will ever meet a lady I will love as much as the sea. I think I am resigned to bachelorhood."

"You are so young to say so. I'm sure time will change all that. Someday someone will walk onto the ship, and you will lose your heart, and you will think of nothing else after that. You have far too much kindness and compassion within you to not share that with a woman."

"Maybe someday, but I don't think for a long time. On the other hand, I think Hugh is seeking a life companion at the time. He certainly was happy to travel to America, and if I may speak plainly, I don't think it was just to purchase property in Chicago."

She put her head down for a moment to hide her noticeable blushing at his frank observation.

"I hope I have not spoken out of turn, but I believe we have an understanding between us that allows me to speak openly," Phillip said in an apologetic tone.

"Of course...you may always do so. I suppose I am not ready to hear such words yet, however flattering they may be. I do so admire your cousin and value his friendship in every way, but I do hope he does not wish it to be anything more than that. As you have said, perhaps someday," replied Madeline.

"Would you like me to share those thoughts with him?" he inquired.

"Oh...no...I wouldn't for the world wish to offend him in any way. I think he knows me well enough to realize that for himself," she said shyly.

"After the business in Whitechapel, I thought you might have been reluctant to have put yourself in a position of possible danger again."

"It is curious. I once thought that also, but it gives me purpose, and that is something I dearly need."

"I hear him now coming down the stairs," said Phillip as he opened the door for his cousin.

"A good cup of tea—always welcome on an afternoon like this," said Hugh.

"Yes, please come and join us," said Madeline.

"May I say you look lovely," he continued.

"Thank you, may I say you both look rather dashing. It is a dreary day, but it will be all the brighter because you are here. I planned on all of us going to the Austin House for dinner. I have been there only once but found it to be quite pleasant. The fine dining, the orchestra, and the large dancing area were notable. It is a gay atmosphere, and I think you might both like it," said Madeline.

"We will reunite, and that will make the evening pleasurable wherever we are," said Hugh.

Peering through the window, they could see Jonathan arriving. Pulling his coat up around him to protect him from the rain, he scurried up the stairs. Hugh went out to greet him as he was carrying packages, and Hugh wished to assist him.

He had brought with him caramel biscuits, two small baskets of fruits and vegetables, along with scented candles for Madeline.

"What a kind gesture," said Madeline. "We would have been more than happy just to see you. You are too generous to bring all these treats for us."

"I hope there is enough to pass along to all of you.

"Where is your father?" asked Jonathan.

"Where he always seems to be...tending to a patient. One of our neighbors went into early labor. She wasn't to deliver for two more weeks," said Madeline.

"I'm sure I shall see him. I hope to enjoy your company for a full month," replied Jonathan.

The men shook hands, and Jonathan bowed slightly to her, giving her a broad, disarming smile.

"This rain, it has followed me everywhere. My last assignment was in Connecticut. It rained every day, but we will not let it deter us from having a lovely evening together," he continued.

Jonathan was slightly taller than Hugh and Phillip, all of them standing around five-foot-ten to six-foot-tall. They all had different shades of brown hair, but Hugh had some waves near his forehead. But that was the only similarity. Jonathan was not the perfectly mannered and groomed gentleman like Hugh. He was somewhat disheveled, paced when nervous, and was anxious always to keep moving—in other words, an American. His words not chosen as carefully chosen as Hugh's, and he was franker in his observations. As a reporter, it sometimes felt like he was always trying to get a story out of people and would ask many more personal questions than Hugh would ever think to do. He had more of the boyish good looks than Hugh, who looked sculpted from bronze. She admired them both, as different as they were because they shared strong characteristics of integrity and kindness.

"The tea is warming and feels soothing on a day like this. I have endeavored to be in asclose proximity as I can to all of you. After consulting with several people, I took a room in what seems to be an exquisite hotel, the Harrison," said Jonathan.

There was silence for a moment as Hugh, Phillip, and she all looked at each other, exchanging glances of amusement.

"What is it?" asked Jonathan.

"My friend, inadvertently, you have put yourself into the heart of a mystery that could not be more suitable for someone like you," said Hugh.

"That couldn't be more wonderful—it will prove highly useful. We must coordinate our efforts now that you have gained us even more access," said Madeline.

"All right...will someone explain to me what you are all talking about," asked Jonathan.

They started speaking at once, each eager to tell Jonathan all the news about the missing girls, the Harrison, and the recent evidence Marilyn had discovered.

"The Auditorium Building story pales in comparison to what you have all told me. Madeline, it seems you have done some first-class detecting and assisted the police. I'd like to interview you about it. If you would like to remain anonymous, that would be fine. Perhaps you and I can visit the Auditorium Building together and then follow up with the interview," said Jonathan.

"I think I'd rather not have my name attached to it, but yes, I would like to tell the story. The coverage of these missing girls should be on the front page, not the fifth or sixth," said Madeline.

"We can continue our conversation at the Austin House. I think we should leave before the storm gets any worse," said Hugh.

The Austin House reputation for lavish surroundings, and enticing clientele of every age, young and old, to its doors because of its beautiful decor and modern dance music, was known to everyone. The dance floor wasn't extensive but large enough for thirty or more people to dance simultaneously. Its decor included gleaming red walls with large oil paintings in ornately carved gold frames. It was high society at its best.

They had just finished ordering when Hugh said, "Isn't that Patrick and Joseph Harrison?"

"It is, and they look to be in a heated discussion. If only I could hear what they are saying," said Madeline.

"That's where I come in. They don't know me. Perhaps I can strike up a conversation with them, or at least eavesdrop on the one they are having," said Jonathan.

Hugh pointed them the two out who were standing against the long, granite top bar.

"What luck to see them and to have Jonathan with us," said Phillip.

"The quiet, rude one, I see him also. He is on the farthest end of the bar, and, of all things, engaging in conversation with a woman. How odd that he has removed himself from his other brothers," commented Madeline.

"I shall be the interloper with that one. He has not seen me either. What is his name?" asked Phillip.

"That one is Christopher. We shall ask the waiter to hold our dinner," said Madeline.

"Here, we are missing everything. I think we might do something about that. My lady...," said Hugh as he escorted her to the dance floor.

While dancing, she could position herself nearer to the Harrisons. She didn't even hesitate to accept—feeling comfortable in his arms only because she was playing a part.

"Mr. Scott, it has been a long time since I have found myself on a dance floor. I do hope you will forgive me if I am not as adept as I once was."

"They are playing a waltz. It is a most convenient choice as we can easily glide past the area where Patrick and Joseph are standing," replied Hugh.

"You will follow my lead, won't you?" Madeline asked.

"What do you mean?" asked Hugh.

"Please keep dancing. You'll see," she replied.

She then wiped her brow and said, "Forgive me, I do feel a little lightheaded. Do you mind if we stop for a moment?"

She conveniently stopped within earshot of Patrick Harrison's conversation. Jonathan had easily placed himself on the other side of Joseph, offering to buy him a drink.

The two brothers did not notice them at all, and with her back toward them, she knew it was unlikely that they would recognize Hugh, even though he had been present at the hotel when they had first seen the brothers.

"Who would have thought our lovely dinner would turn out like this? None of us even sitting at our table, and all of us playing at this game," said Madeline.

"It is difficult not to get involved in this intrigue. Whatever our conversation might have been—I do believe this is more stimulating," said Hugh.

"It appears Jonathan has succeeded in engaging Joseph in conversation," she said quietly.

The band stopped playing for their scheduled break, and without the noise distraction, Madeline could hear Patrick say, "I tell you, she knows something and will not leave it alone. And the other one put in his place. How dare he behave like that!"

"Lower your voice," said Joseph. "Enjoy yourself, dance with one of these fine ladies."

Patrick commented sarcastically, "The ladies, oh yes, they follow me around everywhere. I have to pay for my friendships. You and Christopher have always had it easy, but not me."

"Then, I will dance. Try not to get into any more trouble. You know Christopher is already angry with you," said Joseph.

They moved slightly away from her, but Jonathan remained near them.

"I can't hear what they are saying anymore," said Madeline.

"We can't very well keep nudging down the bar to hear them. I think it best to leave it to Jonathan," said Hugh.

They returned to their table, where they could view Phillip standing near Christopher. Phillip had engaged a lovely young woman in conversation.

"Jonathan is returning," said Hugh.

"They're leaving—I know this might sound absurd, but I'd like to follow them. I don't know what their conversation was about, but I'd like to see where they are going," said Jonathan.

"Are you sure, old man, you will be leaving a lovely dinner?" said Hugh.

"It's my nature. It's what I do. I do feel there is a story here. I'll come by your house after and let you know if I find out anything of interest."

With that, he smiled, grabbed a piece of bread from the table, and sipped a bit of wine, and left.

Madeline could see Patrick and Joseph waiting at the hat check area, and now Christopher was walking across the room as well.

"Well, this is not at all how I thought this evening would go," said Madeline.

"Jonathan—he is quite the man. I envy his spirit. I wish I could be more like him sometimes," said Hugh.

"You are both different, but each of you has your own specific strengths. You are steady on and grounded—those are admirable characteristics."

"Phillip has left his young lady and is on his way back to us."

"I saw Jonathan leave, and Christopher soon followed. I confess I wanted to stay and continue talking to the young woman, Sara's her name, but that is not to be today," said Phillip.

"We may as well continue with our dinner, albeit without Jonathan. Phillip, you can tell us what you found out," said Hugh.

"Not much, I am afraid. He spoke very little, just telling the woman next to him how beautiful she was. He said he had a collection of butterflies and that she reminded him of their graceful beauty. It was something an older man might say. I don't think she was responsive to what he was saying, and she seemed uncomfortable. He continued to flatter her and asked her to dance, but she declined. He seemed put off by it but still asked her to join him for dinner. She declined that also, and he now seemed agitated, clenching his fist and hitting it upon the bar. But then he looked up and said, "My brothers, they will be the death of me...". That's when he left to follow his brothers. He obviously saw that they were leaving."

Madeline said, "I think you did discover something of note. For one thing, it confirms my thoughts that perhaps one or more of the brothers have unusual relationships with women. We know so far that they are all bachelor's, despite their aristocratic upbringing and wealth. From what you heard, Phillip, it sounds like the conversation of someone who does not know how to interact with women. I know older men sometimes have a preference for younger women, but his comments were strange."

"What he said about collecting butterflies and then commenting on her resemblance. It is if he may covet beautiful things and wants them in his possession," said Hugh.

"I had hoped to dance perhaps with all of you, and maybe even go on to another club. However, since Jonathan has disappeared, I think we might go back to the house to wait for him."

"I agree. He has taken on a lot for someone who just arrived in a new place, with no bearings of where he is or what he might face. I wish I had gone with him," said Hugh.

"Jonathan is capable, and we probably worry for no reason, but since we agree, we may as well return to the house," said Madeline.

Her father was awake and in the dining area sipping his coffee and smoking a cigar, his one and only vice that he partook of sometimes after a long week.

"But, where is Jonathan?" Father asked with a concerned look on his face.

"Father, it is a strange tale indeed that we have to tell, but we hope that he will arrive soon."

"I will get us some of that lovely cherry pie Mrs. O'Malley left for us. I do believe we also have a bottle of champagne father bought for just such an occasion," said Madeline.

While she was in the kitchen gathering the refreshments, she heard Hugh and Phillip tell her father all that had happened. She could almost see him from the kitchen, shaking his head.

"I am not surprised that Jonathan threw himself into the chase. He struck me like that from the first when I met him in London—the bold type. I don't suppose anything could happen by just following behind a couple of middle-aged, stuffy men," commented father.

"I wish I could say I agree with you, Father, but after all the odd things that have happened, I don't know. I hope you are right, and they are nothing more than eccentric men with too much money for their own good," said Madeline.

They were conversing about the fine supper they had at the Austin and reminiscing about London when her father said, "It's almost midnight, and I'm an old man. I would like to remain to see Jonathan, but I am afraid I can't keep my eyes open."

Phillip stood and said, "I thought I heard something. It was something—like a moan of sorts. Listen."

"Yes, I hear it too," said Hugh as he opened the front door, and he and Phillip made their way outside.

Then Madeline heard Hugh cry out, "Madeline, please bring your father."

Her father heard Hugh and ran out, followed by Madeline.

Just two doors down, lying against one of their neighbor's bottom stair, was Jonathan with a wound on his forehead and a trickle of blood running down his cheek. He was holding his stomach and seemed dazed.

"It's all right," Jonathan said. "I probably look worse than it is. I almost made it to your doorstep. In my confusion, I gave the cabbie the wrong street number. I think I was a bit disoriented, so I walked the rest of the way, but I was only off by a few blocks. I'll be all right if you will give me a hand up."

"Come, let's take a look at that forehead," said Dr. Donovan.

Hugh and Phillip helped Jonathan inside and onto the living room divan. The doctor grabbed his medical bag and began treating the cut on Jonathan's forehead.

He moved slightly and let out a low moan.

"It is my back that I wish you would look at."

The physician gingerly removed Jonathan's shirt; Madeline thought perhaps she should leave, but then decided not to. After all, she had assisted her father in treating many male patients who had removed more than just a shirt.

Across Jonathan's back was a long, raised red mark, appearing as if a rod struck across it. The swollen skin had a three-inch section that was openly pierced and bleeding.

"There is a small section that will require a few stitches. Madeline, will you assist me?"

While Madeline and her father set about the business of treating Jonathan, Hugh asked, "What happened? Did one of those brothers attack you?"

"To tell you the truth, I am not sure what happened. I followed the brothers as they began walking down the street, not paying any attention to their surroundings. I easily followed behind them without their observance. They spoke about whether they would return to the Harrison or continue their night out by going to another hotel. They said something about an art fair going on somewhere.

They stopped to hail a cabbie. I moved a little closer to them to try to hear the address they gave. I was still keeping my distance, trying to remain in the shadows when I felt a sharp stinging across my back. I fell over onto the steps of the home I was standing near and hit my head on the edge of the staircase step. I began to lose consciousness, but I remember someone trying to go through my coat. I yelled out, and I then heard someone open the door to a house. After that, the person ran off. I wasn't able to see their face. A resident came out and helped me inside their home. I was not functioning very well for the next hour or so. They tried to send me to a hospital, but I didn't believe my injuries warranted that. Now you know all that I know."

"Do you think it was an attempt to rob you?" asked Phillip.

"I suppose that is as good as any other assumption. In this business, I often find myself in compromising situations, and I've had my garments all tailored with an additional pocket under the silk lining of my coats. It is not easily accessible with the quick search the assailant did. I know he reached into my coat pocket, but there was nothing there," said Jonathan.

"Do you want to spend the night with us? You may have my room," said her father.

"Thank you, but no. I am even more curious to get back to the Harrison. It was luck that I have a room there and might be able to observe them or better yet—gain their trust and have a conversation with them."

"May I come back with you?" asked Madeline.

"At this hour, Madeline, what are you thinking?" asked father.

"I'm thinking what better time when it's late, and they would not expect us to be around the halls. The Harrison's don't know one of our own has a room there. I would like to see the second floor. No one can gain access to it without a room key. It's after midnight. I think it couldn't be a better time to see who might be lurking around the hotel at this hour."

"I think it's a grand idea," said Hugh.

"Don't think I'm not coming with you," said Phillip.

"In that case, I suppose there is safety in numbers. For someone who was a timid child, you have turned out to be a little bolder than I would wish," he said as he hugged Madeline.

"Do not worry, Father, I'm sure we won't be later than two or so."

Chapter 11

The Third Floor

There were still a few people mingling in the lobby of the Harrison, and some checking in, but it was the quietest Madeline had ever seen the hotel.

A man checked their room key before letting them into the hotel elevator designated only for guests.

"It is a rather nice suite. The accommodations are as fine as anything I have seen in New York," said Jonathan.

The main room was open and roomy, with the additional luxury of a fireplace. There was a small table for dining. On it placed biscuits, fruit, and a bottle of wine. Fine paintings decorated the walls, along with plush furniture with the Eaton trademark.

"It is without equal," said Madeline. "It seems strange that there is an underlying current of something wicked going on within such beautiful surroundings."

Jonathan was visibly struggling, and Hugh commented.

"Perhaps you should stay here, Jonathan. I think you would be more comfortable lying in those silken sheets in your bed than prowling the halls."

"Yes. As much as I would like to accompany you, I believe I cannot. I will leave the door unlatched so that you may come and go as you please. I'm sure I will not sleep and will leave the door open to the bedroom suite."

"It is similar to the third floor—the hallways wind and appears to have not been constructed like any hotel I have ever seen. Shall we meet back here in one hour?" asked Madeline.

"Yes, that should be sufficient time. I will take the area of rooms numbered 1A to 50A," said Phillip.

"All right, I will then take the B group, and Hugh may have the letter C," said Madeline.

Madeline watched her friends quietly slip away down the adjacent corridors. There was no activity to speak of; she heard a few muffled voices and someone softly playing the violin. She passed only two people, a young couple holding hands, paying no attention to her at all. She felt safe for the moment. Still, she had taken a small knife with her, hidden inside her boot, as she once had when walking the streets of Whitechapel.

The late edition of the *Tribune* lay outside the door of what she presumed were guests of the hotel. Whenever she passed a room that did not have a paper lying beside its door, she twisted the doorknob in the hopes she might find an unlocked room. She continued until she came to a door with no number, only the letter B, but found it locked. She attempted to use a hairpin to unlock the door. Someone once told her that this trick was feasible, but as she jiggled the pin in the hole, she did not feel the lock give way. She was kneeling on the floor, peering through the keyhole to see if anything was visible, but the hallway area was too dark for her to see anything clearly. She then accidentally dropped her hairpin. There on the floor, just barely visible to the eye, was a skeleton key, sticking out from under the threshold of the door. Using her knife to guide it out, she pressed the key into her hand as if it were golden.

Holding her breath, she turned the key in the lock. As it opened, her heart raced, and she could feel her palms instantly begin to sweat.

Inside was a narrow staircase, not more than three feet across. There was dust on the stairs, and cobwebs dotted the entire length leaving her to believe that the hotel staff did not use this area.

Tip-toeing up the stairs as quickly as she could in the dark, she reached the exit door. There was a small landing area, where scraps of paper accumulated on the floor. She could not see what, if anything, was written on them but placed them in her satchel. When she bent to pick the papers up, she saw droplets of red. She wondered if the stains on the floor might be blood. However, she dismissed this idea as she felt that someone certainly would have cleaned the area if it had been the result of malice.

She opened the door as slowly as she could to avoid any sound. She found herself back on the third floor, where she had interviewed the Harrison brothers.

She had no bearing on where she might be, although there were kerosene lamps to light the hallways. Some of the doors had markings, and some did not. She turned several doorknobs, discovering them unlocked. She thought perhaps as this was the hotel's private area, they believed there was no need to lock the doors. As she did not see a light coming from under the doors, she thought it safe to open.

Room HJB's only light came from the moon directly shining through its panoramic windows. It made the room come alive with an eerie yet beautiful glow. She assumed this was Joseph's room for in it was an intricately designed collection of every type of butterfly displayed in ornate glass cases upon the walls and some placed in glass boxes on marble pedestals. Every detail in the room appeared like a museum. The butterflies displayed in such an elaborate matter that one would think they were as valuable as a famous work of art. She thought that she would love to have seen this room in the daylight and marveled at every bit of the extraordinary display.

Emerging from the room, she went down a different hallway, careful to remember how to find her way back to the stairwell that led back to the second floor. She then found a series of three doors set so close together she could not imagine what could be behind them. When she opened the middle door, she clapped her hand over her mouth to stop her scream. A figure was staring at her; within inches of her face...it was her. It was nothing more than a full-length mirror behind the door. She looked for evidence that the mirror was on a panel or something that could slide back to reveal another area, but there was none. The other two doors had nothing behind them but a wall. She felt this was the kind of thing one saw at a replication of a haunted house or some such foolery; it made no sense.

Moving down another hallway, she entered the next room. It was yet another collection of objects, but this had none of the surreal beauty of the other room. HCW, as the room letters read, was a collection of weaponry. It was chock-full with guns, of every shape and size, but there were also knives, including Indian tomahawks, mounted against the wall. An entire wall was decorated with swords and displayed the English coat of arms for the Harrison Heritage. It was majestic in a way, she thought, and probably would have been more appreciated by one of her male friends. She heard the sound of a chime and looked up to see a clock on the small desk in the corner had struck one. They had agreed to return in one hour, so she made her way back to the second floor, anxious to tell of what she had discovered. She did not replace the key but kept it with her.

She breathed a sigh of relief when she saw Jonathan's room. Entering, she saw Jonathan had returned to the main area. A glass of bourbon in his hand, he sat making notes in a leather journal.

He looked up and said, "You are the first to return. Come sit by me, and tell me what you have learned."

"I think I will have the strangest tale to tell. I can't imagine Hugh or Phillip having discovered anything like what I did."

Jonathan grimaced as he sat up, straighter in his chair. "That's quite a statement. Go on."

She went on to tell him about stumbling onto the hidden stairwell and finding herself on the third floor.

"After seeing the butterfly collection, I went on to open another door a short distance away. This time, I almost let out a scream as I saw someone behind the door until I realized it was me. It was a full-length mirror behind the door and nothing else. I searched for a latch to see if there was something behind the mirror but could not find one. However, I did not have sufficient time to deliberate there and then found a weapon collection."

"That is incredible, and what was that you said about the markings on the door. Their meaning, I feel, is easily understood, the HJB. I think it indicates Harrison, Joseph, and B for the butterfly collection—it identifies their rooms."

"Yes, that sounds reasonable. The mirror...is yet another sign of how eccentric the brothers are. What does that mean exactly...eccentric enough to..."

"My thoughts exactly...eccentric enough to commit murder? It would be preposterous. They have everything... everything they need or want, including prestige and power. It would make no sense."

"But murder makes no sense. What is in the mind of the murderer is hidden so deep, it even can elude them. They may not be in control of their actions if they are mentally disturbed."

"But they in no way appear to be so, at least not that I can see."

"I am making my observations from what you have told me. I would like to see for myself this third floor."

"I have the key to the stairwell. If you are feeling better tomorrow, we can try again."

"Will you have a look at my back? I feel it may be bleeding still."

He removed his shirt, now stained with red, and she could see another area of the skin had ruptured and was now bleeding. She laid the hotel towels across his back, putting pressure to stop the bleeding.

"Your wound…it is a perfect marking of a walking stick. I cannot imagine it could be other than that."

"It did have a sharp stinging, and the slap it made across my back had a whip-like sound. I believe you are correct. I had a look at the wound in the bathroom mirror."

"May I pour you a glass of wine and bring you some fruit?" asked Madeline

"Yes, that would be most welcome. I feel that I underestimated my condition. The pain has got the better of me, and I have just sat here hoping to sleep, but unable to do so."

"I will have Father give you something for the pain and sleep. I will bring it by tomorrow. I have been permitted by the Harrison's to have their assistant, Alfred, accompany me while questioning the business owners. It will give me the perfect opportunity to come by and also visit you. I thought about asking to bring you along, but perhaps it is better than the Harrison's don't know we are acquainted. It might work to our advantage. If they think that you know me, they will be on their guard around you."

"Perhaps, after all, you should lock the door to my room."

Madeline walked towards the entrance to be met by Phillip.

"I saw Hugh. He is right behind me," said Phillip.

"I was just about to latch the door. This place makes me uneasy," said Madeline.

She waited for Hugh to come around the end of the hall and enter with Phillip.

They gathered around the fireplace, comforted by the warmth and glow it brought, each bringing with them a glass of wine and a small plate of fruit.

"I am glad to return," said Hugh. "The shadows play tricks about the walls, and I kept thinking someone was following me. I turned back several times to see if I was correct but saw nothing."

Then he asked, "Were you able to find out anything?"

"Nothing of interest...the halls were quiet, with a few people still up. I could hear muffled voices, but nothing usual at all. It was rather disappointing."

"How about you, Phillip?" continued Hugh.

"I think I saw Lady Mary. She was with a man...they were stumbling into a room. I think they may both have had too much to drink. She called me "Sonny" and asked me to help them in their room. They were trying to push a large suitcase. It wasn't closed properly and appeared stuffed with female clothing. Her suite was magnificent; she even had a chandelier in the main quarters. She must have thought I was hotel staff because she tipped me. I was about to decline but just thought it better to have her believe I was."

Madeline retold her story, and Phillip wanted to return immediately to take a peek at the third floor. Still, they all decided they had been fortunate enough already to have not been noticed and would try again at another time.

The three bid Jonathan good-night and left for Erie Street.

It was almost three in the morning when they arrived. Madeline was surprised that her father was not up pacing, but he probably resigned himself that she was safe in the company of three strong young men.

"I am sure we are all exhausted. It turned out to be a memorable evening, even if not for the reasons we had thought it would be. I look forward to seeing you gentlemen tomorrow," said Madeline.

The day proved fruitful, and a happy one at that, for her friend had arrived from New York safely and was more than willing to take part in her investigation. She was dismayed by his assault, but he seemed to be taking it in stride. She hoped tomorrow would bring even more clues into the disappearances.

Chapter 12

The Skeleton

"Would you like me to come with you and examine Jonathan?" asked her father.

"I think I would like to bring him back here instead for dinner. Hugh and Phillip can join us. Mrs. O'Malley will return this afternoon, and I will leave a note that we will have guests."

"All right, if you are certain."

"You did a fine job of suturing. I don't think the additional bleeding was anything significant enough that it could not wait to have the wound looked at."

She did not tell father about what had occurred, saying only that they had a pleasant visit with Jonathan.

"Give my best to Jonathan," said the doctor.

"I will, Father, I will," she said as she left to board her awaiting carriage.

She deterred immediately from her destination of going directly to Jonathan's room when she saw Alfred.

"Mrs. Donovan, I have been awaiting your visit. I should have thought you would have come the very next day. You were so adamant about your request," said Alfred.

"I'm afraid I've had a recurrence of a malady I have. I do suffer so with headaches, and when one afflicts me, I find I must pass the day in solitary reading a good book."

"Yes, women do tend to be distressed with such things. We must treat them as the fragile creatures that they are."

"You are so observant and kind."

She wasn't sure if she could fool Alfred. He seemed too bright a young man for such a simple ploy, but she wanted to appear non-threatening. She had thought better of her bold approach, believing it not to be in her favor and would now try the submissive, curious only, young sleuth.

"If you have a seat, I have something I must do for Lady Mary, but I will return shortly."

"You must care for her very much. You seem so attentive to her."

He replied, with an indiscernible smile, "I care for everyone at The Harrison and aim to please."

He turned away, and she looked to see if Marilyn or Nancy were at the cafe. She didn't see them, but Vincenzo and Joanie were painting, appearing every bit the show people and in their element. They were an attraction all into themselves. Her black silk dress, dotted with small roses, came high up her neck, accenting her long neckline. Joanie stood...adorned with black feathers across her hair and dangling, teardrop red earrings. They sparkled brilliantly in the light of the sun streaming into the lobby from the skylights. They stood dipping their brushes in bright-colored oils, painting portraits, and amazing everyone with their skill. Vincenzo appeared in Italian Renaissance garments, his chiseled face glowing in the attention he received from his audience.

"Vincenzo, are these beautiful outfits as a result of your mysterious benefactor?" asked Madeline.

He stopped for a moment and looked quizzically at her, "I am certain I do not know what you are speaking about?"

She realized she might have spoken of something that was not her place to know about. She tried to fabricate an answer.

"Miss Joanie has told me you have sold many paintings to some unknown purveyor of art."

"That is not at all true. What is this silliness! I told Madeline about your secret meeting. What is the harm in that?" said Joanie, tightening her lips together.

"I'm afraid my dear, Joanie, does not always know what she is saying and embellishes many things. You know how French girls are, especially the wickedly, foolish, young ones," he laughed.

Madeline sensed by his actions and the way he turned his back on her, continuing to paint that perhaps she had said too much about something she did not understand.

"It is true. I make up fantasies to keep myself from going completely mad. Our benefactor is a sweet old lady who has bought not two but three paintings from my beloved," said Vincenzo.

"You both look as if you should be painted and set into a fairy tale book," said Madeline. "Could I trouble you to look at these photographs of the missing girls?"

Joanie attempted to browse through the photographs, but Vincenzo barely glanced at them, saying, "People come to look at us, our eyes on our canvas. I'm afraid I notice little else."

Her question revealed a side of Vincenzo she had not seen before. He had always been more than amiable and true to his Italian nature; broad smiled and socially engaging.

⚜

She walked by the various shops and then returned to the French cafe, where she usually sat with Marilyn and Nancy. Lady Mary was outside on the patio, playing cards with her same gentleman friend. When a half-hour passed, and Alfred had still not returned, she decided to see if Lady Mary might speak with her.

⚜

"You're that girl, the one who keeps showing up. I know my Alfred said you mean me no harm, but I don't know...I just don't know," said Lady Mary.

"May I sit?" asked Madeline.

"As you can see, I'm spending my time with my fine friend, Mr. Willie Lancaster. Besides Alfred, he's one of my best companions."

"She's a great lady, and I am sure did not intend to be rude, but is perhaps too forthcoming. After we finish this game, we plan a lovely stroll in the park...perhaps another time," said Willie.

She was not surprised that they put her off but wished she could find out more about her. She definitely appeared to be a woman of means, as each time she saw her, she had worn expensive jewelry and wore the finest gowns.

"Alfred, come over and have a cup of tea," said Lady Mary as she saw him walk over, not caring that she had just refused Madeline the same courtesy.

"Perhaps later, I have promised to take Mrs. Donovan around to the businesses so she may question them about the poor young girls who have gone missing," said Alfred.

"Humph...I thought so. You are up to no good, young lady. You will find yourself in trouble one day...mark my words, you will," said Lady Mary.

"Now Mary," said Willie, "She seems a fine young lady. Do not fret. Let us go for our stroll."

"Where would you like to begin?" asked Alfred.

"I suppose the hat shop. If they were here, it would be an irresistible place to go."

They began their investigation with disappointing results. Most of the owners said so many people came through daily and were inclined to forget if their mother came in. The only person who thought he might have seen both Felicia and Wanda was a jewelry store owner who thought they had been in to have some jewelry appraised but wasn't sure. She observed Alfred through the interviews to see if he had any reaction at all but could discern nothing. He was consistently charming to everyone.

"Is that all for today, Miss?" asked Alfred.

"I do have one favor to ask. When we were last together, and Lady Mary screamed in the room down the hall, you said the room she was in was a fine library. I was wondering if you might show me such a room."

"You mean you would like to see if there is anything amiss in the room to make her scream, as you do not believe she sprained her ankle. Actually, you would be correct, and I will show you why she reacted that way. Come with me."

She was grateful that Alfred had become so cooperative and hoped to find out as much as she could from him about the Harrisons.

When they neared the library, she could hear the brothers arguing in the same room they interviewed her in.

"Pay no mind to that. They always quarrel, but it is about the running of the business. At the end of the day, they bond as all brothers do," said Alfred.

The room, like the others she had secretly seen, was elaborately decorated. The bookshelves themselves were carved and inlaid with ivory. Marble lions, as well as other animals, served as bookends. Stained glass windows gave the room a majestic feel, similar to walking into a grand cathedral.

"If you like, you may take a book or two with you to read. Their collection is one of the finest I have ever seen. I'm sure the brothers would not mind. Around this back area is what our Lady Mary was frightened by."

Secured on a silver pole, hung a skeleton.

"May I ask why they would have such a thing?"

"They are eccentric. They enjoy studying different things. One of the brothers had dabbled in medicine, Patrick, and he still is fascinated by such things."

Although unbeknownst to Alfred, she already knew about the skeleton, still its dangling, white bones startled her. It was terrifying that once, this was a breathing person full of life. Now reduced to bones, its function now hanging on display, for someone's personal amusement, seemed garish. She noted that the skeleton did not look like the ones she had seen while attending university. It seemed so parched white. She also observed that the deceased had linear cracks on their wrist and ankle. By the pelvic bones, she discerned that it must have been a woman.

"Tell me about them, the Harrisons. They are fascinating," said Madeline.

"They are private people. I can tell you they are generous and treat their staff properly. They take great care if someone is in trouble or needs financial assistance. But their personal life must remain so; it is not my place to speak about them."

"Yes, I understand. You have been a most gracious host, Alfred. Thank you for taking me around."

They said their good-byes, and she left the hotel and strolled to the park. She did not wish to have Alfred see her with Jonathan.

While walking back to the hotel, she spotted Jonathan outside purchasing a newspaper. He was across the street conversing with Little Tony, one newsman to another. They were both laughing, and Madeline smiled to see such an innocent sight.

"Jonathan," she called out.

He looked up and waved while walking towards her.

"I wasn't well enough to go out, but certainly anxious to read the daily news. I wish I had access to the New York Times, but I will have to go to a newsstand for that. I had been watching the clock waiting for you to come by. I am glad you are here. Will you have lunch?"

"May we have the meal in your room? I would like it if no one sees us together if possible."

"Of course, I agree. We will order room service."

They walked together but did not converse and tried to appear as strangers. Inside Jonathan's room, now cleaned, had fresh fruit, biscuits, and coffee placed on his table. The fire was crackling, the suite looking every bit the picture on a postcard.

"I want to interview you about all this, Madeline. Let me get my notebook, and you can start at the beginning. I have some general idea from your letter of what has transpired, but I need the full picture. I think our readers would appreciate a story like this rather than a piece about the sights. Although I still will be doing that, I'd like to begin with these disappearances. Besides, for the next day or so, I think I would like to allow my back to heal somewhat."

"Oh...yes...here is the medicine from father. It is an opiate, so do be careful about how much you take."

"The pain I am in right now, I feel anything that can alleviate some of my distress will prove a blessing."

It was still difficult for her to be around the white powdery substance that could end one's suffering for a while and bring wonderful peace. She watched as Jonathan almost immediately began to sit up easier and relax his face once he had taken just a small amount. She wondered if she would ever be free of her desire for opium and had to fight the impulse to ask Jonathan for a dose for herself.

"So tell me about all the girls who are missing. Do you have all their names?" asked Jonathan.

"The first one I knew of was Maria Falco, and then came Wanda Gapinski and Felicia Zugaj. Three other girls reported a short time ago are Julianne Davis, Elizabeth Ross, and Sara Anderson. All of the girls are between twenty and twenty-eight years of age. And except Maria, they are all blonde. The two that are deceased are Maria and Wanda."

She went on to fill in as many details as she knew of, including the finding of the rings, and the presumption that someone pushed Maria in front of the carriage.

"So the police know about the rings. That is the most telling part of this mystery. Perhaps the rings are a promise of better things to come, or the perpetrator's sick mind that he loves them or some such thing."

"The police do know, but it has not even been reported in the news about it, and as far as I know, Louie has not been questioned about it. I agree it is a most significant find."

"I will try my best to see if I can learn any more about the brothers. If there are in the building, I will try to speak with them."

"Will you return to dine with us tonight?"

"I will write up this article and send it off, and then I will see you this evening."

It was a beautiful day, and she decided to walk home, but then saw Patrick and Joseph across the street headed in the opposite direction. She quickly stepped up her pace to catch up to them. They headed into the market area where little notice of her would come amongst the crowds of people browsing through the wares for sale.

Patrick had stopped to purchase an antique knife, and when the young woman handed him his purchase, he held onto her hand, remarking how soft her skin was, "Excuse me, sir," she said as she abruptly pulled her hand back. Joseph shook his head at his brother but said nothing.

They moved a little further as Joseph filtered through some hanging silk ties. Once again, Patrick purchased an item resulting in a woman's rebuke due to his lingering touch.

"You and Christopher have the luxury of having women vie for your attention. You are never in want of a soft hand to hold and a woman's admiring gaze. It is intolerable."

"Patrick, you cannot hover and cling like a wounded animal begging for attention. You must treat women like the sweetness they are. Embrace their beauty from afar, do not confront it and try to devour it."

"You may say that because you have never had to beg, but look at me. I do not have your looks, or Christopher's. I fear I will never take a wife."

Joseph patted his brother on the shoulder, saying, "Brother, do not wallow in such pity, yet another unattractive feature to a woman. Be more aloof; consider the possibility of less steak and more salad to trim your look. You will be successful, I guarantee it."

The men turned and proceeded back to The Harrison. Madeline had a new impression of the brothers. Perhaps Patrick was needy and a little crude, but they both had behaved like many brothers and men she had known before. Their pleasant manner and their conversation about women did not seem anything short of normal.

Walking back home, she was perplexed, vowing to herself to obtain information about Christopher, the most elusive of the brothers.

She leisurely walked and was almost home when she heard a voice calling out to her, "Mrs. Donovan..."

She turned to see Joanie Sobon briskly walking towards her. "I thought it was you. I have to tell you about Vincenzo.

You looked at him as if he had grown horns. No...my Vincenzo, he is the best man I have ever known. He tells me that the person who pays him the money says he must keep all a secret, or he will not be allowed to paint, and no money. Now with the money, we have many beautiful things and will return to Paris before Christmas."

"I will not mention it again, nor speak of it to anyone. It is his and your business alone. I believe too that he must be a fine young man to have a remarkable woman like you by his side."

She smiled, shook her hand, and waved good-bye.

Hugh and Phillip were at her home with her father, all three sitting outside on the porch, enjoying the pleasant afternoon.

"Where is our friend, Jonathan?" asked father. "Is he still unwell?"

"He is better but needs to write and submit his article to his paper for the afternoon deadline. He interviewed me about the disappearances.Some people in Chicago read the Times, no doubt, but not enough to make a difference unless a local paper picks it up. He will be here for dinner, and we can discuss it further."

"I will put out to sea in two days; I hope we may see the Auditorium and perhaps venture back to the hotel. I would dearly love to see the third floor," said Phillip.

"If Jonathan is agreeable, maybe we could go back and try again tonight, but this time, bring a torch along for each of us," said Hugh.

While Phillip stayed with her father, she and Hugh took a walk through the neighborhood.

"It has been such a joy since you have come to Chicago, and now with Jonathan here, I feel a certain serenity I have not known for a long time. I will miss our Phillip, but with you building a home here, I'm sure we will see him," said Madeline.

"I meant to speak to you about that, but it has seemed inconsequential to everything else that is happening. I have decided on Oak Park, the scenic atmosphere of a grand neighborhood is quite appealing. I am hoping you will like it and spend many hours with me there."

She could feel herself blushing at his remarks and didn't know how to respond to his words.

"Of course...I always welcome your company," was all she said.

She felt he was about to say something further than thought better of it and just touched her hand lightly and spoke once more about the investigation.

When Jonathan arrived later that day, father redressed his wounds before they all dined together on roast beef and creamed potatoes. Sipping wine after dinner, father said, "So you are once again off to the Harrison."

"Yes, it is at the heart of all of this. Jonathan, did you encounter Christopher?" asked Madeline.

"I did see him without his brothers. He was in the barbershop getting his shoes shined, so I ventured in for a haircut. I started talking to the barber about what a fine hotel it was, going on grandly, and hoping to have his ego prompt him to say he was one of the owners. He said nothing, "but the barber said, 'Sir, you're looking at the owner.' " After that, he did converse with me, but it was only cursory and seemed to bother him to make an effort. I suppose he would be more one to watch than to engage with. He did, however, take note whenever a lovely girl walked by in his lobby, even whispering to a man who was with him about the two blonde ladies seated at the French cafe. I bent my head over to look, and they were lovely. I think they might have been twins."

"The girls you are speaking of, I cannot imagine that it would be anyone but Marilyn and Nancy. They are the young ladies who are helping me. Marilyn is the chemist who found the drugs in the chocolate. It is disturbing and sends a chill through me that one of the Harrisons took any interest in them. I suppose I am just foolish, still..." said Madeline.

"No, there was something peculiar in the way he looked at them. Peering at them, staring a little too long, but nothing else in his manner was odd. He behaved like many men of wealth that I come across, arrogant, aloof, and feeling above the rest of us," said Jonathan.

"Do you think that I should mention it to Marilyn?" Madeline asked her collective audience.

"I wouldn't," said father, "It is what older men do, look at beautiful young girls. It may make them feel odd when they are there and prevent them from enjoying themselves."

"I suppose. They are shy and studious, and I do not want to frighten them or make them feel uncomfortable while they are there," said Madeline.

"Then we return to the third floor. This time I want to see something of these collections," said Phillip.

Chapter 13

Vincenzo's Folly

Once again, they waited until almost midnight before returning to the hotel so that there would be fewer people around to see them all together.

In Jonathan's room, they strategized on how best to achieve their goals. They decided to all go together to the stairwell, one by one leaving in intervals. Hugh insisted that he accompany Madeline this time, and she consented, happy to have him with her.

She found it unlocked, so apparently, no one knew of the lost key. The second-floor hallway where they entered the stairwell was empty, and they ascended without incident.

Somewhere on this third floor, she thought, *the brothers reside.* They would have to be certain they did not open a door that would enter into the rooms. They all believed that the brothers most likely would not retire without latching their doors, concluding that it was probably safe to enter the unlocked ones.

Madeline took Hugh to the room where she believed the library was, but she realized it was some type of laboratory once inside. They spoke in whispers, "Did you see this place before?" asked Hugh.

"No, I thought this was the library. The outer door looked similar. It had an English coat of arms on it as this one does. It looks as if someone has been conducting experiments of some kind. There are notes on the table, and the faint odor of chemicals."

"I wonder which brother dabbles in this. From what we know about them, I would guess Christopher."

"There is a walking stick against the wall, but I have seen them all with such sticks."

They both walked over to it, Hugh picking it up gently to see if there were any revealing marks.

"Look, there is a splinter down the one side. Do you think it possible...?"

"That it could have been used on Jonathan? The shape of the top is a wolf's head. We must look again at Jonathan's back to see if the markings might match."

"If it is the case, and they are somehow involved, they would have the money and power to cover up their involvement. I think it would be very difficult to apprehend them."

Leaving that room, and then proceeding down another hall, they came to the library. Madeline showed Hugh the skeleton and he motioned to her that hidden behind the last row of books was an elevator.

They tried several other doors but found the rooms to be sparsely furnished and of no particular interest.

Hugh touched her on the shoulder and pointed down the hall. Casting a shadow on the floor was the light from beneath one of the doors. He grabbed her hand, and they retreated to the stairwell. As they turned the corner, they heard the door open and two male voices speaking. She and Hugh entered the first unlocked door that they came to and stood side by side without moving. When her eyes adjusted to the light, she saw many beautiful dolls, some as tall as four feet high or so, and some just three or four inches in height. There was an elaborately decorated dining table with some of the dolls placed at the table settings. It would have been a little girl's dream room.

Neither of them spoke, but she was pressed against the side of him, the warmth from his body touching hers. The last time she had been so close to him was in the streets of Whitechapel, in a doorway while chasing Jack. Now again, it had an unexpected effect on her. She wished she could reach up and place her arms around him and have him hold her—maybe for a long while and just feel his breath upon her face. She often wondered what it would be like to feel loved again and if someday that love could be between her and Hugh.

As the two men walked past their room, she felt her hand began to tremble. Hugh placed his hand over hers, holding it firmly. She immediately calmed down and pressed her ear to the door to listen, hoping to hear something.

"He does as he pleases, no matter who it hurts. And unlike you, Joseph, Christopher always seems to point out that I am adopted and an outlier to the family fortune. I never feel like a brother when he is with me. I feel like an interloper. Why must he peer at me in such a way, as if I am an embarrassment to the family?"

"Patrick, why must you always assume things that are not true? He cares for you as I do."

"There are so many reasons for us to be cautious, now more than ever."

"You mean about the money? Nonsense. The hotel is doing fine, and what is money if not used to please us? Come; let us have a glass of cognac before retiring."

When they could no longer hear the footsteps, they reentered the hall and hurriedly returned to the stairwell. They did not speak again until they were safely on the second floor.

"I am happy they have gone. I imagined the two of us in shackles," said Hugh.

"What a delight the Harrisons would take in making us pay for our trespassing on their property."

Jonathan and Phillip were already in the room.

"It was something to behold. I am happy I was able to see it with my own eyes," said Phillip.

"Which room did you see?" asked Hugh.

"The butterfly collection...I've never seen anything like it, even in a museum. He took great care with every detail. I also saw the three doors with nothing behind them. I took some time to see if there was a way that the mirror panel could move, but I did not see any. After that, I heard someone coming down the hall and decided it would be best to return," said Jonathan.

"We heard the brothers, too, and it is why we returned," said Hugh.

"I heard voices also, but they were not just male. One was female," replied Phillip.

"I wonder if it was Lady Mary," said Madeline.

"Or perhaps they have brought one of their admired ladies up to dine with them," said Jonathan. "I entered a room that looked nothing more than a closet and then found there was an opening in the floor. When I lifted the hatch, I was amazed to find the entrance to a staircase. I thought it very odd; as there already is the stairwell we had entered. I assume it also went down to the second floor, but I did not descend."

"Were you able to see anything else?" asked Phillip.

"I saw the room with the weaponry—a fine display of weapons as I have ever seen. They spared no expense on their collections, it seems. I suppose for people with unlimited funds, it is not unusual to spend their money on any folly that suits them," replied Jonathan.

"So what is the consensus? Do any of these things mean they are potential murderers?" asked Madeline.

"Although they seem an odd sort and obviously have means and opportunity to commit crimes, I haven't seen anything so far that would convince a jury they were guilty of anything. It would not stand up to prosecution in London," said Hugh.

"I too feel as if we have discovered all manner of strange things about them, but none points to anything of a criminal nature. What little we do know of them, it appears their business does not hold their interest, and they seek other ways to fill their time," said Madeline.

"Their third floor is as mysterious as could be found in a Sherlock Holmes mystery. What could be the purpose of all those doors, some with nothing behind them? I suppose if you are rich, and it fancies you, you just go about that business of pleasing yourself in any way, no matter how odd," said Phillip.

Madeline and Hugh went on to tell them of their narrow escape at being caught by Patrick and Joseph and of overhearing the brothers' conversation.

They said their good-byes with a promise that tomorrow they would be on holiday visiting the Auditorium Building before Phillip had to depart.

They were all tired and anxious to return home. Phillip had the additional task of organizing and packing his things for the return trip to London. Hugh stayed behind for a moment with her on the steps of her home.

"It is always interesting being around you, Madeline. It seems this choice of career will lend itself to some adventurous times. I am happy I was with you. I felt in some small way that perhaps I was of use to you."

The late hour and his nearness once again tempted her to lay her head upon his shoulder and whisper, "I need you, stay with me." but she did not. She only said, "Thank goodness you were there. It calmed my nerves. I would not have wished to have encountered the Harrisons, alone and in the dark."

He watched her safely enter her home, and then he proceeded up the stairs to the upper flat.

She wondered if she was getting closer to finding out anything of significance. She wanted to speak to Jonathan in private before their outing to the Auditorium and thought she might see him early the next day. The night once again brought her nightmares of being chased and then held against her will in a dirty alley. She awoke, knowing she was safe, but somewhere one of the missing girls might be living what she only dreamt about.

When she arrived at the hotel in the morning, Jonathan met her downstairs to gain entrance to his room. Her father had given him additional medication. He seemed much improved after taking it, behaving with even with fewer inhibitions than he usually had—and he didn't have many.

"I'm glad you've come. I wanted you to see my article and speak with you about the case. My editor wants me to continue on with the story. He said to go ahead with the other piece about the attractions, but he wants me to give this story priority. Perhaps the trip to the Auditorium can wait till another day."

"Phillip will be disappointed. Maybe he and Hugh can go, but I'd like to keep an eye on what's going on around here. I saw Lady Mary again last night after you left. She and her gentleman friend were in the hall, this time having a bit of a tussle about something. That young boy—I think you said his name was Alfred—suddenly appeared and literally pulled them into a room, warning them to be quiet. Then I swear I saw Christopher come around the corner, and his hand looked covered in blood. I went down the hall after he left, and the droplets were still there. Where do you think they led to?"

She shook her head as if to say she hadn't the slightest idea, and he added, "The stairwell—they stopped right at the door."

She shook a little, so he placed his hand on her shoulder. "My friend, are you sure this is what you wish to do for a career? After everything you have been through, this is a grim business."

"It is, and I will get stronger and better at it as I go along, so little has been done by the police, even after the discovery of the rings. I have read nothing about it in the paper."

He handed her the *New York Times*, "Yes, I pointed that out in my article, the failure of the local authorities to follow up on what you discovered for them. The finding of the drugged chocolate should have made some headlines, but the story remains buried on the tenth page of the paper."

She read the article and said, "It is a fine piece, I hope enough Chicagoans read it, and it will renew the outrage. I still think most people believe these incidents do not have anything to do with murder, and that is why there is so little noise about it.

"There is one thing I did want to ask you. Would you mind if I looked at your back?"

"I think the wound is healing—I don't feel any intense pain."

"No—that is not the reason."

"All right," he answered as he slowly removed his shirt, still wincing from the residual pain.

"I will clean it. I'm sure that needs to be done," she said.

"There are clean towels in the bath area."

She touched his skin with the hot cloth, noting that there was no evident infection. She wished to view Jonathan's back to ascertain if any remaining imprint left that could be defined.

"Hugh and I had seen a walking stick in one of the rooms. It had the head of a wolf. I was hoping there remained enough of a mark that I might see something on your back, as the area is still red enough to have an outline. I don't know. However, it doesn't look much like the head of a wolf. Do you mind if I sketch it?"

"No, not at all."

Madeline had spent many years studying art, and she hoped someday to return to painting. Capturing the markings on Jonathan's back would be an easy task.

"Anything that might prove useful in the future is worth noting."

When she finished, she helped him with his shirt, and he smiled at her, but this time, it was a more intimate smile.

"Madeline, we make a good team. Our mutual desire to uncover truths and see what is at the bottom of things has created a strong bond. I am happy to be once again working on a mystery with you."

She looked at him again, this time through the eyes of a woman. His eyes so luminescent blue and his enduring Yankee charm were never truly lost on her, but she had kept those thoughts from surfacing. She noticed when she touched him that something stirred in her, and she wasn't sure whether it was because of him or just the nearness of a man's partially unclothed body that made her react so. She knew that she was developing feelings for both Hugh and Jonathan. They each had their own unique characteristics that made them special to her.

"I remember our meeting on the *SS New York* with great joy. If it wasn't for Sherlock Holmes, we might have never met," Madeline said.

She had been reading Arthur Conan Doyle's first published novel, when he had approached her, asking her opinion on it, having been in the midst of reading it himself.

"I think I may not have given up so easily and would have found an excuse to make your acquaintance. We had quite the adventure in London, and it appears are in the midst of one again," said Jonathan.

"I suppose I should make my way downstairs. I am hoping I might meet with Marilyn and Nancy."

"The twin sisters…may I join you?"

"Please do."

Vincenzo and Joanie were setting up their easels in the lobby. Madeline walked toward them while Jonathan saw Christopher Harrison in the barber-shop. He said he would join her in a few minutes, as he would like another opportunity to engage the stoic brother in conversation.

This time Vincenzo greeted her with a warm smile, "Mrs. Donovan, I must apologize for my behavior the other day. Money can be a cruel master. I am doing certain things that depend upon the utmost discretion, and I am afraid I acted poorly. Someday you must allow me to do your portrait."

"May I see what you have done recently?"

"Of course, I am flattered that you should take an interest," replied Vincenzo.

"Here, I will show you as Vincenzo is covered in tips of blue paint," said Joanie.

As she proceeded to move the canvases one by one, Madeline was struck by how talented he was and the brilliance which he captured the essence of the person he was painting. Behind the paintings lay a sketch pad, and Madeline asked," May I see these also?"

"They are but the rough sketches he does before he begins a painting. They will probably be of little interest to you," said Joanie.

"On the contrary, I have also studied art and am extremely interested to see his work."

As Madeline began turning the pages, Vincenzo suddenly looked over and abruptly stated, "No—no, Joanie, not those—no one is to see those."

But it was too late. Madeline was staring down at what appeared to be a rough sketch of Felicia Zugaj and two other unknown girls. She had looked at Felicia's picture enough to recognize her.

"Dear heavens, I believe you have drawn one of the missing girls," Madeline blurted out.

"No, you must be mistaken," said Vincenzo with a look of shock on his face.

"No—I carry all their photographs with me.Look..." she said as she pulled out the picture of Felicia.

Joanie covered her mouth to prevent an even louder gasp. "Vincenzo, it is her. You have made a deal with the devil. I warned you—I knew it could come to no good."

"Is she one of the girls commissioned to paint by the unknown solicitor?" asked Madeline.

Vincenzo stopped painting and wiped his brow with his blue fingertips, giving his now ashen colored face an even more peculiar look.

"Oh...no...what have I done?" he said as his shoulders slumped in agony.

"You must tell me everything, or if not me, the police," said Madeline.

Vincenzo began speaking, the words falling out of his mouth rapidly as if he were finally glad to be rid of the burden of secrecy.

"A man approached me about doing the portraits of some young girls. He said the person wishing the portraits did not want them seen and were only for his private collection. I would paint them in an undisclosed area. I was blindfolded and taken to someplace—I don't know where, but it was a lovely room filled with the chatter of young girls. They appeared happy, and no one seemed held against their will. From what I could observe, they were happy to be there.

"I confess I have not paid any attention to the faces of the missing girls. I never dreamed that this could involve anything but the wishes of an eccentric person. The girls wore masks to cover part of their faces, but I sketched them without the masks on. Although they were told never to take those off, I convinced them I needed to see more of the faces to do them justice."

"Did you ever see the benefactor?" asked Madeline.

"I would not know. The men who did come into the room from time to time were all disguised. They also wore Italian Renaissance costume masks and spoke little."

Jonathan had returned and had heard at least a part of the conversation.

"This is news. I must interview you," said Jonathan.

"No...no, I do not want my shame for the entire world to see," said Vincenzo.

"I agree...you mustn't. It will ruin us," said Joanie.

"I promise you I will not use your name," said Jonathan.

"That means nothing to me. Who but me is the artist in this area? I know of no other. Everyone will know it is me," replied Vincenzo.

"On the other hand, you could become instantly known. It could be to your benefit, and certainly to the benefit of the girls," said Madeline.

"At the end of the day, come to my suite, and I will take down your story. I will not print it until you have given me your permission," said Jonathan.

"We will go to the police," said Joanie. "I can promise you that."

"We shall look forward to meeting with you tonight," said Madeline.

"What a revelation," said Jonathan.

"Let's return to my home so that we may tell the others," said Madeline.

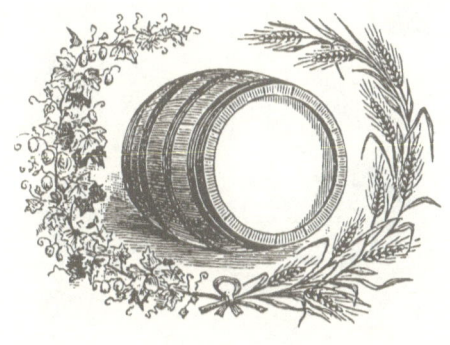

Chapter 14

A Picture of Worth

Hugh and Phillip were surprised to see her returning with Jonathan. It was again a lovely weekend day. Her father and the two young men were outside smoking and conversing with the locals.

After retelling their tale, Phillip said, "It sounds as if we must postpone our trip to the Auditorium."

"It is your last day. If Madeline and Jonathan have other matters to attend because of what has happened, you and I can go," said Hugh.

"Yes, please do...do not let me stop you from going. You will have an arduous journey back to London and should at least have an entire day of entertainment before you go back," said Madeline.

"We shall be at Jonathan's later to meet with Vincenzo, and if you should decide to come by, we can all have dinner," she continued.

After they left, Jonathan confided in her about what transpired with Christopher.

"I asked him if I might inquire as to how he injured his hand, and to my surprise, he answered quite frankly that he and his brothers dabbled in taxidermy and that it was a simple slip of the knife on his part."

"We know that is true because we have seen the stuffed birds, but we will probably never know if that is truly how he cut his hand."

They spent the rest of the day questioning anyone who would stop to speak to them in the market area and the surrounding streets about the missing girls. It was the same story that they looked familiar, but like so many other girls who strolled down these streets.

By late afternoon, they were both tired and parched, "Would you like to have some refreshments?" asked Jonathan.

"Yes, you must try the pastries at the French cafe. They are a sweet sin. It is my favorite place to stop for tea," answered Madeline.

They could see Marilyn and Nancy from where they stood, and when they waved at them, Jonathan asked, "Those are the girls Christopher was eyeing. Are those your friends?"

"They are," Madeline answered as she waved back to them.

They approached the young women, Madeline stating, "This is my friend, Jonathan Franks, from New York."

She thought again about what Jonathan saw, and once again decided not to speak of Christopher Harrison's apparent attraction to the two. She also refrained from telling them about Vincenzo, believing it was a private matter.

"Where are your other friends?" asked Nancy.

"They have gone to the Auditorium, where some say the other girls were. Besides the obvious reasons to see it—for I hear it is a wonder—I would like to browse around and get an assessment of it. We had planned to visit but decided to attend to some business instead," said Madeline.

"We have also planned to go," said Marilyn.

"Be careful. You know both of you are striking and blond-haired, and that fits the description of most of the missing girls," said Madeline.

"I'm sure both of you, however, appear to have your wits about you and would not be in danger. Madeline has told me of your assistance through the use of chemistry—quite impressive," said Jonathan.

Nancy said in an odd tone, "Yes, we always do the right thing. Sometimes it is a great burden to be so conscientious, but my sister ensures that we stay on the straight and narrow...always. I have yet even to have the taste of this absinthe I have heard so much about. So, Mr. Franks, you can be sure we will keep our wits and do nothing other girls our age would do."

Madeline was somewhat stunned by sweet, demure Nancy's sudden burst of frankness. Marilyn looked at her sister as if she was appalled.

"My sister sometimes scolds me for being somewhat over-protective, but we are all we have in the world. Our life depends on our doing the right thing—our finances, everything, is such that we must always be careful, and sometimes that does not allow us the luxury of frivolity or entertainment," said Marilyn.

"I'm sorry. I don't know what came over me," said Nancy, once again assuming her shy demeanor.

"We will go to the Auditorium. I promise you that, sister," said Marilyn. "Do not look so sad. I am not upset that you spoke up. I may very well have protested the trip, but now I will not."

"And next time we meet, we shall all enjoy absinthe together, and I shall not take no for an answer. I certainly owe you both a dinner for all you have helped me," said Madeline.

They smiled in agreement as the twins bid their farewells to her and Jonathan.

"Shall we walk?" asked Madeline, "Or are you still in pain?"

"We can walk, but I think I might move rather slowly," he replied.

"I believe this is the most significant clue yet that may create the path to whoever is holding these girls. I'd like to get a past issue of the paper to see if there are pictures of the other missing girls and if they might be in the sketch," said Madeline. "My Uncle Hank generally keeps his papers piled high in the corner of his room for months. He likes to compare horse races and follow sports. I will try to get that information from him."

"Be careful not to get your hopes up, though. Remember what Vincenzo said; they blindfolded him, and the men were in disguise. He did not know where he was."

"Yes, but he still has a wealth of information whether he believes he does or not. He must have observed enough to gives us more to go on. Painting a portrait takes a great deal of time. I suddenly feel better, as if something good has happened, and maybe there is hope that we will get to the bottom of this."

They returned home—Madeline seeking out her friend, Uncle Hank, who was more than accommodating. Mrs. O'Malley made a late lunch for all of them while they pored over the old newspapers, looking for a photograph of the latest missing girls.

"Tell me, what is the news?" asked Uncle Hank.

Madeline went on to relay all the latest developments to Uncle Hank and her father.

"It sounds like you have made a breakthrough," said her father.

"Whenever I take my walks or am in the market, I think of these poor girls and keep my eye out, especially when my path crosses the Harrison," said Uncle Hank. "Here...I have found one. Her name is Sara Anderson."

"No...she does not look like any of the girls I saw in Vincenzo's sketch—at least to my recollection. I will take all the newspaper photos we find with us this evening when we meet with Vincenzo. We can compare them to his sketches and his memory, in the hopes they look familiar to him," said Madeline.

"How is it that with all the talk about the missing girls, this man did not know Felicia?" asked Uncle Hank.

Jonathan said, "When I am investigating a story, I am never surprised at what clues or facts are missed, not just by the average person, but also by the authorities. If he had only briefly seen the photos, the chances that he would have made the connection, especially if his only thoughts were his completion of their portrait, were probably slim."

"I can certainly see that about Vincenzo. His world revolves around his work, striving for success, and Joanie Sobon, his girlfriend," said Madeline.

"I suppose I can understand that. When I am at work, or at the end of a long workday, we all go to a bar near the Stockyards; I don't pay attention to anything else but the beer in my hand," said Uncle Hank.

They continued until they were able to find the photographs of the other two girls, Julianne and Elizabeth.

"They're all blonde," said Uncle Hank.

"Yes, it seems the person—or persons—we seek has an affinity for blond ladies," said Madeline.

"I feel comforted that my auburn-haired daughter may not be at risk," said her father.

"But the first missing girl, Maria, wasn't she dark-haired? I believe the person may prefer blondes but may also stalk a lady with any hair color if the opportunity arises. It is more likely that his main interest is that they are beautiful," said Jonathan.

"Yes, Maria was a stunning girl," said her father. "What a terrible loss. I hope your meeting with Vincenzo proves to bring more information that may track this killer and bring the black heart to justice."

He asked if anyone would like wine and received affirmative answers from all at the table. Hugh and Phillip arrived and joined in.

"Did you have an enjoyable day?" asked Madeline.

"It was a marvel. I believe they said it was the tallest building in Chicago and that Frank Lloyd Wright also contributed to the design. It was amazing, but crowded with people wanting to get a glimpse of this latest testament to Chicago's claim to be a must-see city for any traveler," said Hugh.

"If someone intended to lure away a young lady in such an atmosphere, I would suppose it might easily go unnoticed," said Phillip.

They went on to discuss their meeting with Vincenzo. "It is your last evening, Phillip. I don't know if you wish to come with us back to The Harrison and be part of our meeting or if you have other plans," said Madeline.

"I would not likely want to miss that. I will return to Chicago again, now that my cousin will have a home here. I can see the sights any time, but this, I am intrigued and will gladly come along."

This time, it was not as easy to navigate through the hotel with their small group, especially now with Vincenzo and Joanie in their company. Patrick and Joseph Harrison were in the lobby and watched the group. They nodded to her, and Joseph managed a slight smile.

Before they entered the elevator, Alfred came up to greet them. "I see you must be having some celebration. Can I send you up some champagne?"

Thinking quickly, she replied, "Yes, you may. Vincenzo has agreed to paint a portrait of my friends from London so that I may have a remembrance of them," said Madeline.

"I will do so, and there will be no charge. You may come tomorrow if you wish to pursue your interviews further. I will have the most of the afternoon available," said Alfred.

"I will check my schedule, but I believe I will take you up on your offer," replied Madeline.

After Alfred left, Vincenzo said, "This is how I make my living through this wonderful place. I hope I have not jeopardized my standing here. They looked at us as if we were criminals."

"I understand, but just think if it was your Joanie who was one of the missing girls. It is of the utmost importance that you follow through with this. You may well be the only person who had made contact with any of the girls before they perished," said Madeline.

"Do you think all the girls in the painting are dead? No...you cannot mean that!" gasped Joanie. "Is it all that serious?"

"I'm afraid so. You are doing the right thing," she replied.

Once in the hallway, their number alone caused the few stragglers to turn and stare at them. Before they reached Jonathan's room, Lady Mary and her friend, Willie, saw them.

"I see you are now staying here. How odd indeed that if you think mischief goes on in this hotel, why would you wish to stay here?" asked Lady Mary to Madeline, while staring at each of them as if they were under suspicion.

"Not at all. It is purely a business transaction. The talented Vincenzo will be painting my friend's picture. He will be doing the preliminary sketch today. We wished to watch as we are in such admiration of his work."

Willie took the old woman's hand and steered her away.

"I'm watching you, young lady!" said Lady Mary, spitting out the words, and then wiping her mouth with her gloved hand. Willie shook his head as if to apologize to Madeline. In what seemed like a dragging motion to get her away from them, he took Lady Mary by the arm. She wondered how this cantankerous lady could have such a friendly friend, as she did not seem to have the capacity for friendship, except for Alfred and the Harrison brothers.

They gathered together in the room, placing Vincenzo's sketchbook on the dining table along with the pictures from the newspaper of the missing girls.

"There is no doubt that one is Felicia," said Jonathan.

"Yes, it is her. She has an unusually crooked smile that I found endearing," said Vincenzo. "The others, I do not remember seeing them. They are not the same girls in my sketch, as you can see."

"Then they were the only ones in the room with you?" asked Hugh.

"Yes, besides a man who sat in the corner most of the time. He spoke little and wore an elaborate costume mask and gown to conceal his identity, but he seemed to enjoy observing us," said Vincenzo.

"Could you describe him as best you can?" asked Madeline.

"It was as if he was our guard; I didn't pay much attention to him. From what I remember of him, he seemed rather ordinary. He wasn't very tall and was perhaps a little plump."

"Tell us anything you can remember at all about your time there," she continued.

"It was a pleasant time. The girls were happy and carried on with one another as if they were sisters. I never had the impression that anything was amiss. The suite had velvet and silk, fresh flowers everywhere, and chocolate and wine were in abundance."

"Chocolate?" asked Hugh.

"Yes, we always had more than enough."

"How did you feel when you were there? Did you have a particular feeling of well-being?" asked Madeline.

"I did. That is why I never thought in any way that these girls were in danger. I welcomed my time there. It was most pleasant."

"We think perhaps the chocolates laced with drugs... perhaps opium," said Madeline.

"Opium?" he asked. "I do not partake of drugs. I don't suppose I would have known...I just remember having a feeling of contentment while I was there."

"Yes, perhaps that is why you had such an experience of happiness and why the girls also did."

"Do you remember anything else? Were you taken up an elevator, or were you on the ground floor?" asked Jonathan.

"We went up the stairs, but I could not say whether we landed on a second or third floor. It seems there were many steps, but again, nothing I paid attention to at the time."

There was a knock on the door, and when Jonathan appeared, Alfred was there with the champagne. "I took the liberty to bring it to you myself. I hope you are enjoying your stay at The Harrison," said Alfred.

"Thank you, I find it a most interesting place," said Jonathan.

Alfred waited at the door, looking in at all of them, "Is there anything else I can get you? Would you like me to start the fire?"

"I think we can do that," he replied.

"It is no trouble, no trouble at all," Alfred said as he moved past Jonathan and over to the fireplace.

Madeline thought it evident that he had gained entrance to see what was happening in the room. Vincenzo immediately took up his sketch pad, and Hugh sat in the red velvet armchair, with Phillip standing behind him. Everyone worked in concert as if they had preplanned their actions. They all seemed aware, as she had, of why Alfred was there.

"May I see your sketches?" Alfred asked.

"Oh...I am sorry. It is just an artist's quirk, but I never show my unfinished work. Please come down to my area in the lobby later, and I will show you my latest painting," said Vincenzo.

"Good evening," Alfred said as he left the room.

"What do you think that was all about?" asked Phillip.

"Alfred is the brother's assistant. I suppose they have sent him to see what we are about. Whether it is just curiosity, or that they have something to hide is what we need to find out," said Madeline.

"Let's not waste the champagne," said Jonathan as he poured a glass for everyone.

Hugh asked, "You will take your sketch to the police?"

"After I have finished work tomorrow, I promise you that," said Vincenzo.

"Do you suppose the other girls in your sketch are all missing?" asked Phillip.

"I hope not," he said forlornly.

"It does seem peculiar that there have been no further reports of any missing girls, at least none that I know of," said Madeline.

"The police will know the answer to that. Can I see your sketch again?" asked Jonathan.

Madeline also stood beside him, looking at the artist's drawing. "Yes, they are lovely, as is the setting they are in. I would also not think anything was amiss if this is what I saw," said Madeline.

"If I am to pack and be ready for my return trip, I am afraid I must leave," said Phillip.

"We shall all go together," said Hugh.

"I will get back to the article I am writing," said Jonathan, "but I hope to see you all tomorrow. I would like to go with you to see Phillip off."

"That would be grand," said Phillip.

When the elevator door opened, there stood none other than the three Harrison brothers, Lady Mary and Willie.

They hesitated as they came face to face with them. "Come in, there is room enough," said Christopher in an authoritative voice that made her feel like a school-child.

They stepped in, and Joseph said, "Vincenzo, what is this, a new sketch. I must see it."

And before Vincenzo could even protest, Joseph had it in his hands. "Look, he captures the two men—very good indeed."

The collective audience browsed through his sketches, with Madeline fairly transfixed on their expressions.

"Now there's a lovely one...," Lady Mary pointed to one of the sketches, but the book turned away from Madeline, so she did not know what they were looking at.

She thought she could feel everyone's tension besides

her own, and when the door finally opened into the lobby, they all rushed out.

When they were out of earshot of the brothers, Vincenzo said, "I suppose there was no harm that they saw the sketches. If anything, they knew our business to be true when they saw the sketch of Hugh and Phillip."

"They did not seem to have any particular reaction after they viewed the book," said Madeline.

"I also saw nothing of note," said Hugh.

"Tomorrow, I will go to the police," said Vincenzo.

"We also have a prior engagement. We will see Phillip off. I hope to see you, perhaps the next day," said Madeline.

"Till then...," said Joanie as they left the Harrison.

Chapter 15

Marilyn's Dilemma

When they arrived at the station, she was grateful to have Hugh, Jonathan, and her father with her to say good-bye to Phillip. She already missed him, and he had not even left. Since the death of her family, she had experienced inordinate anxiety whenever someone she cared for left them for a long journey, and without knowledge of when they would see them again.

Phillip was the steward who attended to her on the *SS City of New York* and was the person who had cultivated her relationship with both Jonathan and his cousin, Hugh.

Phillip smiled at her, that kind, endearing smile. He always seemed to know just how she was feeling.

"Madeline, be careful. My only solace is that I know my cousin and Jonathan will look after you, as I know you will do the same for them. I am returning to my mistress, the sea. I will miss you all, but I will write to you often," said Phillip.

He leaned over and kissed her cheek, and she responded by embracing him and then holding his hands for a long moment.

"Good-bye, my dearest boy. Take care and come back to us soon, perhaps at Christmas," said Madeline.

"We'll see," said Phillip, and he shook the hands of the men before boarding the train back to New York and his awaiting destination aboard ship.

"We have all grown so close, it seems as if he just arrived, and now he is leaving," said Madeline to Hugh.

"He is young, and this is the perfect career for him. His wanderlust prevents him from staying for too long in one place. That may change when he is older, but he will be back," said Hugh.

"I know. He is so dear to me, and I have him to thank for introducing me to you and Jonathan," said Madeline.

During the carriage ride back to Erie Street, Madeline said, "The *helloes* are so wonderful and bring such joy, but followed by the good-byes that tear at the heart."

"Sometimes I worry about him, but mostly I envy him to be so young and without fear, living each day so gloriously on the shoulders of a great ship," said Hugh.

"You are right. I have always been one who finds it's more difficult to embrace the now, and not worry so about the future. I will endeavor to do better," said Madeline.

"I think I will spend the day at the Auditorium and maybe go to Hull House to begin my research for the articles I am obligated to write," said Jonathan.

"And I have a meeting with my architect. Shall we all meet for dinner?" asked Hugh.

Even her father agreed to join them. They would return to the Austin House, where they had enjoyed a fine meal earlier that month.

She spent the rest of the day making notes in her journal, walking in the park, and visiting the Falco family to inform them of the progress she had made. She now believed that the Harrison brothers, one or all, somehow played a part in the disappearances of the girls. Louie Falco told her that the police had detained several neighborhood men, but they released the men because of a lack of evidence with which to hold them.

Later that evening at the Austin House, the band was playing, and her father asked her to dance. "You would do well to consider one of those fine men for more than just casual friendship."

Something about the way he said it, as if she had never married Russell, and didn't already have a perfect family, made her wince.

"They both mean a great deal to me, and truthfully, if I no longer saw them, I would be very sad, but I would survive. They both deserve more than a broken woman who could never truly give them the love they deserve or the children."

"All right, we shall not speak of it again. I see it is still too soon. I just thought the way you and Hugh got on that maybe..."

"No, Father...not yet. Time is a strange bedfellow, and who knows, tomorrow something may happen to change my mind. Today what I care most about is finding out what happened to those girls. I had half hoped to see one of the Harrison brothers here."

"Of late, you seem unable to enjoy yourself at all, and are always thinking about this matter."

"I can't help but think of myself in this beautiful place, dancing with the most handsome man in the room, and that somewhere a woman, perhaps just like me, is in the utmost distress."

"Hugh is motioning to us; I believe our dinner has arrived."

"I see you both are doing the same thing, looking for the Harrison brothers," said Hugh with a slight laugh, addressing Madeline and Jonathan.

"It is second nature to me, I confess. Especially after what happened last time, the wound still smarts on my back. I hoped to have better luck this time, and that I might have the chance to follow along again, but with the idea to see if someone is behind me," said Jonathan.

"Wait, I think we are in luck. It is Joseph, and if he is here, Patrick is probably not far behind," said Madeline.

"Which one is it?" asked her father, who had not met any of the Harrisons.

"He is the tall one with the spectacles sitting at the back table. He is with a woman," said Madeline.

"She looks to be much younger than him," said her father, "But he is not unattractive, and with his wealth, I suppose I could see the possibility."

"There are others that join them; Alfred and Lady Mary just sat down," said Jonathan.

"Interesting...I think I may just pay my respects," said Madeline.

"Are you sure you want to do that?" asked Dr. Donovan.

"I know Alfred well enough that I can intrude. If they are rude, I will not be hurt," she replied, smiling.

"Hugh, could you order me an absinthe while I am gone?" asked Madeline.

He nodded, and though she might have felt a twinge of guilt, the nervous tension she had felt these last days had given way to her resolve.

She walked by casually as if she had accidentally come upon them, "Alfred, good evening, and also to you, Mr. Harrison," said Madeline.

The gentlemen rose from their table and greeted her. "It's Mrs. Donovan, isn't it?" said Joseph.

"I am flattered that you remember my name. This is a lovely place, almost as lovely as the Harrison," she said.

"Now, you flatter me. Would you like to join us?" asked Joseph.

"No, thank you. I am here with my Father and friends."

She continued to stand there, waiting for Lady Mary to speak, but the woman ignored her. Then Alfred said, "Allow me to introduce my very good friend, Margaret Downing, whom I hope one day to marry," he said with a loving look at the girl.

"A pleasure; Alfred is certainly a charming man. I wish you well and a pleasant evening," said Madeline.

She returned to her group and said, "It is not as interesting as we had thought. The young lady is not with Joseph, but with Alfred."

"Perhaps, that is a good thing. What of Lady Mary?" asked Hugh.

"She did not say a word, not even a greeting. I truly believe she thinks I mean harm to the Harrisons.

"There were three walking sticks set beside the table, but two rounded, and one had a bird's head. I don't think they would fit the shape of your wound, Jonathan."

"Would you and Hugh like to return with me to the hotel?" asked Jonathan.

"Yes, at least we know part of their group are detained here," said Hugh.

They dropped her father off at home and proceeded to the Harrison.

It was still early, nearly seven in the evening, and the hotel was unusually busy. She thought perhaps because it was Friday, and people were inclined to seek out entertainment.

When they walked into the lobby, several people began walking toward them—Vincenzo, Joanie, and Marilyn.

"Madeline, I must speak with you," said Marilyn.

"I also wish to speak to you," said Vincenzo.

"Vincenzo, you can come over here and talk to with us while Madeline speaks with Marilyn," said Jonathan.

"Can we walk outside?" asked Marilyn, her hand shaking. "I have been to your house, and when you weren't there, I waited for you here."

"Good heavens, what is it that has you so upset?"

"I have been to the police, but I needed to talk to someone."

"Yes, go on."

"Yesterday, we did go to the Auditorium. My sister was happy, the happiest I have seen her in quite a while. She carried on as if she had not a care in the world. We both went to different areas that we wanted to see, agreeing to meet back at the entrance, but she never returned."

"No—no, it cannot be, not Nancy. She is demure. I cannot even imagine her speaking with a stranger, let alone succumb to their advances, especially after what has happened."

"I too felt that way, but she was talking yesterday about how interesting it would be to find out what happened to the missing girls, and other peculiar things such as how exciting it would be to discover the truth. I don't know what possessed her, but now she's gone. The police were methodical as if taking a census. They did little else but ask a few questions and state they would get in touch with me if they have any word about her. Madeline, I am frightened. I can't stop shaking."

"I know. I understand. There will be a new urgency to our search. Marilyn, do you have someone to stay with?"

"Yes, I have an aunt. I will go there now. I don't know what to do with myself."

"You are welcome at my home anytime. You can stay with us if you need to. I will see you tomorrow here for lunch, and I promise we will do all we can to find her."

She hugged Marilyn and wiped a tear from her eye. She thought, *No, not sweet, innocent Nancy.*

Vincenzo was still speaking with Hugh and Jonathan when Madeline approached them, visibly shaken.

Hugh said, "Madeline, what has happened?"

He took her hand and said, "Come over to the table and sit."

"We will speak of it when Vincenzo has finished his story," she replied.

"I was just telling the gentlemen, Miss. I am sorry to say, but my sketchbook is gone. I have always placed it where I can find it. I hide it behind some of my paintings. Sometime yesterday, when I was painting in the lobby, someone stole it."

"The only people who knew it even existed were the people in the elevator," said Madeline.

"Of course—Joanie and I do go to lunch, but hotel security watches over my things. But it does seem strange, for it has been here all along these past weeks and has never before been disturbed."

"That is truly unfortunate news. Do you think you could recall her face enough to redraw it?" asked Jonathan.

"Perhaps, I will try."

They spoke with Joanie and Vincenzo for a few minutes longer, then walked away to converse in private.

"Even if he could redraw the sketch, it would not have the details necessary or the evidentiary properties the police would need. If he told them he drew it from memory, and he would have to tell the truth about it, I do believe they would dismiss his findings," said Madeline.

"Madeline is correct. Within the law, it would hold no bearing, I'm afraid. The original may have proved useful, but I suppose whoever took it has already destroyed it," said Hugh.

"But still, it has shown the hand of whoever is behind this. One or more of the people on the elevator knows about the disappearance of at least Felicia. Why else would anyone take the sketches? They did not want anyone to see those sketches of Felicia and the girls in that room," said Madeline.

"There is still the supposition that an admirer of Vincenzo's work may have taken it as a souvenir," said Hugh.

"Perhaps, but I think we all agree that would be the most unlikely of the scenarios. We must add Willie to the suspects. I imagine Lady Mary would have told him what transpired on the elevator, and I'm sure he would take it for her," said Jonathan.

"Now, tell us what news from Marilyn has so disturbed you," asked Hugh.

"I suppose it is the worse news. Nancy has gone missing. They were at the Auditorium when they decided to separate, with both agreeing to meet later. Nancy never returned. I truly believe she is in danger, and now more than ever, this hotel must give up its secrets so that Nancy may be found unharmed."

"That is terrible news. That shy young lady, I cannot imagine anyone could convince her to go along with them. I would have thought she would be too cautious," said Jonathan.

She went on to tell them about her conversation with Marilyn and what Nancy had said.

"So our young lady has a bit of a daring streak in her," said Hugh.

"Still, I think she would only go if she thought she was in no danger. Perhaps she knew the person. What if it was Lady Mary who she spoke with? She wouldn't have had a fear of harm," said Madeline.

"We need to go back to the third floor. Are you game?" asked Jonathan. "I would like to see the library, and perhaps take a look at the exit in the room and see where it leads."

"All right, you and Madeline go together, and I will see if I can discover anything elsewhere. Let's see if the skeleton key still fits," said Hugh.

"If it does, it means they don't believe anything has gone awry, or they would have changed the lock," said Madeline.

"It's almost ten; I think we have waited long enough. If we see there are lights under any of the doors, we will return...agreed?" asked Jonathan.

They nodded and made their way down the two corridors till they came to the forbidden stairwell. She held her breath as she turned the key, hoping it still worked.

It did. They smiled at each other in silence as they crept back into the darkened staircase and up to the third floor.

It was still, with only a few kerosene lamps dimly lit. Hugh motioned that he would go the other way as Madeline led Jonathan to the library. As they approached the door, she thought she could hear voices in the distance. Jonathan heard the same thing as he motioned his hand toward the hall. She hoped they would be safe within the library for now.

They had a torch with them but were reluctant to use it now that they had heard the voices. The moonlight once again was a friend and guided their steps. Jonathan could see the elevator now and walked toward it. She motioned to the hanging skeleton. He continued on to the elevator, and she followed.

"It's no good. It needs a key," whispered Jonathan.

"It would be nice to know where it goes to, but I believe the noise from us using it would alert anyone who was awake."

"You're right. I might try to find the closet with the stairwell and see if that might be an alternative way to get to the basement floor."

They both grabbed several books from the shelves around them. Seating themselves on the floor, they browsed through as many as they could reach from their position.

"Did you see the skeleton?" asked Madeline.

"Briefly. With their obsession with collecting things, I suppose it might not be that odd."

"Do you see these books? They are about famous collections of different things."

"Except for the ones stashed behind the chemistry books, there are about adoption. They must be Patrick's."

She turned each of the three books over in her hand. The titles depicted the internal struggle in dealing with being an adopted child. They made sure they put these back exactly as they had found them.

"I'd like to see if we can get to the staircase. Are you ready?" asked Jonathan.

She nodded her head, yes, but as they walked toward the door, she accidentally touched the skeleton with her shoulder, so she reached up to steady it. She was about to move on when she grabbed Jonathan's hand to stop him and signaled that she wanted a moment. Although it was dark in the room, the light was strong enough from the moon that she could see the skeleton quite well. Suddenly, she clasped her gloved hand over her mouth. She gently touched the skeleton again and walked around it. She felt dizzy and leaned against Jonathan.

"Madeline, what is it? Are you faint?"

"We must go. I will speak to you when we are clear of here."

"This way," he said.

They tiptoed, looking for lights under the door, but did not see anyone. Entering the narrow opening of the stairwell Jonathan previously found, they began their descent. But even though able to use the torch, the darkness was pervasive. They knew they had passed the second floor level and were now going into what they believed must be the lower level of the hotel.

What they saw upon arrival in the basement shocked them both.

Chapter 16

Barrels of Death

The first thing they were aware of was the noxious odor coming from the area. It looked like nothing she had ever seen. There were several dead rats caught in traps that lay scattered around the room. She supposed that it was not unusual that a hotel would have a problem with rodents; most of the city residents had the same problem.

She also saw several barrels of what she believed to be lye.

"It does appear they are making their own soap for the hotel," said Madeline.

"Be careful; don't get too close. Look over at that barrel; there are animal skeletons."

"Do you think they put the dead rodents in there?"

"I suppose they might use that method of disposal. It appears like a macabre dungeon down here."

"I know the brothers are involved in taxidermy, and I do believe the procedure involves the use of lye to clean the skeleton. It may be that."

"I think you might be right. The skeletons are small, bird-like."

"It also may be used for murder," she stated, clenching her fist as she spoke.

"What do you mean?"

"Let's leave this desolate place. I will speak to you back in your suite."

Hugh was there, sitting by the fire and sipping on a glass of wine.

"This is a strange place, and I am happy you are both back safely. I don't know why, but I had the strangest feeling as if you were in danger."

"It felt like the very hand of death was on my shoulder," said Madeline.

"I have a bottle of absinthe if you would rather have that than the wine," said Jonathan.

"Yes, that would be lovely."

She had returned to drinking a bit more alcoholic beverages than she had promised herself to have but believed the nature of what she was doing would probably prompt her to do so. For now, she felt she had it under control.

"Did you find anything useful, Hugh?" asked Jonathan.

"That can wait. I want to know what happened. Madeline looks as if the underworld has accosted her. Your face is ghostly white."

"I kept thinking I was mistaken, but I know I wasn't. When we were in the library and looking to see if we could access the elevator, I brushed past the skeleton. Of course, I had seen it before and would mean nothing except," she hesitated, "Except it's not the same skeleton."

"What?" they both said in unison.

"Do you remember, Hugh, that I had paid particular attention when looking at it? It had such starkness about it, not like others I have seen in university or a medical facility. It was so parchment white. I remember examining her wrist and ankle, and both had visible fractures. This skeleton did not. I looked at it several times, thinking it was because of the poor lighting, but it was a skeleton from another person."

"And what purpose could it be to change skeletons, of course, unless...could I dare say it, unless it is a skeleton of a murdered missing girl," said Jonathan.

Jonathan said what she was thinking. "I hesitate to say it, but I believe it could very well be true, especially in light of our other discovery," said Madeline.

"What is that?" asked Hugh.

"We took the staircase Jonathan found earlier and followed it to the basement. There were barrels of what we believe to be lye. They contained floating skeletons of dead animals in one, and in another area, the lye was used for soap making. I assume for the hotel," said Madeline.

"Of course, someone could easily dispose of a body in the lye, but why hang the skeleton in the library?" asked Hugh.

"Perhaps it is just a place to put it in plain sight before the disposal of the skeleton. I know there is a market for the purchase of skeletons by hospital research facilities, doctors, and even learning centers such as a university," said Jonathan.

"Now, there is no doubt that within The Harrison resides a murderer," said Madeline.

"Who is it that you think might be the one?" asked Hugh, directing his question to both Madeline and Jonathan.

"All of the three brothers stand out as suspects, but then there is Lady Mary and her cohort, Willie, and the assistant Alfred. There is still the possibility of a staff member that has access to the basement and third floor," said Jonathan.

"I am not certain yet, because they all seem to be hiding something. If we could discern the motive, we would be closer to the killer," said Madeline. "I think it unlikely that it is a staff member, but still, I don't completely rule it out."

"I didn't have such success as you both had, but I did come upon a room that had a light under it. When I walked by, I heard what seemed to be the laughter of women. It could have been Lady Mary, or it could have just been visitors of the brothers, but I marked the location down."

"Maybe Nancy was behind that door. Imagine if she could be here right under our noses," said Madeline. "I don't know how I will sleep now that I know that sweet girl is missing and after finding the skeleton and its implications."

"With everything we learned, it is still not enough to go to the police with. Everything is circumstantial, and the Harrison's team of lawyers would dismiss all of it," said Hugh.

"Besides, how would we reveal how we obtained the information? They would detain us for possible prosecution. We have to get something concrete," said Jonathan.

"I'd like to talk to Lady Mary again and see if I can't implore her to be more forthcoming about anything she might know, especially in light of Nancy's disappearance," said Madeline.

"Unless, of course, if she is guilty of wrongdoing," said Jonathan. "Then it would only put her on her guard and force her to cover up her part in it."

"I know. I had thought of that too. None of them seem innocent. We will have to tread carefully. I had an idea that we might try to steal the skeleton and bring it to the police, but then how would we prove it had been in their library?"

"There still might be an explanation for that skeleton; someone could have procured it through legitimate means," said Hugh.

"Let's meet tomorrow and see what we can come up to find the killer," said Jonathan.

Madeline and Hugh left the hotel to return home.

"A midnight glass of wine?" asked Hugh.

"Yes, how welcoming the moonlight looks coming through the window, and how beautiful the flowers look gracing the night."

Everyone was asleep. They enjoyed their privacy at the window seat, talking of the day's events.

"Somewhere in this city is my friend, Nancy. I am assuming someone tempted her to go with someone despite the threat to her life. I am not certain why she would do this unless she knew them, and she trusted them," said Madeline.

"It does boggle one's understanding of why she went unless she did not go willingly. However, if she did not, I cannot imagine with all the people there that someone would not have noticed a struggle, or that she would not have called out for help."

"We cannot find her in the river, like Wanda. I feel I must take greater risks in trying to find out what happened."

"What do you mean?"

"I must be bolder in my pursuing the truth, whatever that takes."

She was not certain herself what that would entail, but she felt she needed to insert herself further into the business of the Harrisons.

"You must, at all costs, stay safe. Soon they will break ground in my new home. You must come and see it. Your opinion is important to me, and a trip to Oak Park would be a welcome respite from this turmoil."

"You are right. Since you and Jonathan have been here, we spend our days pursuing leads. We will change that soon, hopefully, as soon as our Nancy is safe."

When she stood at the door to say her good-nights, he unexpectedly walked back through the door and embraced her. She responded and hugged him, grateful for his presence in her life.

Her sleep was troubled as she thought of the skeleton and the barrels of lye that she believed may have been the place of disposal for one or more of the missing girls. She knew that Nancy might not have fully realized what a dangerous situation she had placed herself in. She could have thought she had finally ventured out of her structured, safe life and perhaps knew the perpetrator.

She kissed her children's portrait, hoping she might dream of them instead of the ghoulish scene at the hotel.

When she awoke the next day, she was anxious to tell her father all that had happened.

"Madeline," he said, "you must go to the police with this news." said her father.

"But as Hugh said, Father, it is all supposition. And without informing them that we were illegally trespassing, how could we explain how we came by these facts."

"Yes, I can see that. Then it will be up to you to find something to give to the police that will make them act and take a look at the skeleton before it also disappears."

"Yes. With Nancy now missing, time is of the essence. I am leaving now to see if I can beseech Lady Mary to cooperate in some way."

"If you do not find her to be congenial, I can try to see if I may find out something," said Mrs. O'Malley.

"Thank you. If she will not speak to me, there is a good chance she may trust you. I will let you know," said Madeline.

When she arrived at the Harrison, it no longer appeared to her as the beautiful palace she had once had the impression it was. Now it was the house of some unknown force that had taken away its beauty and replaced it with black death.

Lady Mary and Willie were drinking and playing cards on the patio. They did not even notice her walking up to them.

"Lady Mary, I must speak to you. It is about a very dire situation. I am imploring your help," said Madeline with urgency in her voice that even made Willie take notice.

"What could you possibly want from me other than to pry into the brothers' lives again? And you know I won't do that."

"May we speak in private?"

"No, I hold nothing back from my Willie. Go on, if you must."

"Do you remember the two blonde girls that sit in the French cafe? They were there when we spoke once."

"Vaguely," she replied.

"Nonsense, my lady, you've taken note of them before saying they were a couple of beauties," interjected Willie.

"All right...all right, what if I have?" asked Mary.

"The slender one who wears glasses has gone missing. Her name is Nancy. Her sister is in a state of shock, and we all feel she is in great danger. If there is any possibility you know of anyone in this hotel, the brothers, or others you think might have a hand in this, you must come forward with the information. You simply must—her life may depend on it," said Madeline.

She looked upset, biting her lip and crumpling the cards within her hand.

"I tell you, I know nothing. Besides, they are all my boys, like my own children. I would die for them. I would do anything to protect them," said Mary.

"Including murder?" asked Madeline in a stern voice.

She held her gaze and then said, "Yes, including murder. It's obvious you don't have a family or anyone you love, or you wouldn't be sticking your nose into other people's lives. I've shocked you, well, if you ever loved someone enough that you could say that, you might be fortunate. That's all there is in life is your family."

"Please...think about it. That lovely young girl is being held by someone right now...if she is even still alive. You may be able to save her," said Madeline.

"Willie, take me from here. Please, she is upsetting me."

Willie looked at her with some compassion, saying, "Sorry about your friend, Miss. I hope someone finds her."

Before leaving, she looked over to where the twins always sat. There was no one there. It made her tremble that Nancy might be the victim of foul play perpetrated by one of the Harrisons.

She decided to return and enlist Mrs. O'Malley's help rather than stay and contact Jonathan. She knew she would see him later that day.

"I'll be happy to do it. It must stop, and if that crotchety woman has something to say, I'll get it out of her. I got a bit of the blarney in me even you've never seen me use," said Mrs. O'Malley, smiling, taking off her apron and straightening her hair.

She knew that Lady Mary did not know of her relationship with Mrs. O'Malley and had already trusted her before. She hoped she would return with news.

She sat on the porch, drinking lemonade. It was a usually warm day. A lovely, warm breeze blew, and the children were playing kickball in the street. It was in such contrast to what was happening just a short distance away.

She saw Hugh step out of a carriage and come toward her. It was barely noon, and she hadn't realized he had been away, but she was delighted to see him.

"I've been with my designer. I saw the first few boards go up on my new home. It fills me with joy, and I so wish to share it with you. Would you consider going with me to see it?"

"I will…soon. With this news of Nancy, I cannot bring myself to steer away from the case. I have sent Mrs. O'Malley on a quest to try to pry something out of Lady Mary. I tried this morning but failed to reaffirm my suspicions that she is more than just a close friend to the Harrison men.

"There is one thing of note. Her companion, Willie, his walking stick, it was in the shape of a horn. I do believe that is the type of stick that made the marks on Jonathan. I'm sure there are hundreds of walking sticks like it, but nonetheless, the path of this investigation always remains pointed at a few people."

"May I have a glass of lemonade and join you while you wait for Mrs. O'Malley?"

"Of course," she replied as she stood to go to the kitchen to bring the pitcher of the sweetened drink back to the porch.

"Chicago has turned out to be quite the city. I'm sure you will not lack for cases here," said Hugh.

"I believe that is true if they can bring themselves to trust a woman. I know I will have to prove myself to secure clients.

"This is lovely, just sitting in the afternoon sun, watching the children play and sharing the moment with a friend.

"Oh, there is Mrs. O'Malley. I didn't know she could move so fast," Madeline pointed out as she waved to her friend.

"Come into the house and sit down. I have much to tell you," said Mrs. O'Malley, and then continued on.

"She was a sight. She gladly accepted the bourbon, and like before, did not speak much until she had three or four of them in her. Then she was like a schoolgirl with her first beau. She couldn't get the words out fast enough.

"The nanny that the boys were raised by was...none other than...her. Her mother, sister, and later her daughter, all lived with the Harrisons after her father died—her father worked as the family butler before he passed away. They took pity on the girls and allowed them all to stay. Apparently, the father, like his sons, had an eye for the ladies. Remember when I told you that her sister became pregnant out of wedlock? Well, it wasn't so magnanimous a gesture after all that they took the baby in because the father was the elder Harrison. She was sent away to live with an aunt and tragically died in childbirth. The son she gave birth to was Patrick Harrison. The father arranged the adoption of the boy—and I don't think that Mrs. Harrison ever knew, but either way, she died soon after from pneumonia. She said she wasn't sure to this day if the brothers or Patrick are aware that he is actually their half-brother."

Hugh and Madeline listened with great interest as she went on.

"There's more. Her daughter, Patricia, also was the victim of a Harrison. She conceived a child by Joseph. She ran away after the birth—left on a ship to Europe—and Lady Mary has never seen her again. She doesn't even know if her daughter is alive or dead. But like Patrick, the father once again arranged an adoption of sorts."

"No...you don't mean, Alfred?" asked Madeline.

"Yes, Alfred is her daughter's child, and Lady Mary is his grandmother. She has so much grief in her heart, and even though she resents them for what they did, she is loyal and devoted to them for having cared for the two boys. Alfred, of course, is not as well-positioned as Patrick, but still, he had his education taken care of by them and is guaranteed a position for life at the Harrison."

"Does Alfred know?" asked Hugh.

"She says she has never had the heart to tell him. She thinks he might be ashamed of her because of her lack of breeding or education. She doesn't know how he would take knowing that Joseph is his father and the others his uncles."

"What a web of deceit! It seems it just adds further suspicions," said Hugh.

"As far as the missing girls, even the alcohol did not make her forthcoming about that. She kept saying she would protect them no matter what they had done," said Mrs. O'Malley.

"I'm going back there and see if Alfred will speak to me. If not, I will see Jonathan," said Madeline. "I will see you later for dinner."

Chapter 17

The Twins

While waiting in the lobby for Alfred, Madeline once again looked over at the area where the twin sisters were seen so often working on their papers and sipping their tea. She had attempted to see Marilyn, but her aunt said she was unwell and was resting. The aunt said Marilyn had not been able to eat anything and was in such an agitated state that she could not stop crying.

When Alfred did come forward, smiling as always, he said, "Mrs. Donovan, what is it? You look as if you are troubled."

She spoke to him of Nancy and her sudden disappearance.

"Do you know which girl I am speaking about? Surely, you have seen her. She is all but a fixture at the French cafe."

"Yes, I believe I know the girl. This is quite a serious matter. I agree with you that it has gone beyond a reasonable doubt that the disappearances do not connect somehow. I can now see your opinion about their presence in the hotel. I will do all I can to assist you. I promise you I will make a greater effort to convey your concerns to the brothers," Alfred said.

"There is Christopher and Joseph. Wait here. I will see if they will come over to speak with you," he continued.

She waited, watching the way they interacted. They looked at her several times and then finally approached her.

Christopher spoke first, "I'm sorry about your friend— the hotel will do all it can to help. Bring her picture in. We will show it to our employees. Perhaps someone will have seen her."

"There are so many girls who frequent our establishment; I do not see how anyone will remember just one. But like my brother said, we will endeavor to assist. Alfred can help you now. We are late for an appointment," said Joseph.

"Mrs...I'm sorry I have forgotten your last name," said Christopher.

"Donovan."

"Mrs. Donovan, although I sympathize with this situation, I would like to point out that you and you alone seem to be preoccupied with thinking that there is a criminal who resides in our hotel. The police have not been at our door, but you remain a constant thorn. I hope you will tread lightly."

She wasn't surprised by his comments, as she knew she was an unwelcome burden to them.

"Thank you just the same for your assistance," she said.

Madeline had been there several times, and now the people she spoke with displayed a sense of alarm that perhaps something untoward was truly taking place at the hotel. Alfred took umbrage at this and said, "You see, Miss, this is why the brothers are against you doing this. It may start a panic or have dire effects on business. I think that is enough for today."

In the evening, she told Hugh what had occurred.

Hugh asked, "Are you game to go back tonight? I would like to see the basement and these cauldrons of lye."

"Yes, let's go see Jonathan," Madeline replied.

Jonathan was working on his article about the Hull House and other Chicago attractions but readily agreed to return to the basement.

"One of these days, we will find that the locks changed. I can't believe our luck so far that we have not gotten caught," Jonathan said.

At ten, they made their way to the staircase that took them to the basement, the smell once again overwhelming them all.

"The odor of decay is enough to make one ill. This is bizarre," said Hugh.

The rats in the corner were gone, and additional animal

skeletons—which they assumed were from the rodents—were floating in one of the barrels.

They each went to different areas, looking for something, for anything that might provide a clue as to what had occurred in that terrible place.

Madeline strode around the three large vats of lye, looking around and under each one. She was about to move to another area when she spotted something gleaming on the floor. Kneeling down, she reached into a small crack in the floor, juxtaposed to the bottom of the barrel. Reaching down and picking up the small treasure, she almost yelled out in joy.

She walked as quickly as she could to Jonathan, who was closest to her.

"Jonathan, look, it is the link we have been waiting for. Now the police must investigate this place."

She handed Jonathan the platinum ring that matched the ones Maria and Wanda owned. Hugh now joined them and whispered, "I think we have all we need now. Let's get out of here."

When they were safely in Jonathan's room, she said, "I don't like to say it aloud, but what if a body was in there, and during the boiling process, her ring fell off to the ground?"

"It is a gruesome thought. A few weeks ago, I would have said that it was completely a fantastical notion. But now, I think it may have some validity," said Hugh.

"How will we say we found the ring without admitting what we were doing here?" asked Madeline.

"It is not as good as finding it in the basement, but I can say I found it in the hall near my room. It may not be the truth, but it will serve two purposes. The police will finally investigate The Harrison, and whoever left it there will act. One of the brothers may respond to the finding of the ring," said Jonathan.

"Madeline, take the ring with you. I don't trust it being in this room. You never know if they have been searching my room to see what we have uncovered. I am always careful to keep my notes with me," he continued.

"We will return tomorrow afternoon, and we can go to the station together," said Madeline.

Hugh and Madeline enjoyed their nightly beverage by the window seat. The air was crisp, and the wind had cooled the night, although still warm, they opted for steaming cups of Earl Grey.

"I enjoy our time together, Madeline, despite all that is happening. The ring is the most revealing of all things we have discovered because it points to a direct connection now to the hotel. Whether it's the brothers or someone who resides at the hotel, we know it traces back to there," said Hugh.

"I feel we are the closest we have ever been to catching a killer. I hope that we will find Nancy in time," said Madeline.

They laid the ring on the ledge of the window seat. "It is a thing of beauty. Who would think that such a token of love and commitment would now be a symbol for murder?" said Hugh.

Then unexpectedly, he took her hand and said, "Madeline, have you ever thought there might come a time when you would consider marrying again?"

Looking at him now, at that late hour, with the moonlight shining upon his face and highlighting his lovely black hair, she thought it might be but only said, "It is something I have not given much thought to since Russell passed. I'm afraid it might not be in the alignment of my stars. Something has changed in me that I cannot touch or put a name to, but it is a feeling that the door of love might be closed to me forever."

With those words, Hugh removed his hand from hers and said, "I hope one day that might not be true.

"Well, tomorrow will be a day of note. The police will surely have to act now."

They spoke of their childhood days, and other memories before bidding each other good-night. Somehow this calmed her, and she had a peaceful sleep.

The next day, in the early morning hour of seven, their telephone rang. It was not unusual to get telephone calls because of her father's medical practice. They were one of a very few families that had the luxury of a telephone, but it was a necessity for a doctor. However, they received very few calls other than from the hospital. This morning it was from Marilyn.

"Madeline," she said, her voice barely audible through her tears. "Madeline, it is a miracle. The most wonderful news...Nancy is home."

The shock Madeline felt at those words was this time, a good feeling.

"You must have much to say. I cannot imagine the story Nancy must have to tell. Will you both come for lunch? I will invite Hugh and Jonathan so we can all hear your story."

Marilyn went on to tell her how happy she was that Nancy was safe and home. Madeline could tell by the gasps while she spoke that this was a matter more easily discussed in person. The importance of it could not be understated.

She knocked on her father's door, feeling that she had to tell someone what Marilyn had said. But to her disappointment, her father had already left for his office. She decided to go upstairs to Hugh's flat to tell him the news.

Hugh met her at the door, romantically disheveled; wearing the smoking jacket and silk pajamas she had seen him wear in London during her recovery at his home. Impulsively she embraced him for a long minute.

He responded, asking, "What's all this?"

"You simply must come to lunch today. We will have the most blessed visitor," she said playfully, waiting another moment before revealing her news.

"All right. I know Phillip is out at sea, so I know not who you could mean."

"It will be Nancy."

"Nancy! The missing twin sister?"

"Yes!"

"That is startling news. Let me dress, and I will come right down so you can tell me all about it."

Mrs. O'Malley had the tea brewing and set out some toast and jams for them.

"You must sit and hear the news, just as soon as Hugh gets here," Madeline said.

Hugh arrived, looking still somewhat tousled.

"Excuse my appearance—I could not wait to hear what you had to say."

"It is Nancy—she has returned home. All of our worries are over. Truthfully, after what happened to Maria and Wanda, I did not hold out much hope that she would be found alive."

"I agree with you. That is remarkable. What happened to her?" asked Hugh.

"Marilyn and Nancy will both be here at noon for lunch and tell us all that has occurred."

"Oh my...I must go to the market. I do not have anything suitable for a luncheon," said Mrs. O'Malley.

Hugh excused himself to put himself together properly, and Mrs. O'Malley left, leaving Madeline to her thoughts. She would spend the time writing notes in her journal of the progress that made.

She held the ring in her hand, and then placed it in front of her on the table as she wrote.

The ghastly truth is that someone has lured young girls, apparently preferring blondes, with some enticement method into captivity. I don't believe the girls were frightened at the time of their meeting with the perpetrator. Of all the many girls who have gone missing, two are confirmed dead. But the rest, except for Nancy, remain missing.

I believe the answer lies with the rings. It is a token of love, so perhaps the captor begins by wooing his victim, and then if she does not comply the way he wishes, then and only then, he harms her. Of the brothers, I believe all had the capability of doing such an act. Christopher is arrogant, dictatorial, and bends everyone to his will. I could imagine that he might wish to enslave a beautiful woman. Joseph appears to have an inordinate desire for lovely women, and Patrick wants love, but feels inadequate and may wish to keep women by other means than love. Lady Mary, Alfred, and Willie, I could easily see would be complicit in doing whatever the brothers would want to be done and may have helped lure the girls to the hotel or wherever they are. Nancy may be able to reveal much to us today.

She continued to write, explaining how she found the ring by the barrels of lye and all that had happened. Putting her pen down, she chided herself that she had just finished a glass of white wine. She had poured it without thinking, her nerves jangling from all the news. She could no longer deny that she was once again falling into the arms of addiction. She wondered if she ever again would ever be truly free of her desire to numb the pain of things too powerful for her to accept.

She thought again of her traumas and about what Hugh had intimated. Besides her obvious love that remained for her deceased husband, she had personal life issues that she felt were not conducive to a committed relationship with another man. She always made bargains with herself, saying tomorrow she would defeat the things that plagued her, but those promises slipped away. She did not know if she could confide in anyone—not even Father, Hugh, or Jonathan—about her personal failings. For now, she would give herself up to trying to become a worthy adversary for the demon she was chasing.

Chapter 18

Unexpected Good News

Hugh, Jonathan, Mrs. O'Malley, and even her father postponed an appointment to be there when Marilyn and Nancy arrived. They stood peering out the window for the twin's arrival as if they were bird watchers.

"They're here," Mrs. O'Malley called out, and they hurried back to the dining area.

Everyone greeted both twins with warm embraces and smiles, ushering them into the dining area. The doctor provided an excellent wine he had saved for Christmas, deciding it was a celebratory day.

"I cannot tell you our relief and joy after finding you had returned safely home. You must not keep us in suspense. Tell us what happened," Madeline implored.

After taking several sips of wine and a bit of some

cheese, Nancy began, "You all know I was longing to go to the Auditorium, not just because I wanted to see the place, but also because of the intrigue of the missing girls possibly being abducted from there.

"I suppose because it was daylight, and there were many people, I certainly felt safe. I began a conversation with two other young ladies, when a middle-aged man, clean-cut and reasonably attractive, walked over to us and asked us if we would like to participate in an adventure. Of course, we were all intrigued and asked him to go on. He said if we wanted to hear more, we would have to go with him for a carriage ride. He assured us of our safety and that with three of us, none of us felt we were threatened in any way.

"It was a fine carriage, and once inside, he gave us each a bouquet of roses and pieces of chocolate. Champagne was given to us in the finest crystal glasses I had ever seen. He said if we were to go with him, we would be paid handsomely, but the stipulation that would have to be adhered to is that we must tell no one. We would be blindfolded so that we did not know our destination. He continued to say we would be free to leave at any time should we so desire. However, if we stayed, we would be given enough money that it would exceed a normal year's pay of an average worker. The money would be based on the amount of time we spent there. If someone agreed to a month, there would be a bonus paid in jewelry and a fur coat.

"He took us on a journey that seemed a long time in the carriage, then up some stairs, downstairs, and then up again in an elevator. By the time we arrived, I could no longer perceive whether we were on a top or bottom floor. It was very confusing. Then we were led into a room where our blindfolds were finally taken off. The suite was breathtaking, like something out of a fairytale. An abundance of fruit, flowers, and candy were laid around different tables. Music was playing, and the scent of perfume was clearly in the air. It was like something you dream about when you are a little girl.

"A man dressed in a Renaissance costume finally appeared, and spoke in a deep voice, as if to disguise it. He asked us to remove our boots and wear satin slippers. We complied, not knowing why except he said he likes the sight of petite women. He went on to explain that what he sought was the company of beautiful, intelligent young ladies. All who decided to stay with him would enjoy the best of everything. He only asked in return to hear their laughter and speak with them on any subject they desired, to play cards and chess, and perhaps to hear them play the piano or sing if they were inclined. He said we were all free to go at any time, but the one caveat was that we were never to tell anyone of the transaction. If we complied, someone would see to it that we received additional monies for our silence. The initial gift every girl received was a diamond ring—a most exquisite diamond ring. Here, let me show you," said Nancy.

She withdrew from her satchel a ring, identical to the one found on the two deceased girls, Maria and Wanda.

Madeline had not told Nancy and Marilyn about the rings, but Hugh and Jonathan looked at her now in a knowing way. She wondered if they were thinking the same thing as she, how lucky Nancy was to be alive.

"Excuse me for one moment—I have something to show you," said Madeline.

She returned with the matching ring she had discovered at the hotel.

"Where did you get it?" asked Marilyn.

"I found it in the basement of the hotel," said Madeline, and then proceeded to retell the events that led up to it.

"Now, there should be sufficient evidence with your testimony to get a search warrant," said Hugh.

"We suspect the Harrison brothers might be involved. Do you think the man who was with you could have been one of them?" asked Jonathan.

"I couldn't say. He wore a long gown, like an emperor's robe, that hid his physique, and, of course, he always wore an elaborate face mask. He was tall but not too tall. I believe it could have been any one of them or none of them," said Nancy.

"You did not feel you or the other girls were in danger?" asked Hugh.

"No, I did not," she answered.

"What made you go along?" asked Madeline.

"I know, looking back, that is was a foolhardy action to take, but I wanted to see if I could find out anything, and I knew I fit the age and description of the missing girls. I suppose I could say the monetary concession also enticed me. Look, I received fifty dollars. I don't know when I have had so much money. It will help with my education."

"How did you get away?" asked Jonathan.

"It wasn't a story of getting away. I never felt that I couldn't leave. When I decided to leave, knowing how frantic my sister would be, the other girls joined me. We told them of our wishes, and he wished us well. Then everything repeated itself. After our payment, we were once again blindfolded and taken back to the Auditorium. It was quite the experience, one I will never forget. It was like being part of a fairytale story."

"And one I will have a hard time forgiving you for, despite the money," said Marilyn as she squeezed her sister's hand. "I don't know what I would have done if anything had befallen you."

"But now…what a happy ending. We will have money for many things, and we still may sell the ring and be even more financially solvent," said Nancy.

After another hour of conversation, they agreed they would meet at the Maxwell Police Station at one in the afternoon to tell their strange story.

When the twins left, everyone spoke at once.

"You see, Madeline, the hotel is safe, and you have worried for naught," said her father.

"No, Father. I feel it is just the opposite. I think they allowed Nancy to go free to avert suspicion. All eyes fell on the Harrison after Nancy went missing, and they could not have that."

"Does anyone believe that they may have the girls actually inside the hotel?" asked Hugh.

"I think it would be risky now, but before Madeline started digging into this, I don't think whoever did it was worried. I think the girls are in the hotel right now, at least the ones who managed to stay alive," said Jonathan.

"At last, we shall see the police swarming over the Harrison. If there are girls hidden somewhere behind those walls, they will find them. The basement alone should give us clues to one or more homicides committed," said Madeline.

"It is a gruesome thought to think someone could be capable of such a thing," said her father.

"After Jack the Ripper, I will never believe that any behavior coming from a deranged criminal is not possible," said Madeline.

Jonathan looked at his pocket watch. "It is time to go."

The officer in charge greeted the excited group with curiosity, hearing a quick synopsis of their story before stopping them, and asking them to wait until he spoke to his superior.

A few minutes later, the large man with the darkened, crooked teeth, who they'd come to know as Inspector Roberts hauled them into his office. His sternness immediately made them calm down.

"Now, what's this all about," said Inspector Thomas Roberts. "One at a time. Who is the girl who went missing? I'd like to hear her story."

Nancy retold her story in great detail, as the inspector diligently took notes. He did not interrupt her and let her speak freely. After she had finished, Madeline and Jonathan began talking to him about the rings, the basement, and their suspicions. They were not entirely truthful about how they obtained access to the Harrisons' private quarters, telling the others that they had accidentally stumbled upon the rings. The inspector raised his eyebrows at this part of the story, and coughed several times, letting them know he suspected their story was fabricated.

"Young lady, you know what you did was unwise, and you are fortunate you were not harmed by your actions. As you do not know where you were taken, it may not have been the hotel, but because the rings are the same, it may give us enough to do a search.

"As for the skeleton, I can't imagine someone having the audacity to murder someone and then hang their skeleton in plain view in their own hotel, but we will have it examined," said Inspector Roberts.

They thanked him, and they left—all exhibiting relief that if the girls were being held against their will, that they would be rescued.

Believing it was now in the hands of the police at this stage, the group spent the next two days sightseeing with Jonathan finally traversing downtown to sample the local dining fare.

When the evening found Madeline and Hugh sitting at their familiar spot by the window, she said, "Marilyn left a message saying she was at the hotel when several police officers arrived there. At least we know something is finally being done. I'm certain Jonathan will get his big story now," said Madeline.

"Would you like to go to the hotel in the morning and see what Jonathan has heard?" asked Hugh.

"Yes, I had been planning to. I can only imagine how shocked the brothers were when they were descended upon by the local authorities. Even they cannot keep this out of the news."

"I still find it amazing that Nancy was not harmed."

"I hope she will not be the only one who will be saved. I have this fear that there is so much more we do not yet know."

"We shall soon find out."

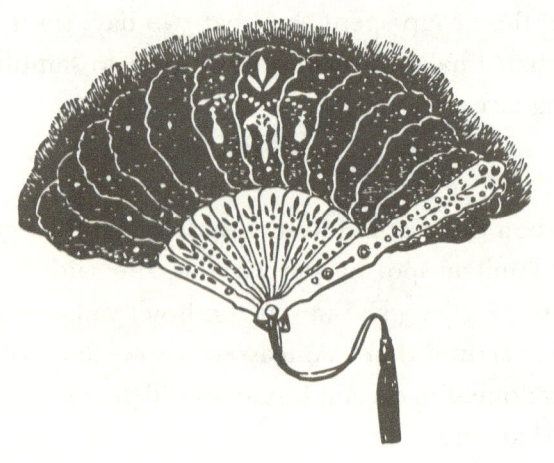

Chapter 19

An Unsettling Development

In the morning, she and Hugh walked to the hotel. When they were within hearing distance, they heard Little Tony yell out, "Harrison under investigation for missing girls... brothers' protest."

They purchased a paper from Tony, who said, "Miss, there been goings on in there all yesterday. I seen the coppers come and go, and the reporters were everywhere. Do you think it's true, Miss, that someone in the hotel took them girls?"

"I don't know, Tony, but I'm relieved the police are trying to find the truth."

When entering the Harrison, they could hear the rumblings of the patrons talking about the girls. Patrick

Harrison was in the lobby, talking to a reporter, and Christopher was speaking with Jonathan. Photographers were taking pictures, and people bustled about trying to find out what was happening.

Marilyn was there alone without her sister, but that didn't surprise Madeline that after Nancy's ordeal, she would choose not to come to the hotel.

"How is Nancy?" asked Madeline.

"Better than expected. She is the center of attention, and everyone wants to know her story. We came yesterday, and the reporters had somehow already found out and surrounded her. However, she only allowed your friend, Jonathan, to interview her. She decided it was too much for her, but I came because I was curious to see if anyone would be arrested."

"I am hoping Jonathan will have that information," said Hugh.

Jonathan nodded to them, and they waited with Marilyn at the French cafe for him to join them.

Within a few minutes, he arrived.

"It is quite the story and not the one you would expect. The police have been through the hotel, from top to bottom, and have turned up nothing. When I spoke to Christopher Harrison, he was furious and threatened to bring a lawsuit against the police for harassment. He told me personally that he believed Madeline had something to do with this, and that he was considering banning her from the hotel," said Jonathan.

Madeline asked, "What about the skeleton?"

"I heard it was nothing more than an ordinary specimen, the same that are displayed in museums," answered Jonathan. "Supposedly, they had the receipt for it, and it had been purchased for some medical supply company. To my knowledge, the police didn't even take it with them for analysis."

"But that is absurd. We saw it with our own eyes. It could not have been," said Madeline.

"We did see it in almost complete darkness. Perhaps we were mistaken," said Hugh.

"And what about the ring? Was that also our imagination?" asked Madeline.

"The police believe any staff member may have dropped it while cleaning down in the basement," said Jonathan.

"This is terrible news—terrible. Now, they will be completely free to do whatever nefarious deeds they are up to. They will know the police will be quite hesitant ever to come back, especially with the fear of a lawsuit," said Madeline.

"I heard Patrick and Joseph saying they want 'that woman' removed from the premises. I'm assuming that woman must be you," said Jonathan.

"I must get back up to the third floor. There is something they missed," said Madeline.

"And the nasty basement—there must be something more there," said Hugh.

"Tonight, then?" said Jonathan. "Be careful that they do not see you coming into the hotel."

They returned at ten, all of them discussing at dinner how appalling the situation was.

"We should have known after Nancy returned, and they realized who she was and that they would be obliged to cover their tracks. It seems they did a very good job of it," said Jonathan.

"It is up to us now to find out the truth about the Harrisons," said Madeline.

This time, the trio stayed together. They agreed to return to the library first.

Madeline was in the lead, and reaching the skeleton, she said, "Look, it is not the same one. This one is yellowed and has no markings of any kind—it is neither one of the skeletons we saw before."

"I think we can all agree on that," said Hugh.

"Whoever changed this skeleton must be the murderer," said Madeline.

"I think you are right. The person knew someone would examine and catch them. But I wonder how it was that they found nothing at all. Where are the girls? Do you think they are all deceased?" asked Jonathan.

"I suppose that is what we must find out," said Madeline.

They proceeded down the hall but found only locked doors. They went back to the staircase that took them down to the basement. The rooms were tidy; even the animal skeletons no longer were there. All that remained were the materials for soap making.

Returning to Jonathan's room, Madeline said, "They know. They must know we have been through the rooms. Obviously, they allowed the library door to remain open so we could see the skeleton. It is like they are taunting us—to let us see nothing is remaining that ties them to a crime."

"Do you think they are working in concert to protect one another?" asked Hugh.

"If that is so, it will prove even more difficult to apprehend who is responsible," said Jonathan.

"There is nothing more to do here. I suppose we must devise another plan," said Madeline wishing Jonathan good-night.

When they arrived at Madeline's home, she declined to participate in their late-night talk and bid Hugh good-night also. She wanted to think about what she should do now. She laid in bed, thinking, and when she couldn't sleep, she lit a candle and started writing notes about the Harrisons. She hoped something would stand out that would place one suspect more in the light.

She decided she would do what she had done in London. She would disguise herself and take a room at the hotel. According to what Jonathan had heard, she knew she was no longer welcome there and might even be banned. It would not be difficult to create a costume for an older woman. She could use her grandmother's gray wig and wear her rather ostentatious jewels. She had bequeathed them to her, but she had never worn them as they seemed inappropriate in the current times. She was sure Mrs. O'Malley could help her with any other items she needed.

When she told her father and Hugh the plan the next morning, neither was keen on the idea, but she insisted that she must do it. Jonathan would be on the same floor, and she could always contact him if necessary.

Chapter 20

Darkness

When she checked in at the hotel, Alfred was just a few feet away from her. No one paid any particular attention to "Mrs. Sullivan" as she named herself. She passed several of the staff that knew her and Lady Mary. No one seemed to recognize her. She was pleased that the first part of her plan was working.

Jonathan was unaware of what she wanted to do, and when he opened his door, at first, he did not recognize her. But when she spoke in a normal tone, he said, "Madeline? I see you have resorted to the days at Whitechapel, although I don't think I ever saw you in disguise there."

He laughed and invited her in.

"So what is all this?" he asked.

"The Falco family was generous in their payment to me.

I have used some of that money to take a room near you. It is but one corridor down and then three doors to the left. I also have procured some skeleton keys from a locksmith and several other useful tools used in the opening of locks."

"If caught, they will prosecute you."

"I won't be, but I will catch whoever is taking these girls."

"I would offer to accompany you, but I will be in Joliet for two days. My editor has asked me to cover a business convention there. Hugh is welcome to stay here so that you may have someone nearby."

"No...I must be able to do this on my own. Of course, Father would be frantic if he knew you are not going to be here, but I must do this."

"I don't feel that good about it myself. There is a possible killer somewhere in this hotel."

"I'm sure I can survive for two days, or what worth could I have?"

"Here is an extra key to my room in the event you change your mind and ask Hugh to stay."

"Thank you, and I hope you enjoy your trip. I'm sure we will have much to talk about when you return."

She returned to her room, knowing that she was on her own now. She shivered a little as she crept along the second floor to the locked stairwell. The hall was empty for the most part, with a few people walking down the corridor. She attempted entry into the door. She placed several items from her satchel onto the floor, so if anyone saw her, she could use the excuse she had dropped her articles and was trying to retrieve them.

She had practiced on her own and her neighbor's door in using the tools to pick the lock, it had been much easier than she imagined. She heard the click and opened the door. When she reached the top of the stairs, she noticed the wooden planks, once stained with what looked like blood, were no longer there.

She entered the library first. Surprise it remained open. She was somewhat apprehensive, believing it might be a trap they had set for her. However, she was too far into it now to turn back. She stepped quietly into the room. Transfixed on the skeleton, she went to examine it again. It was the same one the police had seen. She envisioned that yet another victim could be hanging there in full view. She looked for anything that might look like another entrance or exit into the room. If the Harrison's were so eccentric to create such a place like this, it could be likely there were other secret passageways within the rooms.

She pressed and pushed on the walls and looked behind pictures that hung on the walls. She thought there might be a trap door, but there were tables with books on them that would be difficult to move easily, so she discounted that.

The one odd piece in the room was a pillar with a bust of Benjamin Franklin atop it. She ran her hands over every part of it, finding beneath the marble top a small lever. She moved it, but nothing happened. She then attempted moving the pillar and the bust itself. When she tried to move it clockwise, the bust remained solid but gave way and turned when she moved it counterclockwise. She heard a noise, and when she looked up, she saw two of the bookcases had moved apart to reveal a door behind. The space was narrow, and the door panel needed pushing back for her to enter. Inside, the area was well lit and clean, unlike the other stairwells. There was a handle set upon the wall that she moved to close the bookshelves.

The stairwell descended at a steep incline. She moved cautiously, not knowing what she would face. She could hear the stairs creaking beneath her feet no matter how quietly she tried to maneuver.

When she reached the bottom, an odor arose, the dank, musky smell that most cellars have. The room had the feel and look of an abandoned mine shaft. Strewn everywhere was what she believed to be antiquities of all sorts. Statues, furniture, paintings, and clothing were scattered in large crates and stacked against the walls. As she walked about, she could hear the scurrying of feet—presumably from rats or mice—but she did not see them. She had to cover her mouth to muffle her moans. As she continued to walk through this capacious area, she could see tunnel-like halls that led to other places. She followed the one that was the least obscured.

She went on, marking the area in her mind so that she could find her way back. After she had walked for several minutes, she came upon a site with kerosene lamps on either side of a door. This area was in harsh contrast to what she had just seen. It was swept clean and had candles, fruit baskets, and a case of champagne outside the door.

Finding the door locked, she took her assortment of tools and manipulated the door until it opened. She had become adept at picking locks. She walked for just a short distance when she thought she heard voices. She turned to go down another hall to follow the direction of those voices. She listened closely. She could hear the chatter of female voices and what she believed was a male voice. She stood deadly still, her heart beating with excitement. Behind that door might be one of the missing girls. She stood listening for almost an hour until she finally heard the man say he would return later to wish them good-night.

She moved the wooden bar from the door to release it and opened the door with great anticipation.

Inside were the faces of three girls—who looked at her as if she had come from another world.

She put her finger to her lips, indicating to them to please be quiet.

"Who are you, and what are you doing here?" asked one of the girls in a whispered voice.

"I hope I've come to save your life," she said, holding on to the girl's hand. "You're Felicia Zugaj, aren't you?"

The girl's face showed the perplexed look Madeline had expected. The other girls huddled together around her.

"Yes, I am, but how could you know that? What is this all about, and how did you get through this door?" asked Felicia.

"We must be quick. I will have to explain most of this later, but I believe you are all in great danger. I must get you out of here, and before anyone is aware of it."

"What do you mean? We are not in danger at all. We are happy and treated well. Yes, we are, in a way captive, but by choice. Our month is almost up. Our pay is substantial," said another girl.

"We all sent word to our families through Wanda Gapinski, a friend of mine, that we were safe and would return within the month," said Felicia.

Madeline shook her head and said, "Wanda Gapinski is dead. She was floating in the Chicago River. There is no evidence that it was murder, but it is suspected. And the three of you, your pictures are on the pages of every newspaper as missing persons," said Madeline.

"I believe there are other girls here. Sometimes I thought I heard them coming from another room," said Felicia, now with a look of fright on her face.

"I'm sure they are also in danger," said Madeline. "There are many girls who have gone missing. We believe one of the brothers of the Harrison Hotel may be responsible. That's where you are right now—in the cellar of the hotel."

"We never knew where we are. As you can see, we have lived in luxury and wanted for nothing. You cannot mean the sweet man who comes to talk to us is responsible for harming Wanda?" asked Felicia.

"I don't know, but I wouldn't want to confront him in the case that he, or one of his brothers, might mean you harm," said Madeline.

"Oh, no…he is returning. I hear his footsteps. He wasn't due to come back for another hour," said one of the girls.

"He cannot find me here. I will come back for you, but not alone. I will bring the authorities. Until then, do not let on that anything has changed. Your very lives may depend on it," said Madeline as she slipped through the door and placed the plank of wood back to secure it.

She thought it would be unwise to confront whoever it was, even knowing that there were four of them to mount a defense. But the unknown factor of not knowing how many people might be involved made her believe this was the safest route to take. She had a knife in her boot. Madeline brought with her the Derringer that had once belonged to her mother, but wanted to avoid using it was at all possible. She would return and bring the police with her.

She felt relieved when she saw the antiques and knew she was within a short distance of the exit that would bring her safely back to her room and the authorities. But then, something gripped her heart, and she began to quiver. There—against the wall—alongside one of the statues was a walking stick, not just any walking stick, but one with a horn as the handle, the shape of the figure on Jonathan's back. She was certain it had not been there when she entered the area, as the statue was one of the markings she had used to find her way back. It stood right outside the hall she had entered.

The murderer was there and looking for her. She pulled her gun from her satchel and steadied herself.

She moved in silent steps, looking around her, walking near to the antique furniture so that it would give her some coverage. She heard the feet of the rodents again as she looked around to watch for any movement. She knew she was within a few yards of the door to the staircase and continued walking toward it. Her feet felt numb as she walked as if they had betrayed her and could barely move. She tried to shake off her fear, telling herself the weapon in her hand would protect her. She reached the door, and for a moment, panic set in—a rusted lock bolted the door.

Her way out was gone. Whoever was there had her trapped and knew it. They were playing with her, perhaps watching her right now.

She would now have to keep her wits about her. There had to be another way out; the area she was in was expansive. She thought about going back to the door into the room the girls were in. The person might be watching, but she had to try at least.

She did not dare to turn on her torchlight and walked slowly back to where the girls were. When she was in sight of the door, someone removed the fruits and vegetables, and the door now had a similar bolt attached to it.

She returned into the darkness, now traveling down a different corridor. She looked for an adequate place to hide, believing that she would have an advantage if she had her back to the wall. She placed herself between two stacks of boxes and thought it would give her some protection. For the moment, she would wait and listen.

She had a pocket watch and two pieces of fruit with her. She had thought she might walk to the park later, so she included the snack in her satchel.

Almost an hour had passed, and except for the rats, there was only disconcerting silence. She had hoped the perpetrator would confront her while she had her back against the wall and her gun in her hand. Now she stopped—taking a few bites of her pear to provide herself with some liquid on her tongue.

She knew she would have to leave that place and continue her search for an exit. She prayed the girls were safe.

She moved along the wall to another corridor, and seeing a door, acted quickly to see if it might allow her out of that dungeon. It was open but was just a closet filled with rags and miscellaneous garbage. She now saw two more doors, but they were both secured.

It was still quiet, so she began maneuvering the pick in the lock. She felt like a bird in a cage. Perhaps the murderer was toying with her and would appear at any second. She finally opened the first door. It also was a storage area but filled with lovely clothes. It had a scent of cologne. She tried the second door, and when she opened it—there was what she had always dreaded.

There lay the skeletal remains of two bodies.

She bit her lip so hard to stop from screaming that she

could feel the trickle of blood rolling down her chin. She wiped it away with her white glove and saw the crimson color stain it. Seeing the red slashed across the white, she imagined the fate of these two people, their resting place a locked closet, without even a decent burial. She wondered if they had suffered and if the killer had tortured or defiled them.

She closed the door, walking away with a new determination to try to escape the dungeon and the craven person who did that deed. Then she heard the laughing—a cruel laugh, the kind one remembers in their sleep and wakes screaming. She froze, standing behind one of the large statues. Then she heard a thump of a walking stick hitting the floor, the footsteps that accompanied them so quiet that the stick hitting the floor became louder and louder in her ear.

"Madeline, how clever of you to have found me out," said a gruff, low voice.

She did not recognize the voice. She stood without movement, trying to ascertain how close he was to her.

"You see, you have discovered things that will prove of no use to you, for you will not live beyond this day. But perhaps I will spare you if you will come out and speak to me."

She knew his words were false and that he wanted her to show herself. She still had some advantage; he didn't know exactly where she was. If he walked within visual range, she might be able to fire at him. He did not know she had a gun, and she hoped she would get the opportunity to use it against him.

He was wrong—she was not so clever after all, for she thought it would be Patrick speaking to her. She had long thought that he might have the most compelling motive and insecurities to perpetrate such a crime. She knew he resented his place in the family, not only because of his adoption but also because of him sorely lacking in the looks the other brothers had. But now that she heard him speak again, she knew who it was.

"If only you would have waited a few more days, my sweetheart and I would have been gone to Paris. I have already booked our passage. I have enough money now to care for both of us.

"A few more days...and you would not have been in any danger. It is a pity—for I rather liked you."

She heard a shot ring out, and he said, "You see, no one will come for you. No one can hear anything from the cellar. I have moved the girls to another location. I had planned on leaving them alone, but now you have ruined that and will have their deaths on your head for your interference."

He was getting closer to her, and she thought it was her best opportunity to fire at him. He was moving cautiously, darting behind chairs and other objects, so she did not have a clean shot, but she knew she must do something as she might not get another chance.

As he moved alongside a large stack of boxes, his foot bumped something, and he temporarily lost his bearings. She jumped out from behind the statue and fired.

She grazed him in the shoulder, forcing him to drop his weapon. He now stood with his hand to his shoulder, saying, "Let me go, Madeline, and I swear no harm will come to you or your father."

She was startled by his speaking of her father, and the thought that he might harm him enraged her even further, "Why, Alfred, why? Why did you do those horrible things? Was it truly just for the money?"

"Please...of course not. I fully intended to set the blame on my Father and my uncles. That was perhaps the sweetest part of it. I was certain after I left that one of them would see the noose."

"So you knew all along of your parentage. I don't think Lady Mary knew."

"You mean my grandmother. I knew. I've known for almost a year after I heard her speaking to Willie about it, but I always suspected it. That is why I gave her the money I received from selling the skeletons to make sure she had something to tide her over when I'm in Europe."

He made a sudden move, and she yelled out, "Be still, or I will not hesitate to shoot you. I have killed another madman like you, and I should not regret doing it again."

"Why, Mrs. Donovan...I think I believe you."

Then without her seeing in the darkness, he threw his walking stick at her. She tried to block the stick and automatically fired her weapon, but did not hit her target. Before she was able to recover, Alfred had retrieved his weapon. He was unsteady due to his wound. He fired at her from behind one of the wooden shelves he hid behind.

She thought her only chance now was to run, and run she did. She went down one hall and then another with Alfred calling out to her, almost singing out her name and laughing. She continued checking each door that she saw. He was moving almost as quickly as she was, slowed only slightly by his wound. Finally, she came to a door that opened, and she prayed it was not another storage area. It wasn't. Behind the door were glorious stairs—stairs to her freedom. She ran up with Alfred following right behind her.

When she reached the exit door, she found she was in the basement floor with the vats of lye, almost now as terrifying to her as Alfred, for they represented what he had done. She remembered where the exit door to the second floor was and started for it, yelling now for help, hoping someone might hear her.

She was nearly at the door when the heel of her boot snagged against a potted hole in the floor. With the speed she had been running, it caused her to lose her balance and fall backward, dropping her weapon as she did.

When she looked up, Alfred stood over her, a maniacal look upon his face of joy.

"I knew it was not possible that someone such as you could have outdone me," he said.

With that, he pulled off her wig and threw it into one of the vats. "Did you really think you had fooled me with that ridiculous costume? I was following you all along after I saw you in the lobby. Now, you will see what it feels like to be one of my victims! And, I will get a pretty penny for your skeleton."

He had a hold of her hair now in both hands—dragging her up the steps towards the landing and to the top of a lye barrel. The blood from his wound dripped down against his shirt and then onto Madeline. She could feel the red liquid running down her face, the pain from her being dragged by her hair excruciating, as she fought to get free. She knew her only chance to defend herself would be once they reached the landing at the top of the stairs.

He was pulling her with his back toward her. She pulled her leg up and reached inside her boot for the knife she had placed there. She knew she would only have one chance.

When he pulled her onto the platform, he continued to

push her towards the closest barrel. When he turned, she stuck the knife into his leg, which was the closest part of his body to her. He yelled out, and she pushed him over, his hand now falling over into the barrel of lye. He shrieked with pain, his skin erupting from the toxic substance.

She ran down the stairs and out to the exit, up the stairs, screaming for help. She arrived on the second floor, still calling out, blood-stained and weak.

She began to lose consciousness, but then she saw the face of her friend. "Jonathan, quick, it's Alfred. He tried to kill me. Get him. He is in the basement. He has a gun—be careful."

By now, many residents had come out of their rooms and rushed to help her while Jonathan left running to the basement. Then blissfully, everything went black.

Chapter 21

Until We Meet Again

When she awoke, she was in her room at the hotel. Her father was holding her hand and wiping her forehead with his handkerchief.

"Madeline, this seems all too familiar. My goodness child, you gave me a bit of a fright."

"I'm sorry, Father, but it was necessary. Besides, this time, I am not injured, frightened to death, but not injured."

"I left word for Hugh. He informed Mrs. O'Malley that he would be in Oak Park at the site of his home. I have sent a messenger to tell him what has happened. As you know, Jonathan is at the police station with Alfred. I'm sure he will be there a while, not only because he was with Alfred and will have to give the details to the police because he will have quite a story to prepare.

"I have brought you something to calm you. No, it is not opium. I will give you an injection of morphine. This drug will calm you and believed to have great medicinal benefits."

"Thank you, Father. We will have much to talk about. Did the girls get set free?"

"What girls?"

She went on to explain about Felicia and the other two young girls. Her father said he would go downstairs and bring one of the police officers up to speak with her. He said the lobby filled with policemen.

When the officers arrived, they took her statement. They would enlist the Harrison brothers to search the cellar area and aid the women who remained there.

"I can rest now, Father, knowing they are safe. I think I would like to go home now and get away from this place."

Her home was a blessed sight to her, and she was grateful to be back on Erie Street. She still felt weak. Mrs. O'Malley brought her out a blanket, a glass of wine, and her mystery novel. She lay on the divan near the window seat and tried to relax.

"Father, I would like to have everyone involved to come to dinner tomorrow so that we may tell them what happened. I know Louie and Rosa will want to know, as well as the Gapinski family, and, of course, Marilyn and Nancy."

"Mrs. O'Malley...," said the doctor.

"I heard, Dr. Donovan, we shall have an event tomorrow. I'll go to the market first thing in the morning."

"Will you be all right alone? I have an emergency I have to attend to. One of the children down the street, I believe, has broken their leg," said her father.

"Yes, Father, I will be fine. I am still somewhat in shock from what happened, but so very happy no other girl will fall victim to Alfred. Besides, you have notified Hugh, and I am sure he will be here soon."

She lay there alone, trying to read her book, but the effects of the morphine and the wine had taken hold of her, and she drifted into sleep.

She awoke sometime later to the knock on her door, and her friend, Hugh, calling to her.

"I came as soon as I heard. Are you all right? Have you been harmed?" He asked with a frantic tone in his voice.

His concern soothed her. Taking his hand, she said, "I am better than I have been in a long time—the murderer is in custody. Hugh, it was Alfred, Alfred, the attractive, smart, young man who had everything in the world going for him. Alfred...I thought perhaps he was involved in some way, but I had believed one of the brothers committed the crimes."

"Dear Lord—Alfred! I, too, cannot imagine that it is him. Now, if you feel you are up to it, tell me everything."

She told him some of what happened but stated that she would explain everything at dinner the next day after a full night's rest. Whatever she didn't know, she knew Jonathan would have gathered more information about the crimes through his interviews.

She impulsively kissed Hugh's cheek as he leaned over her to say good-bye. He looked somewhat startled, his eyes warmly looking searchingly into hers. Smiling, he grasped her hands and said, "Take care, my friend. You will be in my thoughts until I see you again. Till tomorrow..."

She continued resting on the divan, sleeping on and off, sometimes waking to Alfred's snarling face. She was about to retire when she heard a carriage outside. Looking out the window, she saw Jonathan. She ran to the door to let him in, anxious to hear what news he had.

"Jonathan…how wonderful to see you."

"It is the hour too late?"

"Under the circumstance, no hour would be too late. I have thought of you all day, hoping you might come by and tell me what you have learned. But first, tell me how you happened to be at the hotel when I thought you were going to Joliet?"

"I attempted it. I think I had gone about five miles before I turned around. I just felt so uncomfortable that you were searching for the killer without anyone even knowing where you were. You will have to tell me later how you found the cellar."

"That is indeed another story. But go ahead, tell me about Alfred."

"Alfred is in the hospital for his gunshot wound and his hand injury from the lye. He waived his right to a lawyer, and all he wanted to do was talk to the press. He didn't want to talk to me at first but then sent for me. He said that since I was the one to bring him in, I could hear his story.

"He ranted and cried and then ranted again. He truly has been a tormented soul, probably all of his life. He killed the girls almost methodically, doing it as a means to have finally the life he so craved…to be with his love, Margaret, and to be away from the Harrisons.

"He said he wanted to speak with you if you were willing to come into the spider's web."

"Me? Heavens, that's extraordinary, but, of course, I will. I will go tomorrow. Perhaps he will explain why this all came to be, that is if he even knows. His problems must be deep rooted."

"Indeed."

Jonathan went on, and they conversed for two hours until she insisted he stay the night and sleep in the spare room. He looked weary and in need of a peaceful night, as she did. Tomorrow she would tell the story to the group.

She awoke at five, and if she could have gone to see Alfred at that moment, she would have. She was anxious to discover why he wished to see her. To the world, young, agile, intelligent Alfred had everything to live for. More than anything, she wanted to know the underbelly of this nightmare scenario.

Lighting a candle, she began the arduous task of documenting everything that had happened the last few days in her journal so that she might use it as a reference.

At just eight, when she knew she would be allowed into the hospital, she arrived. At first, the man guarding his room would not let her in. She would be permitted to converse with Alfred as long as an officer stayed in the room with her.

When she entered his room, he was warned again that his words could be used against him, but he motioned for her to come in. He waved the one bandaged from the damaging lye, and this was not lost on her.

"Madeline, come sit by me."

"No, she must remain on the other side of the room," said the officer.

"What a pity. You know I should hate you for ruining everything, but somehow I believe I will survive. Perhaps we will meet again someday,"

The officer laughed and said, "The only thing you'll be meeting, sonny boy, is the noose."

"I think not; there is no noose that could take me. Someday we must all die, but I will not die by the noose, I can promise you that."

The officer laughed again and said, "Get on with it. You only have a half-hour allotted to you."

"Madeline, I will tell you a story about a boy—just like any other boy—wanting love, a home, and a family, and what happens when those things never become yours."

Alfred went on to tell her his defense of why he had to commit the crimes he did. His pain was so justifiable to him that he failed to show only momentary regret for what he did to his innocent victims.

"Everyone has their life's tragedies, Alfred. As much as you would like to believe you are alone in life's miseries, we all suffer. Now you have inflicted untold suffering to so many who were innocent in every way. I hope you may someday at least find it in your heart to repent for what you did."

As she turned to leave, he said, "Until we meet again, Madeline, may you rest as uneasy as I will. If it weren't for you, I'd be in Paris with my Margaret. Yes, until we meet again."

When she stood, she felt one of her feet give way and had to steady herself against the wall. Even with the police officer sitting five feet from her, she felt as if she was on a desert island with a madman.

Chapter 22

The Final Analysis

When she arrived home, Jonathan had departed for the Harrison. He had to prepare his article for the Times and also to continue with his interviews. He would return later for dinner.

The hotel would be abuzz with activity. Jonathan wanted to be there to hear all that was going on in the aftermath of Alfred's apprehension…but for Madeline, her job was now over. She felt no compulsion to revisit the hotel.

Hugh appeared early in the afternoon to assist her and Mrs. O'Malley in preparing for the evening's guests. They spent the time talking about the progress made at his home in Oak Park and the upcoming dinner. They did not discuss Madeline's dramatic encounter with Alfred, agreeing that they would wait till the evening. She would then reveal all that she had come to know about his gruesome actions.

Champagne and wine were provided, along with several liqueurs. When the guests began to arrive, Hugh and Madeline ensured everyone had a glass in their hand. Somehow she believed the business they would be discussing might set easier if they were all somewhat relaxed.

Mrs. O'Malley prepared a sumptuous meal of beef, dumplings, and other delicacies. She had gone to the bakery and brought an assortment of jellies and cakes. After they had all dined and thanked Mrs. O'Malley for her superb effort, they turned to her and requested she begin her story.

"Thank you for coming. Those of you who have suffered a terrible loss because of Alfred may find it difficult to hear the details. Still, I have asked you here to allow you to learn everything that I know about his motives and his apprehension."

Mr. Gapinski said, "It will be difficult—we all agree, but we choose to know, so please go on."

Louie and Rosa nodded in agreement, and so she began.

"There were some things I surmised, but I learned directly from Alfred yesterday at the hospital many of the facts I am about to tell you.

"Many years ago, Lady Mary, her daughter, sister, and mother lived with the Harrison family. She was the boy's nanny. Her mother was the family's cook, and her sister performed the duties of a maid and assisted her mother in the kitchen. She said her sister was the beauty of the family, and the Harrison's father had an eye for her. He promised her many things, saying the boys' mother was ill and that someday he would marry her. When she became pregnant, they sent her away. She died in childbirth, and the old man did show some genuine remorse at her passing and arranged to adopt the child. That child was Patrick.

"Alfred learned of these things by listening in on Lady Mary's conversations as a child and going through her things whenever she was inebriated and didn't pay close attention to him. He was closest to her, as she treated him like family. In his earlier life, he held no real resentment for the brothers. However, he did not learn of his own blood connection to the family until about a year ago. That is when his hatred and plans to hurt them took root.

"Lady Mary's daughter, like the sister, had become pregnant by yet another Harrison, Joseph, and Alfred was the result of that pregnancy.

"Joseph, however, did not wish any further involvement with her, agreeing only to adopt the baby and financially support him. However, Joseph did not give him his name or rightful place in the family. He gave her a monetary supplement, and she disappeared. Neither Lady Mary nor Alfred has ever seen her again.

"Alfred had been stealing small things from the brothers for years, but not for himself—to give money to Lady Mary. He didn't know then that she was his grandmother, but he thought of her that way.

"He knew that Joseph had a weakness for the ladies and that he carried his passion to extremes by offering young women money to spend time with him. He and Patrick chose those who he thought might be desperate for money and might agree to his terms. Whether they stayed a day or a month, he gave them each a platinum ring to signify his connection to them. He swore them to secrecy and hid his identity."

At great length, she described how the girls had to wear blindfolds and their treatment once they arrived in the cellar.

"Maria, like many of the girls, according to Alfred, agreed to go and was swayed by the promise of the easy money. The ring alone, she thought, would bring enough money for her to start her own bakery here in Chicago. But, after only a few days, she thought better of it and decided to leave. Unlike the others, she noticed the peculiar reaction everyone had after eating the chocolates. Alfred overheard her speaking to one of the girls about taking the evidence with her to the authorities. Alfred had Willie tie her up until they decided what was to do. Willie thought Alfred might harm her and told her he would release her if she promised not to go to the authorities. He snuck Maria out, but then he found information in her bag, notes about what happened. He became afraid and wanted to take her back to the hotel. She bolted from the carriage. He then chased after her. He told Alfred he hadn't meant to harm her, just warn her. But when Willie had caught up with her...the carriage came rushing up, and he pushed her in front of it. He had done it in a state of panic, believing that he and Alfred would go to jail. Willie never knew that Alfred murdered the girls; he only thought he was stealing from them.

"Joseph had several locations besides his hotel, where he looked for beautiful women. They chose the ladies from those seen at the hotel or the Auditorium. That is why the hotel had so many events that attracted women, such as the fashion shows.

"What Joseph didn't know was that after he paid the girls their money, and released them to Alfred, who'll be returning them to the Auditorium or some other location, that many of them never to be seen again. Alfred did not harm all of them, just those given the greater amounts of money. He left with them, stole whatever money Joseph had given them, and then suffocated them. He felt that was the most humane way to kill them and to preserve the body intact. He then placed them in the lye vats to strip the human remains and sold the skeletons.

"Wanda, unfortunately, like Maria had decided to leave and was overheard by Alfred talking about how bizarre the situation was and that someone should be told about it. When Wanda proclaimed she wished to leave immediately, Alfred was not inside the hotel. Joseph then enlisted Patrick to take her. But Alfred saw them outside the hotel and took his place as the driver.He charmed her into going for a ride in the park with him. Alfred gave her enough opium to make her woozy and disoriented. He stopped at the river, telling her the night air would make her feel better. They got out of the carriage and walked by the river, and it was easy enough for him to push her then. She was probably too drugged to have put up much of a fight or survive the waters.

"He never took the rings from any of the girls because he knew that the diamonds were imitation, unbeknownst to the recipients. It would have taken an expert to tell. When I saw the rings, I thought they must be very expensive.

"It was then that Alfred believed the situation had become too dangerous to continue.He thought he would either be found out by the brothers, by the police, or by the efforts of our snooping. He had deliberately been kind to me, hoping that I should never suspect him.

"Although he had hoped for an even bigger cache, he was content with the money he had and booked his passage for him and Margaret.

"Poor Margaret believed him nothing less than a prince and had agreed to run away with him without telling anyone."

"Was it just about the damned money?" asked Louie, his face reddened with rage.

"No, it was more than that. The money was a way for him to escape, but he left a trail, thinking the brothers' arrest would occur for what he did. He believed that if even one of them were prosecuted, the hotel would not sustain the scandal, and they would lose everything. He said he always felt slighted by the brothers but still was grateful for what they had done until he learned he was Joseph's actual birth son. He felt that he should have had the prominence of being part owner. He resented Patrick, for although he too was adopted, he stood to inherit. Alfred received none of the things that Patrick had, which made him bent on revenge. He also knew that they did not provide for Lady Mary, as she thought they did. Most of the money she received to be able to remain in her luxury accommodations came from Alfred. He told her the money was from the brothers to spare her from the hurt it would have inflicted if she knew they actually had done little to help her.

"He had taken enough money to be able to marry Margaret and live abroad, at least for a few years. He already had booked his passage and had false passports for the two of them.Chances are he would have left the country before anyone found out the truth.

"Willie is in custody for his part in this, and of course, the brothers are being investigated. However, the only action that was prosecutable was to give the girls drugs without their knowledge. Everything else was done with the girls' consent. They did not hold them against their will; they were always free to go at any time."

"What part did Christopher and Patrick play in this?" asked Marilyn.

"Patrick only wanted to continue to favor Joseph, so he helped his brother hide the goings on in the cellar from Christopher. There were only the four of them that even knew the cellar existed. All the brothers wanted to keep the existence of the cellar unknown to the police. Patrick and Joseph, for obvious reasons, and Christopher because some of the items stored in the basement were contraband from other countries, had to hide their worth from the internal revenue service," said Madeline.

"Did he say why he assaulted Jonathan?" asked Hugh.

"I can answer that. I asked if it was him who hit me across the back, and he said it was. He said he had been at the Austin all along with Margaret and saw me go after the brothers. He was afraid I would catch them in the act of soliciting women and ruin his plans prematurely. He wanted to be certain I couldn't continue to follow them," said Jonathan.

"Christopher was the only one who played no part in this at all. He is the serious one who was always busy with the running of the hotel. He sensed his brothers might be up to something and tried to keep a watchful eye on them but never caught them doing anything. He did not know the girls were in the cellar. Alfred brought things up from the cellar for him, and he never went down there," said Madeline.

Marilyn asked, "What about Lady Mary?"

"Alfred said she did not know about what was happening. I am sure she will be shocked to find out what her grandson did and to lose her friend, Willie at the same time.

"Alfred even took the clothing from the girls that he thought might fit Margaret and stored it in the cellar. He wanted to have the trunk filled with the dead girl's clothing shipped to Europe. He was planning on giving the clothing to her as a wedding gift," said Madeline.

"Do they know how many girls he may have killed? And who was the unidentified man who took us in the carriage?" asked Nancy.

"Jonathan said they found the receipts to the places he sold the skeletons to, and they will follow the trail from there. They found as many as eight receipts, but they believe there to be more as he may have dabbled in murder before building the Harrison when the brothers were in Detroit.

"As far as Joseph's part in getting the girls to the hotel undetected, according to what Alfred said, he hired a different man to pick the girls up each time. The man then proceeded to some unknown destination near the hotel where he was paid and let go. Patrick, in disguise, then took the carriage the rest of the way."

"So Joseph and Patrick were aware they had been with the missing girls. Why didn't they tell the police? And what about the first girl that I told you about, the one in the stockyards—was she also his victim?" asked Uncle Hank.

"Scandal. They felt no remorse in not conveying their knowledge because, as far as they knew, the girls were all still alive when they saw them last. They felt whatever happened to the girls did not have anything to do with them. Christopher already had diminished some of their authority. They thought he would be very displeased with their actions and what it might do to the hotel's reputation if he learned of this.

"I asked Alfred about the girl thought to have committed suicide. He did not lay claim to killing her, but the police will reopen that case to be certain," replied Madeline.

She and Jonathan discussed the other particulars of the case, including finding the secret passage into the cellar.

It was a bittersweet meeting for all. They expressed their relief that Alfred could harm no one else, but they found his actions so horrifying that many wept as she told the story.

When everyone had gone, and only Jonathan and Hugh remained, they sat together; true friends now bonded forever.

It was almost ten—her father and Mrs. O'Malley were still sitting at the dining table talking. Jonathan, Hugh, and Madeline went outside to walk in the cool, moonless night.

"Thank goodness you are safe. I think you took too great a risk. You may have been killed," said Hugh.

"I may have, but I believe this is my life now, and what I choose to do. I will get better at it," said Madeline.

"You've had a successful outcome to your first case, Madeline. Congratulations! What a story I accidentally fell into; I can't wait to get back to New York and tell the account of what happened at that seemingly lovely hotel," said Jonathan.

She impulsively hugged them and said, "I don't know if I could have done it without you both. You two are part of my life now, a most welcome part."

A light rain trickled down their shoulders, and Hugh said, "After you."

She took his arm and had started up the stairs when a young man ran past them to the front door.

"May I help you?" Madeline asked.

"I'm looking for Dr. Donovan. I have an urgent telegram for him."

"He's my father. Please come in."

Her father tipped the boy, took his glasses out, and read his telegram. When he finished, he scratched his head and then handed the telegram to Madeline, saying, "This is a quandary. What will I do about my practice?"

"What do you mean, Father?" asked Madeline.

"Read the telegram. It's from Belle Mayfair. Do you remember her?"

"Of course."

Aunt Belle Mayfair was a grand, Southern woman who hailed from New Orleans. Like Uncle Hank, she was not actually her aunt, but a close friend of her father and mother. When her parents were on their honeymoon and traveling through New Orleans, they had accidentally met Belle and her family. They had been dining in one of the eateries at the time. When Belle's daughter began choking on a piece of meat, her father, who sat near her, saved her daughter's life.

In return, Belle, who was quite wealthy, assisted with the finances needed to establish his first medical office. Her father had always been extremely grateful for her generosity and credited her with his early success. They became fast friends, and through the years, the doctor had advised her on many medical issues that her family had.

During her childhood, she remembered Belle's visits as a cause for celebration. Her charm and wit kept everyone listening to her stories and clamoring for her attention. She

www.ingramcontent.com/pod-product-compliance
Lightning Source LLC
Chambersburg PA
CBHW020256200626
46816CB00001BA/317

had made it a point to come to see them at least once a year for many years. Madeline thought she might be eighty now. It had been ten years since they had seen her, but they still corresponded regularly.

> *August 1st, 1889*
> *Dear Brian:*
> *I have been remiss in not coming to see you, but I have ol*
> *bones now, and they do not allow me to do the things I once*
> *enjoyed. The plantation is no longer the fine place you once saw;*
> *has withered as I have. However, we still carry on. But, now to r*
> *request, you once saved my life by saving my child's life. There*
> *trouble at our homestead. You are the only one I feel I can trust, s*
> *ask you to save my life once again. Please come to Belle Magnol*
> *Your faithful friend,*
> *Belle*

After reading the telegram aloud to Jonathan a Hugh, she asked, "Gentlemen, have you ever been to N Orleans?"